PENGUIN

THE SUNDIAL

SHIRLEY JACKSON was born in San Francisco in 1916. She first received wide critical acclaim for her short story "The Lottery," which was first published in *The New Yorker* in 1948. Her novels—which include *The Sundial*, *The Bird's Nest*, *Hangsaman*, *The Road Through the Wall*, *We Have Always Lived in the Castle*, and *The Haunting of Hill House*—are characterized by her use of realistic settings for tales that often involve elements of horror and the occult. *Raising Demons* and *Life Among the Savages* are her two works of nonfiction. She died in 1965.

VICTOR LAVALLE is the author of the short story collection *Slapboxing with Jesus*; three novels, *The Ecstatic*, *Big Machine*, and *The Devil in Silver*; and an e-book–only novella, *Lucretia and the Kroons*. He has been the recipient of numerous awards, including a Whiting Writers' Award, a United States Artists Ford Fellowship, a Guggenheim Fellowship, a PEN/Open Book Award, an American Book Award, and the key to Southeast Queens. He teaches at Columbia University.

SHIRLEY JACKSON

The Sundial

Foreword by
VICTOR LAVALLE

PENGUIN BOOKS

PENGUIN BOOKS
Published by the Penguin Group
Penguin Group (USA) LLC
375 Hudson Street
New York, New York 10014

USA | Canada | UK | Ireland | Australia | New Zealand | India | South Africa | China
penguin.com
A Penguin Random House Company

First published in the United States of America by Farrar, Straus & Cudahy 1958
Published in Penguin Books 1986
This edition with a foreword by Victor LaValle published 2014

LIBRARY OF CONGRESS CATALOGING-IN-PUBLICATION DATA:
Jackson, Shirley, 1916–1965.
The sundial / Shirley Jackson ; foreword by Victor LaValle.
pages ; cm.—(Penguin classics)
ISBN 978-0-14-310706-4
I. Title.
PS3519.A392S9 2014
813'.54—dc23
2013034518

Printed in the United States of America
1 3 5 7 9 10 8 6 4 2

Set in Sabon LT Std

For Bernice Baumgarten

Contents

THE SUNDIAL

Foreword

In 2007 my girlfriend and I went to see the latest Coen brothers' film, *No Country for Old Men*, at a movie theater near Union Square in New York. The place was jammed, but we got decent seats. We'd been dating for a year by that time. Emily and I knew each other pretty well, but it had still been only a year, and it occurred to me, and I'm sure to her, that you could spend that long dating someone and still not know her, understand her, on some essential level. You're enjoying your days together but also waiting for that moment when you see a flash of the soul, the person's true essence, so you can decide if this relationship is truly serious. I wasn't thinking about this stuff consciously as the lights dimmed and the movie started, but it was there in the atmosphere of our relationship. Time to get serious or get gone. Then the predawn imagery of Texas—rough, lovely open country—appeared on the screen. Tommy Lee Jones spoke in a voice-over as the images played on. ("I was sheriff of this county when I was twenty-five years old.") The audience, Emily and I included, grew quiet.

Toward the end of this astounding film Tommy Lee Jones, who has been playing a weary old lawman, sits at the kitchen table of his home with his wife. By this point *No Country for Old Men* has morphed from a riveting crime drama into a parable about death, the one inescapable fate. Death in one form or another finds whomever it pleases in the film, and it will not be reasoned with, escaped, or outgunned. By the time Tommy Lee Jones sits in that kitchen his weariness seems well earned. His character has hoped that his earnestness, his competence, his goodness will spare him the destiny that has come for so

many others. He tells his wife about two dreams he's had the
night before. The second one is both chilling and resigned.
The lawman finally grasps that the end will come for him, as it
did for his father, as it does for every woman and man.

While Tommy Lee Jones was reciting these dreams, I found
my eyes drawn away from the screen for a moment. Something
was moving through the theater. I looked to my left, and there
I saw a boy, probably nine or ten years old. He looked tall, but
that was just because he was very thin. He had the reddish
brown skin and large eyes of an Ethiopian, that striking beauty
that can seem almost otherworldly in certain contexts. Certain contexts like right then in that dark theater.

The boy walked up the aisle, scanning the room. His head
swiveled left and right. His large, bright eyes seemed to pan
across every face in the theater. All the while Tommy Lee
Jones's voice thundered on about his spectral dreams.

Emily, to my right, must have noticed my distraction. She
inched forward in her chair. She was looking at this boy now
too. Her instinct was to help him. She guessed, as I did, that he
must've been looking for his seat in the dark, scanning for the
empty chair where he'd probably just been sitting with his parents. But what parents would bring their nine- or ten-year-old
boy to a Coen brothers' movie? Especially this one. The boy's
age made him seem as out of place as his appearance made
him seem from another world. I looked up at the screen and
Tommy Lee Jones had finished his speech and now he sighed
and his eyes looked wet with the sudden *knowing* of what his
second dream meant. At that moment Emily raised her left
hand to wave to the boy, the one scanning all our faces with
those impossibly bright eyes. But I grabbed her hand and
pushed it back down onto the handrest.

"Don't call to him," I whispered. I knew she couldn't understand, and yet I said it.

Emily looked at me in the dark. Our faces were only slightly
visible in the light cast by the movie screen. She narrowed her
eyes.

"Because he's death?" she said.

It's the moment I knew Emily would be my wife.

So why did I just tell you that anecdote?

I'm trying to relate what it felt like the first time I read Shirley Jackson's fiction. What it feels like each time I've read her work since. I didn't grow up in a small New England town like the one in *The Sundial*. I was raised in an apartment building in Queens, not in a sprawling, slightly sinister mansion like the one where the Halloran family resides. And the La-Valles sure didn't have some storied patriarch whose name we uttered like a prayer, as the Hallorans so often do in this book. And yet when I open *The Sundial,* I feel the same sense of kinship, of recognition as I did in that movie theater when my soon-to-be wife seemed to read my mind.

The Sundial shares some of the characteristics of Shirley Jackson's most famous works of fiction. There's the enormous, imposing estate, as in *The Haunting of Hill House*; the once great but now diminished family, as in *We Have Always Lived in the Castle*; and even the doom-laden atmosphere of her classic short story "The Lottery." So what makes *The Sundial* stand out? Why is it worth reading? Because *The Sundial* is funny as hell.

This may surprise some readers. An eerie work of suspense by one of the great American masters of literary unease couldn't also make you laugh so loud you wake your sleeping wife, could it? If you accept the caveat that by *funny* I don't mean "light" or "silly" or "cheerful," then the answer is an easy yes. *The Sundial* is written with the kind of humor that would make a guillotine laugh.

The novel begins, after all, with the family returning from a funeral for Lionel Halloran, the heir to the Halloran estate and all its fortune. Lionel was pushed down the main stairs in the mansion and fell down dead. Who did the ghastly deed? His own mother. As the extended family returns home, here's the conversation between Lionel's widow and the couple's ten-year-old daughter, Fancy.

Young Mrs. Halloran, looking after her mother-in-law, said without hope, "Maybe she will drop dead on the doorstep. Fancy dear, would you like to see Granny drop dead on the doorstep?"

"Yes, mother." Fancy pulled at the long skirt of the black dress her grandmother had put on her.

I'm not spoiling anything by quoting this horrifically hilarious exchange because it occurs in the first two paragraphs of the book! In that moment I imagine Jackson peering over those round-framed glasses in her famous author photograph, her eyes gleeful, because things are going to get so much worse.

The Hallorans, and their extended hangers-on, become a kind of cult when one of them, Aunt Fanny, receives prophetic messages from her long departed, much revered father. He has appeared to his only daughter to warn that the world is soon to end. All those in the Halloran home must prepare for the coming doom. Shut the doors and windows, close themselves off from the cursed world. Prepare to become the last of the human race. In quick time the family members are drawn into paranoia and conspiracy. They come to believe the prophecy. They have been chosen to inherit the earth. Jackson proceeds to illustrate, in rich detail, just how sad such a fate would be. The whole world ends, and *this* is all that's left? Jackson spares no one her precise, perceptive eye. Sadder still is how much I recognize myself, from my worst moments, in one character or another. What saves me from despair is Jackson's wit, her deadpan demolition of human foibles. For me, that kind of reading experience is essential, and when I discovered Shirley Jackson, it was as if she'd understood what I wanted, what I needed, and set it all down on the page long before I was even born. That recognition is profound, life changing, whether it comes in a darkened movie theater or between the covers of a novel.

Shirley Jackson enjoyed notoriety and commercial success within her lifetime, and yet it still hardly seems like enough for a writer so singular. When I meet readers and other writers of my generation, I find that mentioning her is like uttering a holy name. The grins we share. The blush of reverence. She doesn't appear to us in prophetic dreams but in her books.

VICTOR LaVALLE

The Sundial

I

After the funeral they came back to the house, now indisputably Mrs. Halloran's. They stood uneasily, without any certainty, in the large lovely entrance hall, and watched Mrs. Halloran go into the right wing of the house to let Mr. Halloran know that Lionel's last rites had gone off without melodrama. Young Mrs. Halloran, looking after her mother-in-law, said without hope, "Maybe she will drop dead on the doorstep. Fancy, dear, would you like to see Granny drop dead on the doorstep?"

"Yes, mother." Fancy pulled at the long skirt of the black dress her grandmother had put on her. Young Mrs. Halloran felt that black was not suitable for a ten-year-old girl, and that the dress was too long in any case, and certainly too plain and coarse for a family of the Halloran prestige; she had had an asthma attack on the very morning of the funeral to prove her point, but Fancy had been put into the black dress nevertheless. The long black skirt had entertained her during the funeral, and in the car, and if it had not been for her grandmother's presence she might very well have enjoyed the day absolutely.

"I am going to pray for it as long as I live," said young Mrs. Halloran, folding her hands together devoutly.

"Shall I push her?" Fancy asked. "Like she pushed my daddy?"

"Fancy!" said Miss Ogilvie.

"Let her say it if she wants," young Mrs. Halloran said. "I want her to remember it, anyway. Say it again, Fancy baby."

"Granny killed my daddy," said Fancy obediently. "She

pushed him down the stairs and killed him. Granny did it. Didn't she?"

Miss Ogilvie raised her eyes to heaven, but lowered her voice in respect for the sad occasion of the day, "Maryjane," she said, "you are perverting that child's mind and very possibly ruining her chances of inheriting—"

"On this day," young Mrs. Halloran said, putting her mouse face into an expression of reproachful dignity, "I want it clearly understood by all of you, everyone here, and remembered always, *if* you don't mind. Fancy is a fatherless orphan today because that nasty old woman couldn't *stand* it if the house belonged to anyone else and I was still a wife, a beloved helpmeet." She breathed shallowly, and pressed her hands to her chest. "Pushed him down the stairs," she said sullenly.

"The king, thy murdered father's ghost," Essex said to Fancy. He yawned, and moved on the velvet bench, and stretched. "Where are the funeral baked meats? The old woman can't be planning to starve us, now she's got it all?"

"This is unspeakable," said young Mrs. Halloran, "to think of food, with Lionel barely cold. Fancy," and she held out her hand. Fancy moved unwillingly, her long black skirt swinging, and young Mrs. Halloran turned to the great stairway. "My place now is with my fatherless orphaned child," she said over her shoulder. "They must send my dinner up with Fancy's. Anyway I believe I am going to have more asthma."

WHEN SHALL WE LIVE IF NOT NOW? was painted in black gothic letters touched with gold over the arched window at the landing on the great stairway; young Mrs. Halloran paused before the window and turned, Fancy toiling upward still, entangled in her skirt. "My grief," young Mrs. Halloran said, one hand on her breast and the other barely touching the wide polished handrail, "my lasting grief. Hurry *up*, Fancy." Together, young Mrs. Halloran leaning lightly upon the shoulder of her daughter, they moved out of sight down the hall, into the vastness of the upper left wing which, until so recently, they had shared with Lionel.

Essex looked after them with distaste. "I should think Lionel would have welcomed the thought of dying," he said.

"Don't be vulgar," said Miss Ogilvie. "Even with me, please remember that we are employees, not members of the family."

"*I* am here, however, if you please," Aunt Fanny said suddenly from the darkest corner of the hall. "You will of course have overlooked the fact that Aunt Fanny is here, but I beg of you, do not inhibit your conversation on *my* account. I am a member of the family, surely, but that need not—"

Essex yawned again. "I'm hungry," he said.

"I wonder if it will be a proper dinner? This is the first funeral since I've been here," Miss Ogilvie said, "and I'm not sure how she manages. I suppose we'll sit down, though."

"No one will waste a minute's thought if Aunt Fanny stays safely in her room," Aunt Fanny said. "Tell my brother's wife," she said to Essex, "that I will join her in grief after dinner."

"My first funeral, too," Essex said. Lazily, he stood up and stretched again. "Makes you sleepy. You think the old lady's locked up the gin in honor of the day?"

"They'll have plenty in the kitchen," Miss Ogilvie said. "But just a teensy one for me, thanks."

"It's over," Mrs. Halloran said. She stood behind her husband's wheel chair, looking down onto the back of his head with no need, now, to control her boredom. Before Mr. Halloran had become permanently established in his wheel chair Mrs. Halloran had frequently found it difficult to restrain her face, or the small withdrawing gestures of her hands, but now that Mr. Halloran was in the wheel chair, and could not turn quickly, Mrs. Halloran was always graceful with him, standing protectively behind him and keeping her voice gentle.

"He's gone, Richard," she said. "Everything went off beautifully."

Mr. Halloran had been crying, but this was not unusual; since he had been made to realize that he would not, now, be vouchsafed a second run at youth he cried easily and often. "My only son," Mr. Halloran said, whispering.

"Yes." Mrs. Halloran forebade her fingers to drum restlessly upon the back of the wheel chair; one should not fidget in the

presence of an invalid; in the presence of an old man imprisoned in a wheel chair one ought not to be impatient. Mrs. Halloran sighed, soundlessly. "Try to be brave," she said.

"Do you remember," Mr. Halloran asked, quavering, "when
he was born, we rang the bells over the carriage house?"

"Indeed we did," Mrs. Halloran said heartily. "I can have
the bells rung again, if you like."

"I think not," Mr. Halloran said. "I think not. They might
not understand, down in the village, and we must not indulge
our own sentimental memories at the expense of public opinion. I think not. In any case," he added, "the bells are not loud
enough to reach Lionel now."

"Now that Lionel is gone," Mrs. Halloran said, "I am going
to have to get someone to manage the estate."

"Lionel did it very poorly. At one time the rose garden was
perfectly visible from my terrace, and now I can only see hedges.
I want the hedges all cut down. At once."

"You are not to excite yourself, Richard. You were always a
good father, and I will have the hedges trimmed."

Mr. Halloran stirred, and his eyes filled again with tears.
"Do you remember," he said, "I wanted to keep his curls?"

Mrs. Halloran put a little wistful smile on her face and came
around the wheel chair to look at her husband. "Dear Richard," she said. "This is not healthy for you. I know that Lionel
loved you better than anyone in the world."

"That's not proper," Mr. Halloran said. "Lionel has a wife
and child, now, and his father must no longer come first. Orianna, you must speak to Lionel. Tell him that I will not have
it. His first, his only duty is to the good woman he married,
and his sweet child. Tell Lionel . . ." He stopped uncertainly.
"*Is* it Lionel who died?" he asked after a minute.

Mrs. Halloran moved around to the back of the wheel chair
and permitted herself to close her eyes tiredly. Lifting her hand
with deliberation, she put it down softly onto her husband's
shoulder, and said, "His funeral went off very well."

"Do you remember," the old man said, "we rang the bells
over the carriage house when he was born?"

Mrs. Halloran set her wine glass down very quietly, looked from Essex to Miss Ogilvie and said, "Aunt Fanny will be down for dessert?"

"Adding the final touch of jubilation to a day of perfect happiness," Essex said.

Mrs. Halloran looked at him for a minute. "At such a remark," she said finally, "Lionel would have found it necessary to remind you that you were not here to be ironic, but to paint murals in the breakfast room."

"Orianna *dear*," said Essex with a little false laugh, "I had not suspected you of fallibility; the one painting murals in the breakfast room was the *last* young man; *I* am the young man who is supposed to be cataloguing the library."

"Lionel wouldn't have known," Miss Ogilvie said, and turned pink.

"But he would have suspected," Mrs. Halloran said agreeably, and then, "Aunt Fanny is at the door; I hear her little cough. Essex, go and let her in, or she will never bring herself to turn the doorknob."

Essex opened the door with a flourish; "Good evening, Aunt Fanny," he said. "I hope this sad day has agreed with you?"

"No one needs to worry over me, thank you. Good evening, Orianna, Miss Ogilvie. Please don't bother, really; you know perfectly well Aunt Fanny is not one to worry over. Orianna, I shall be glad to stand."

"Essex," said Mrs. Halloran, "set a chair for Aunt Fanny."

"I'm sure the young man would rather not, Orianna. I am accustomed to taking care of myself, as *you* have surely discovered."

"A glass of wine for Aunt Fanny, Essex."

"I take wine only with my equals, Orianna. My brother Richard—"

"Is resting. He has had his dinner, Aunt Fanny, and his medicine, and I promise you that nothing will prevent your seeing him later in the evening. Aunt Fanny, sit down at once."

"I was not brought up to take orders, Orianna, but I suppose you are mistress here now."

"Indeed I am. Essex." Mrs. Halloran turned easily in her

chair and leaned her head back comfortably. "I want to hear how you wasted your youth. Only the scandalous parts."

"The path gets straighter and narrower all the time," Essex said. "The years press in. The path becomes a knife edge and I creep along, holding on even to that, the years closing in on either side and overhead."

"That's not very scandalous," Mrs. Halloran said.

"I am afraid," Aunt Fanny said, "that this young man did not have what we used to call 'advantages'. Not everyone, Orianna, was fortunate enough to grow up in luxury and plenty. As of course *you* know perfectly well."

"The statistics scratch at your eyes," Essex said. "When I was twenty, and could not see time at all, the chances of my dying of heart disease were one in a hundred and twelve. When I was twenty-five and deluded for the first time by a misguided passion, the chances of my dying of cancer were one in seventy-eight. When I was thirty, and the days and hours began to close in, the chances of my dying in an accident were one in fifty-three. Now I am thirty-two years old, and the path getting narrower all the time, and the chances of my dying of anything at all are one in one."

"Very profound," said Mrs. Halloran, "but still not altogether scandalous."

"Miss Ogilvie," said Essex, "treasures in an ebony box stolen from the music room and hidden under the handkerchiefs in the top right hand drawer of her dresser the small notes Richard Halloran wrote her four years ago, before, although it is perhaps rude to mention it, he took to his wheel chair. He left one every evening for her, under the big blue cloisonné vase in the main hall."

"Good heavens," said Miss Ogilvie, pale. "*That* could not be what she means by scandal."

"Do not trouble yourself, Miss Ogilvie," Mrs. Halloran said, amused. "In his capacity as librarian Essex has become accustomed to spying on all of you. He brings me very entertaining stories, and his information is always accurate."

"A moment of truth," said Aunt Fanny tightly. "Coarse and vulgar I said *then*, and coarse and vulgar I say *now*."

"I would not have stayed on—" Miss Ogilvie began with difficulty.

"Of course you would have stayed on. Nothing could have dislodged you; your mistake," Mrs. Halloran said kindly, "was in supposing you could dislodge *me*. Aunt Fanny's mistake, in a word."

"This is needless and disgusting," Aunt Fanny said. "Orianna, if I might have your gracious permission to retire?"

"Stay and finish your wine, Aunt Fanny, and Essex will think of more scandalous stories for you."

"The path gets narrower all the time," Essex said, grinning. "Does Aunt Fanny remember the evening when she drank Lionel's birthday champagne and asked me—"

"I believe I am going to be ill," Aunt Fanny said.

"You have my gracious permission," Mrs. Halloran said. "Essex, I am not pleased. *You* must be above suspicion, even if Aunt Fanny is not. Fanny, if you *are* going to make some demonstration, please get it over with; I want to have my walk before we play backgammon, and my schedule has already been much disturbed today. Miss Ogilvie, have you finished your wine?"

"You are going to play backgammon?" demanded Aunt Fanny, distracted. "Tonight?"

"It is *my* house now, Aunt Fanny, as you have reminded me. I see no reason why I should not play backgammon in it."

"Coarse is coarse," Aunt Fanny said. "This is a house of mourning."

"I am sure that Lionel would have foregone dying, Aunt Fanny, if he thought his funeral would interfere with my backgammon. Miss Ogilvie, *have* you finished your wine now?" Mrs. Halloran rose. "Essex?" she said.

The character of the house is perhaps of interest. It stood upon a small rise in ground, and all the land it surveyed belonged to the Halloran family. The Halloran land was distinguished from the rest of the world by a stone wall, which went completely around the estate, so that all inside the wall was Halloran, all outside was not. The first Mr. Halloran, father to

Richard and Aunt Fanny—Frances Halloran she was then—
was a man who, in the astonishment of finding himself suddenly extremely wealthy, could think of nothing better to do
with his money than set up his own world. His belief about the
house, only very dimly conveyed to the architect, the decora-
tors, the carpenters and landscapers and masons and hodcar-
riers who put it together, was that it should contain everything.
The other world, the one the Hallorans were leaving behind,
was to be plundered ruthlessly for objects of beauty to go in
and around Mr. Halloran's house; infinite were the delights to
be prepared for its inhabitants. The house must be endlessly
decorated and adorned, the grounds constructed and tended
with exquisite care. There were to be swans on the ornamental
lake before the house, and a pagoda somewhere, and a maze
and a rose garden. The walls of the house were to be painted
in soft colors with scenes of nymphs and satyrs sporting
among flowers and trees. There was to be a great deal of silver,
a great deal of gold, much in the way of enamel and mother-
of-pearl. Mr. Halloran did not care much for pictures, but
conceded a certain few to the decorator; he did, however, insist upon one picture of himself—he was a practical and a vain
man—to be hung over the mantel of the room the architect,
inventing madly, was calling "your drawing room." Mr. Halloran did not care for books, but he bowed to the incredulous
smiles of the architect and decorator, and included a library,
which was properly stocked with marble busts and ten thousand volumes, all leather-bound, which arrived by railroad
and were carried carton by carton into the library and unpacked with care and set in order on the shelves by people
hired to do the work. Mr. Halloran set his heart upon a sundial, and it was ordered from a particular firm in Philadelphia
which was very good for that kind of thing, and Mr. Halloran
himself selected the spot where it would go. He had half hoped
that the inscription on the sundial—left to the discretion of
the people in Philadelphia who knew so much about that kind
of thing—would be "It is later than you think," or perhaps
even "The moving finger writes, and having writ," but through

the fancy of someone in Philadelphia—and no one ever knew who—the sundial arrived inscribed WHAT IS THIS WORLD? After a while Mr. Halloran quite fancied it, having persuaded himself that it was a remark about time.

The sundial was set into place with as much care as the books had been put into the library, and properly engineered and timed, and anyone who cared to ignore the little jade clock in the drawing room or the grandfather clock in the library or the marble clock in the dining room could go out onto the lawn and see the time by the sun. From any of the windows on that side of the house, which was the garden front looking out over the ornamental lake, the people in the house could see the sundial in the middle distance, set to one side of the long sweep of the lawn. Mr. Halloran had been a methodical man. There were twenty windows to the left wing of the house, and twenty windows to the right; because the great door in the center was double, on the second floor there were forty-two windows across and forty-two on the third floor, lodged directly under the elaborate carvings on the roof edge; Mr. Halloran had directed that the carvings on the roof be flowers and horns of plenty, and there is no doubt that they were done as he said.

On either side of the door the terrace went to the right for eighty-six black tiles and eighty-six white tiles, and equally to the left. There were a hundred and six thin pillars holding up the marble balustrade on the left, and a hundred and six on the right; on the left eight wide shallow marble steps led down to the lawn, and eight on the right. The lawn swept precisely around the blue pool—which was square—and up in a vastly long lovely movement to a summer house built like a temple to some minor mathematical god; the temple was open, with six slim pillars on either side. Although no attempt had actually been made to match leaf for leaf and branch for branch the tended trees which bordered the lawn on either side, there were four poplars, neatly spaced, around the summer house; inside, the summer house was painted in green and gold, and vines had been trained over its roof and along the pillars supporting it.

Intruding purposefully upon the entire scene, an inevitable focus, was the sundial, set badly off center and reading WHAT IS THIS WORLD?

After the first Mr. Halloran had his house, painted and paneled and brocaded and jeweled and carpeted, with sheets of silk on the beds and water colored blue in the pool, he brought his wife, the first Mrs. Halloran, and his two small children to live there. Mrs. Halloran died there within three months, without ever having seen more of the sundial than the view from her bedroom window; she did not go to the center of the maze nor visit the secret garden, she never walked into the orchard to pick herself an apricot, although fresh fruit was brought her every morning in a translucent blue bowl; roses were brought her from the rose garden and orchids and gardenias from the hothouses, and in the evenings she was carried downstairs to sit in a chair before the great fire in what Mr. Halloran was by now frankly calling the drawing room. Mrs. Halloran had been born in a two-family house on the outskirts of a far-off city where most of the year seemed wintry, and she felt that she had never been warm in her life until she sat before the great fire in her drawing room. She could not bring herself to believe that in this house she would never see winter again, and even the eternal summer in her room, of roses and gardenias and apricots, did not reassure her; she died believing that snow was falling outside the window.

The second Mrs. Halloran was Orianna, Richard's wife, who had made a particular point of behaving with appreciation and docility while her father-in-law was alive. "I believe," she told Richard once, after they had returned from their honeymoon in the Orient and settled down in the big house, "I believe that it is our duty to make your father's last years happy ones. After all, he is your one living relative."

"He is not at all my one living relative," Richard pointed out, puzzled. "There is my sister Frances, and my Uncle Harvey and his wife in New York and their children. And I am sure I have other second and third cousins."

"But none of them has any control over your father's money."

"Did you marry me for my father's money?"

"Well, that, and the house."

"Tell me again," Mrs. Halloran said, looking down at the sundial in the warm evening darkness.

"'What is this world?'" Essex said quietly, "'What asketh man to have? Now with his love, now in his colde grave, Allone, with-outen any companye.'"

"I dislike it." Standing in silence, Mrs. Halloran reached out and touched a finger to the sundial; there were faint noises of leaves stirring and a movement in the water of the pool. In the darkness the house seemed very far away, its lights small, and Mrs. Halloran, touching the sundial, moved her finger along a W, and thought: without it the lawn would be empty. It is a point of human wickedness; it is a statement that the human eye is unable to look unblinded upon mathematical perfection. I am earthly, Mrs. Halloran reminded herself conscientiously, I must look at the sundial like anyone else. I am not inhuman; if the sundial were taken away I, too, would have to avert my eyes until I saw imperfection, a substitute sundial—perhaps a star.

"Are you warm enough?" Essex asked. "You shivered."

"No," said Mrs. Halloran. "I think it has turned quite chilly. We had better go back to the house."

Walking, Mrs. Halloran caressed with her soft steps the fine unyielding property she walked upon; she was not unable to perceive the similar firmness of Essex' arm under his sleeve, and she felt the very small tensing of his muscles as equally a response to her perfection and a little gesture of protection; this is all mine, she thought, savoring the sweet quiet stone and earth and leaf and blade of her holding. She remembered then that she had decided to send Essex away and thought, smiling a little, poor Essex, unable to comprehend that the essence of the good courtier must be insecurity. Now I own the house, she thought, and could not speak, for love of it.

In the big drawing room Richard Halloran sat by the fire in his wheel chair, and Miss Ogilvie sat, pointedly remote, at a table far away with Aunt Fanny. Miss Ogilvie was holding a book and Aunt Fanny was playing solitaire; she had clearly not felt herself entitled to turn on an adequate light, and both she and Miss Ogilvie bent, squinting.

"Orianna," said her husband, when Mrs. Halloran and Essex came in through the tall doors from the terrace, "I was thinking about Lionel."

"Of course you were, Richard." Mrs. Halloran gave her scarf to Essex, and went to stand behind her husband's wheel chair. "Try not to think about it," she said. "You'll have trouble sleeping."

"He was my son," Richard Halloran said, patiently explaining.

Mrs. Halloran leaned forward. "Shall I move you away from the fire, Richard? Are you too warm?"

"Don't badger him," Aunt Fanny said. She lifted a card to hold it pointedly toward the light and look at it. "Richard was always perfectly capable of making his own decisions, Orianna, even about his own comfort."

"Mr. Halloran has always been such a forceful man," Miss Ogilvie added fondly.

"We rang the bells over the carriage house for his first birthday," Mr. Halloran explained across the room to Aunt Fanny and Miss Ogilvie. "My wife thought we might ring the bells again today—as a sort of farewell, you know—but I thought not. What do you think, Fanny?"

"By no means," Aunt Fanny said firmly. "In deplorable taste. Naturally." She looked at Mrs. Halloran, and said "Naturally," again.

"Essex," said Mrs. Halloran, not moving. "I wonder if we should have them ring the bells, after all." Essex, crossing the room with the soundless step of a cat, stood beside her attentively, and Mr. Halloran nodded and said, "Thoughtful. He would have liked it. We rang the bells over the carriage house," he told Miss Ogilvie, "for his first birthday, and then every birthday after that, until he asked us not to do it any more."

"I am afraid, however, that it is too late to ring the bells tonight," Mrs. Halloran told her husband gravely.

"You are right, my dear, as always, Poor Lionel would not hear them, in any case. Perhaps tomorrow will not be too late."

"Lionel was a fine man," Miss Ogilvie said, drooping mournfully. "We will miss him."

"Yes, you must get someone to cut down the hedges," Mr. Halloran said to his wife.

"His father was always everything a boy could desire," said Aunt Fanny. "Richard, are you too warm by the fire? You always disliked being overheated. Although," she added, "the fire is not very high, apparently. At least, it gives almost no light."

"Essex," said Mrs. Halloran, "go and turn on the lamp for Aunt Fanny."

"Thank you, no," Aunt Fanny said. "It is never necessary to consult *my* comfort, Orianna. You are perfectly aware that I ask for nothing at your hands. Or," she added, glancing at Essex, who stood by her, "at the hands of a hired—"

"Young man to catalogue the library," Essex supplied.

"Mr. Halloran," Miss Ogilvie asked, "may I get you a shawl to throw over your shoulders? Perhaps your back is cold? I know one's back so often is, even when the fire is warming one's . . ." she hesitated, "extremities," she said.

"Do you mean feet, Miss Ogilvie?" Mrs. Halloran asked. "Because I assure you that Richard still has his, although they are not often visible. Miss Ogilvie is concerned about your feet," she said down to her husband.

"My feet?" He smiled. "Don't do much walking any more," he explained gallantly to Miss Ogilvie, who blushed.

"Aunt Fanny," Mrs. Halloran said, and they all turned to her, wondering at her voice, "I am happy to hear that you ask for nothing at my hands, because there is something I am going to tell all of you, and Aunt Fanny reassures me."

"I?" said Aunt Fanny, astonished.

"The essence of life," said Mrs. Halloran gently, "is change, you will all, being intelligent people, agree. Our one recent change—I refer, of course, to the departure of Lionel—"

"It *was* Lionel, then," Mr. Halloran said, nodding to himself before the fire.

"—has been both refreshing and agreeable. We could very well do without Lionel. I am now convinced that a thorough housecleaning is necessary. Richard will stay, of course." She put her hand on her husband's shoulder and he nodded again, gratified. "Essex," said Mrs. Halloran. "I wonder if we have not detained you past your time?"

"The library—" said Essex, putting his fingers against his mouth and staring.

"I think I shall let the library go for a while," Mrs. Halloran said, "and get someone to paint murals in my dressing-room. You will, of course, receive a small settlement to start you on some small scholarly pursuit."

"The path," Essex said tightly, "gets narrower all the time."

"So wise of you," Mrs. Halloran said.

"I would have hoped—" Essex tried. "I would hope that after—"

"Essex, you are thirty-two years old. It is not too late for you to find a career in life. You might work with your hands. You may of course take a day or so to plan. Miss Ogilvie," and Miss Ogilvie put out her hand blindly and took hold of her chair arm. "I am pleased with you," Mrs. Halloran said. "This is not criticism, Miss Ogilvie. You are a gentlewoman, of a sort too rarely found in the world today; you have been sheltered—you came, I think, just shortly before Fancy was born?—you have been sheltered from the world all your life, and I would not thoughtlessly put you out to live exposed. I think we shall put you into a little boarding house, genteel, of course—you may be positive that it will be genteel, and altogether suitable for your condition of life and your breeding; some watering place? A spot by the sea? In the off season you will play cribbage with other ladies of similar station in life. Perhaps during some warm autumn month you will fall into the hands of an adventurer, carried away by the sound of the sea and the fading merriment on the pier; perhaps even Essex, in his trackless scholarly wanderings, will find you and take your money away from you. You would of course be perfectly safe in the hands of an ordinary adventurer, since the little nest egg I will give you will be absolutely out of your control; I feel that it is only wise."

"This is heartless." Miss Ogilvie sank back in her chair. "I have not deserved this."

"Perhaps not. But you must allow me my impulse of generosity. I insist upon the nest egg."

"And I? Am I to be turned out, too?"

"Dear Aunt Fanny, this is your home. Do you suppose me ungrateful enough to turn you away from the home of your childhood? You have lived here with your mother, with your father—a fine man; I remember your father."

"My mother and father have nothing to do with *you*. My brother—"

"Yes," said Mrs. Halloran. "You went to your first, and only, dance, in the ballroom here; Miss Halloran, you were then; we must not lose sight of Miss Halloran in Aunt Fanny. Equally, however, your brother and I are alone now; we have not been alone in this house since our marriage. There is room enough for you and me in the house, Fanny," Mrs. Halloran said indulgently.

"I have never thought so," Aunt Fanny said.

"Do you recall the tower, Fanny? Your father built it; it was to have been an observatory, was it not? I remember workmen there during my early days in the house. The tower could be made extremely comfortable. You may even take some of my furniture up there; I have no objection to your choosing anything in the house, except, of course, those objects of particular sentimental value; the blue cloisonné vase in the hall will go with Miss Ogilvie."

"I will take my mother's jewelry."

"I daresay that people in this house years from now will begin to talk of the haunted tower." Mrs. Halloran laughed. "Well," she said, "who is left now? It will be lonely here for Maryjane, I know; I am positive that she had a genuine feeling for Lionel, although I would not care to define it any further than that. I think I shall send Maryjane home again. Lionel found her in a public library in the city, so that is where she is going. She had a little apartment at the time, and I shall arrange for her to have her little apartment back again. She will not absolutely have to go back to work in the library, because of course I will be generous. She may even take up again with her old friends as though no time had passed; I am afraid, however, that she must not hope to find a second Lionel. One Lionel in a lifetime is, I believe, quite enough for anyone."

"And Fancy?" said Miss Ogilvie, barely speaking. "I am her governess, I should—"

"Fancy is mine, too, now," Mrs. Halloran said, smiling. "Some day everything I have will belong to Fancy, and I think to keep Fancy with me."

"*I* think you've been joking with us," Essex said, his voice flat, and without life. "It's one of your jokes, Orianna. You want us all to be frightened, and beg, and then you will laugh and say you were joking—"

"Do you really think so, Essex? Then I will be interested to see how far my joke will go before you beg. Richard?" Mr. Halloran opened his eyes and smiled. "Bedtime," he said cheerfully. Mrs. Halloran turned the wheel chair. "Goodnight," she said; "Goodnight," Mr. Halloran said, and Mrs. Halloran had pushed the wheel chair almost to the door before Essex ran to open it for her.

Miss Ogilvie was crying, not noisily, but obtrusively; she had cried slightly when Lionel died, but her tears then had been more formal, and she had kept her nose from turning red. Aunt Fanny sat in patient grimness, staring into the fire. Her hands were folded in her lap; when her brother and sister-in-law left the room Aunt Fanny had said "Goodnight, Richard," and had not spoken since. Essex walked, because when he was still he saw himself; "Cringing," he said, "fetching and lying and spying and outraging, and turned away as I deserve. Aunt Fanny," he said, "Miss Ogilvie—we are contemptible."

"I always tried to do what was best," Miss Ogilvie said miserably. "She had no right to speak to me so."

"It was true," Essex said. "I was shallowly protected; I thought I was clever and quick and invulnerable, and that is not a very good protection; I thought she was fond of me, and I made myself into a pet monkey."

"She could have broken it more gently," Miss Ogilvie said.

"An ape, a grotesque little monster."

"Be quiet," said Aunt Fanny, and they turned to her, surprised. She was looking toward the door; it opened, and Fancy slipped in.

"Fancy," said Aunt Fanny, "your grandfather would not like you to be downstairs so late. Go at once to your room."

Disregarding Aunt Fanny utterly, Fancy moved to the fireplace and sat crosslegged on the hearth rug. "I spend a lot of time in here," she said. "When you're all in bed, mostly." She looked directly at Miss Ogilvie. "You snore," she said.

Miss Ogilvie, goaded, almost snarled. "You ought to be spanked," she said.

Fancy ran her hand richly along the soft hearth rug. "It's going to belong to me when my grandmother dies," she said. "When my grandmother dies, no one can stop the house and everything from being mine."

"Your grandfather—" Aunt Fanny said. "My brother—"

"Well," said Fancy, as one explaining to an unreasonable child, "of course I know that it really belongs to Grandfather. Because it belongs to the Hallorans. But it doesn't really *seem* to, does it? Sometimes I wish my grandmother would die."

"Little beast," said Essex.

"This is not properly spoken, Fancy," Miss Ogilvie said gravely. "It is very rude of you to think about your grandmother's dying, when she has been so kind to you. And it is very rude to steal about the house at night spying on people and then making comments on—" She hesitated. "You ought to behave better," she said.

"Furthermore," said Aunt Fanny, "you had better not count your riches before you get them. You have plenty of toys."

"I have my doll house," Fancy said suddenly, looking for the first time squarely at Aunt Fanny. "I have my beautiful little doll house with real doorknobs and electric lights and the little stove that really works and the running water in the bathtubs."

"You are a fortunate child," Miss Ogilvie said.

"And all the little dolls. One of them," Fancy giggled, "is lying in the little bathtub with the water really running. They're little doll house dolls. They fit exactly into the chairs and the beds. They have little dishes. When I put them to bed they have to go to bed. When my grandmother dies all *this* is going to belong to me."

"And where would we be then?" Essex asked softly. "Fancy?"

Fancy smiled at him. "When my grandmother dies," she said, "I am going to smash my doll house. I won't need it any more."

Essex lay absolutely still in the dark, thinking that if no sound or movement could be heard outside the door he would be safe; always, when he held himself this still he hoped that he might be really dead.

"Essex," Aunt Fanny whispered, tapping softly, "Essex, please let me in?"

At first, sometimes, Essex had tried to answer her. "Go away, Aunt Fanny," he would say; "Aunt Fanny, go away from here." Now, however, he knew that he was safer if he did not speak or move; he might even be dead.

"Essex—I'm only forty-eight years old. Essex?"

I am enclosed in the tight impersonal weight of a coffin, Essex thought; there is thick earth above me.

"Orianna is older than I am. Essex?"

I cannot turn, cannot move my head; if my eyes are open I do not know it; I dare not move my hand to feel the holding wood around me.

"Essex? Essex?"

I will try to speak into the deafening silence; I will try to move and turn my head and raise my hands and I will be held tight, tight.

"Let me in, Essex—you can stay on in the house with me."

It was very early in the morning, so early that there was no clear light. On the terrace and on the long lawn it was dark, and only a certain knowledge that the sun rose every morning

could give any hint of brightness. Aunt Fanny, who had sat all
night inside her dead mother's bedroom, and Fancy, who had
awakened and stolen softly away from her sleeping mother, met
and startled one another on the terrace. At first each of them
saw only a dark figure, and then Aunt Fanny said "Fancy?"
whispering, "what are you doing out here?"

"I was playing," Fancy said evasively.

"Playing? At this hour?" Aunt Fanny took Fancy's hand and
led her down the terrace steps. "Come away from the house,
Fancy; we'll go into the gardens. What were you playing?"

Fancy smiled provokingly. "Just playing," she said.

"Who told you all of this would belong to you someday?"
Aunt Fanny asked suddenly, stopping her walk to stand and
look down at Fancy. "Your mother? It must have been. I suppose your mother thinks she has a claim. Let's walk down the
side path, dear; Aunt Fanny likes the secret garden early in the
morning. Now, a little girl ten years old with a mother and a
grandfather and an Aunt Fanny to look after her shouldn't be
always thinking about what she is going to get someday. We
all love you, you know that? Aunt Fanny loves you."

It was almost too dark to see the path, but Aunt Fanny
could see Fancy's face turned to her, curiously. She does not
have the family charm, Aunt Fanny thought, and sighed. Then
Aunt Fanny stumbled, and thought, perhaps it is still too dark
to go down these side paths, but now it was as far to go back
as to go on. Looking upward, to see if it was getting any
lighter, Aunt Fanny made small sounds of irritation. The gardeners were growing careless with these walks far from the
house; perhaps they knew that only Aunt Fanny habitually
came along these ways, because the hedges beside the path had
not been clipped smooth, making a straight green wall on either side; indeed, when Aunt Fanny looked up she could see
that the hedges had been allowed to grow almost wild; were,
in fact, in some places meeting overhead, darkening the path
and giving an air of gloom to a walk which should have been
agreeable and refreshing. "My father," Aunt Fanny said aloud,
"would not have tolerated this; Fancy, look there: the turnings
of this walk should be perfect, lending themselves to a gentle

easy saunter, and here we are slapped and confused. I wish," Aunt Fanny said, "that my father could see what has been done to the gardens."

"There's a gardener," Fancy said.

It was not until that moment, Aunt Fanny thought, that the faint depression she had been feeling deepened and centered and became conscious; walking in the gardens had always made Aunt Fanny feel happy, but when Fancy pointed out the gardener Aunt Fanny at the same time recognized that they had somehow strayed off the side path and were lost, perhaps even wandering onto someone else's property, although, as she told herself at once, they had not gone through the wall so it was really all right; certainly they had not been gone ten minutes from the house, and the Halloran property did not end ten minutes from the house in any direction.

"Fancy," she said uneasily, "I really think we had better go back," but Fancy had run on ahead. There was light now, of a sort, but it was growing misty, and, with the green branches now reaching most frighteningly over her head and the faint touches of mist curling around the tips of leaves and through the branches and even almost hiding Fancy's feet as she ran, Aunt Fanny became, quickly and most pressingly, nervous, and, worse, bewildered. "Fancy," she called, "come back at once," but Fancy, as in a dream, ran on, always too far ahead to catch, running ankle deep through the mist, turning and even laughing as she ran ahead between the hedges; "Fancy," Aunt Fanny called, hurrying, "come back."

Then she too saw the gardener; he was standing on a ladder some distance down the path, and he was clipping the hedge. Aunt Fanny was perplexed, wondering how Fancy could have seen him before, so far back among the twisting curves of the path, but Fancy was running to him now, laughing, and Aunt Fanny, gasping, hurried on. Fancy caught the bottom of the gardener's ladder and spoke to him, laughing, and the gardener turned and looked down at her and nodded and pointed. When Aunt Fanny came up he turned back to the hedge and raised his clipper again. "Fancy," Aunt Fanny said, pulling at her, "come away at once. We do not run and laugh before the

gardeners," she said severely but softly, "Fancy, we always observe decorum; I am displeased that you should have run away
from me."

"I wanted to ask him the way," Fancy said. She was walking
quietly now, her cheeks faintly flushed from running. "Didn't
you think he was funny?"

"I hardly noticed, Fancy. One does not—"

"Dressed funny, I mean? And his hat?"

"I said, Fancy, I do not—"

"Look at him, then." Fancy stopped, and shook at Aunt
Fanny. "Look and see how funny he is."

"Look back on a gardener? I?" Aunt Fanny gave Fancy an
irritable little pull. "Fancy, behave yourself."

"He's gone now, anyway." Fancy moved slightly ahead and
then said, "Why, here's the garden; I didn't know we were so
near it." She moved between the arching branches overhead,
the mist moving around her ankles, and Aunt Fanny, annoyed
and frightened and tired, hurried to keep up with her; it would
not do to let Fancy stray too far. A little girl and a defenseless
woman, Aunt Fanny thought with sudden acute fear; strange
gardeners around (and there *had* been something funny, Fancy
was right—was it the turn of his head?), and neither of them
sure of the way back.

"Please wait, Fancy," she called, and followed, into the garden, and stopped. This was not her secret garden, this was
not the garden which ought to have been at the end of the
path they had taken, this was a garden so secret that Aunt
Fanny wondered, shocked, if anyone had ever seen it before.
Fancy, half-hidden in the mist, was dancing on the grass, and
there were flowers, dull in the mist, but showing sullenly red
and yellow and orange. Distantly, clouded, Aunt Fanny saw
the hard whiteness of marble, and then through a break in the
mist a narrow marble pillar. "Fancy," she cried out, moving
forward and holding her hands guardingly before her, "where
are you?"

"Here," Fancy called back.

"Where?"

"In the house."

The voice died away and Aunt Fanny, tangled in mist now, began to cry helplessly. "Fancy," she said.

"Aunt Fanny," but it came from far away.

Stumbling, Aunt Fanny went forward, hands out, and touched marble, but it was warm and she took her hand away quickly; hideous, she thought, it's been in the sun. Then she thought, why, this could be the summer house and I am only turned around; we could have strayed from the path and come into the garden by another way and *that* would be why it looked strange; this is certainly the summer house and it is silly of me to cry and stumble and be frightened. I shall go into the summer house, she thought, and sit down quietly on the bench, and when I have recovered myself I shall either call until Fancy finds her way to me—the wicked girl, to run away so—or I shall wait until this mist clears a little—and it *must*, of course; it is an early morning mist, a trifle; the sun will sweep it away; I have been in fogs many times worse than this and never been frightened; it was only because it was unexpected; I shall sit in the summer house until I am able to go on.

For a minute she stood very still with her eyes closed, trying to remember precisely the secret garden so that she might go into the summer house correctly in the mist. I must not fall down, she thought, because I shall not be able to get up again; if I fall down it will really be quite serious; I would have to call for help.

"Fancy," she called, "Fancy!"

Moving blindly, trying, although she could not, to watch her feet, trying not to stumble, she moved carefully and with extreme slowness around the summer house, remembering distinctly the pillars, the dark bushes on all sides, the four poplars around, the two low marble steps. If I sit in the summer house in the secret garden, she was telling herself reassuringly, if I go into the summer house from the secret garden, if I go into the summer house through the secret garden, I need only take four steps across the marble floor, four small steps across the marble floor and from the other side of the summer house I can look out over the long lawn and up the far lawn and past the pool and I will see the sundial and then the house.

If I get into the summer house even the mist cannot stop me from seeing the house, and I can go down the two low marble steps on the other side and out onto the lovely long lawn and go straight, right down the middle of the lawn, even through mist, past the sundial, and go to the house.

Fancy, she realized, had probably gone that way already. Fancy was almost surely halfway home.

She stumbled, and put out her hand to catch herself against the marble pillar, but the mist cleared briefly and she saw that she had caught hold of the long marble thigh of a statue; standing soberly on his pedestal, the tall still creature looked down on her tenderly. The marble was warm, and Aunt Fanny drew her hand back and screamed "Fancy, Fancy!" There was no answer, and she turned and ran madly, putting her feet down on flowers and catching herself against ornamental bushes; "Fancy!" she screamed, taking hold of an outstretched marble hand beside her, "Fancy!" stopping just short of a yearning marble embrace, "Fancy!" and turned away crazily from a marble mouth reaching for her throat.

"Aunt Fanny?"

"Fancy! Where are you?"

"In the house."

"Please come back, Fancy; please come back." She was by a marble bench. Its back and sides were stained and uncared-for; there was a crack running clearly down one leg, there were dead leaves lying along the seat and heaped in the corners. Thankfully Aunt Fanny sat down; the bench was warm, and she moved, huddling herself together, sitting only on the edge of the bench. This is unspeakable, she thought; am I in the family graveyard? Why is this happening?

Unexpectedly, she thought of Essex—the path gets narrower all the time, she told herself—and was reassured. He will laugh at me, she thought; I must control myself. She forced herself to sit up primly on the edge of the marble bench, repressing firmly the nausea she felt at its warm pressure, and she smoothed the black linen of her dress across her lap, and tucked in her hair, which had somehow come loose, and crossed her ankles decently, and took her black-edged handkerchief from her bosom and dried her eyes and wiped away the dampness and grime from her face. Now, she thought; I may go mad, but at least I look like a lady.

A certain unfamiliar humor had come upon her with the thought of Essex; if he were here, she reflected, we would be sitting together on this marble bench and no one could see us in the mist. We would be in a deeply hidden garden—she could catch, now, the heavy sweetness of roses—and on a fair low seat, the marble warm beneath our hands. Distantly, she heard the music of a fountain, the touch of water upon itself, the low murmur of the fall. It came, perhaps, through the lifted curved hands of a marble nymph, running down her arms and over her shoulders and breast and clothing her in water falling softly, falling on and on. Then it might overflow one wide pool and fall on, down, into the reaching stone arms of a satyr who pushed upward to catch both hands full of water and let it fall gently against the arched backs and lifted heads of the dolphins who held him. Then, past the frozen dolphins, across the wide pool and on, down and down, into a great cup held by two maidens, overflowing the cup, going always past their stone smiling faces, their hard curls, on down and down over rocks and marble lilies, under and around marble fish and between the long legs of stone birds, necks always bent, heads always turned curiously. Far, far beyond, in a long sweet movement from the high curved hands of the nymph past the satyr, over the dolphins, between the maidens, leaving behind the lilies and the rocks and the fish and the birds, the moving water must be caught and imprisoned at last in a final narrowing agonizing eddy, twisted and trapped and forced down, pushed underground to run secretly and flow, perhaps, into the ornamental pool before the house, colored blue, and moving only faintly under the wind.

Roses, she thought: I would like to give Essex a rose. She put her head gently back against the marble bench, tears on her cheeks, and listened to the drops of water singing as they went down the fountain ("Frances, I have waited for you so long . . ." "Impatient, Essex?" "Impatient? Say rather mad . . .

burning . . ."). She stirred, and smiled, and lifted her hand in tender protest, and looked upon the marble jeering face of a fiend, set into a shrine beside the bench, roses growing low against his head, dead petals caught between his thrusting teeth.

"Fancy," she called, screaming, "Fancy, Fancy!"

The moving water in the fountain called "Fancy, Fancy" faintly, and the tortured marble face was warm.

"Aunt Fanny?"

"Please help me. Please come; please hurry!"

"I'm in the house."

"Hurry!"

"I'm coming. I'm holding out my hand. It's all right, Aunt Fanny, I'm right here."

And Aunt Fanny, turning, took hold of Fancy's hand, and it was warm marble; far away, she heard Fancy's mocking laughter and her voice singing.

Somehow, sobbing, Aunt Fanny came through the mist and into the summer house and in four wide steps was running down the lawn toward the sundial in the darkness, and then she heard a voice. It was huge, not Fancy at all, echoing and sounding around and in and out of her head: FRANCES HALLORAN, it came to her, FRANCES, FRANCES HALLORAN. Twisting as she ran, moving wildly, she put out her hands; FRANCES HALLORAN, the voice went on, FRANCES.

FRANCES HALLORAN: she was gasping dreadfully for breath, one shoe lost and the grass unexpectedly wet under her stocking: FRANCES HALLORAN, and then she stopped absolutely. There was something there in the darkness hard by the sundial, not a statue, not Essex: "Who?" Aunt Fanny said, cold.

"Frances Halloran—" Remotely.

This was fear so complete that Aunt Fanny, once Frances Halloran, stood with nothing but ice to clothe her; *was* there something there? Something? Then she thought with what seemed shocking clarity: it is worse if it is not there; somehow it must be real because if it is not real it is in my own head; unable to move, Aunt Fanny thought: It is real.

"Frances?"

Aunt Fanny moved one hand, blindly. "Father?" she said, without sound. "Father?"

"Frances, there is danger. Go back to the house. Tell them, in the house, tell them, in the house, tell them that there is danger. Tell them in the house that in the house it is safe. The father will watch the house, but there is danger. Tell them."

Am I hearing this? Aunt Fanny thought lucidly, and then, fumbling, "Father?"

"The father comes to his child and says gently that within himself there is no fear; the father comes to his child. Tell them in the house that there is danger."

"Danger? Father?"

"From the sky and from the ground and from the sea there is danger; tell them in the house. There will be black fire and red water and the earth turning and screaming; this will come."

"Father—Father—when?"

"The father comes to his children and tells them there is danger. There is danger. Within the father there is no fear; the father comes to his children. Tell them in the house."

"Please—"

"When the sky is fair again the children will be safe; the father comes to his children who will be saved. Tell them in the house that they will be saved. Do not let them leave the house; say to them: Do not fear, the father will guard the children. Go into your father's house and say these things. Tell them there is danger."

Aunt Fanny, formerly Frances Halloran, put her hand down onto the sundial and found it warm. "Father?" she said into the sudden bright sunlight, but there was nothing there. "You were never so kind to me before," said Aunt Fanny brokenly.

Then, screaming for Essex, she fled, and crashed against the terrace door and wildly pounded it open, to stop in complete silence, staring madly at the astonished faces around the breakfast table, eyes wide, mouths open, regarding her.

"I want to tell you," Aunt Fanny said and then—to the embarrassed surprise of everyone in the room, none of whom had ever had any occasion to believe that Aunt Fanny was capable of a single, definite, clear-cut, unembellished act—Aunt Fanny fainted.

2

Essex carried Aunt Fanny into the drawing room, since it was the nearest place with a couch to put her on; Miss Ogilvie followed, panting, with a glass of water, Fancy tagged curiously, Maryjane brought two aspirin from the bottle she always carried in her pocket, and Mrs. Halloran, finishing her coffee without haste, came into the drawing room at last to find Aunt Fanny, surrounded, on the couch, turning and twisting her head and murmuring incoherently.

"Chafe her wrists and loosen her stays," Mrs. Halloran suggested, seating herself in an armchair from which she could observe Aunt Fanny, "burn a feather under her nose. Raise her feet. Please do not neglect any possible attention; I would not have Aunt Fanny think that we took her malaise lightly."

"Something has clearly frightened her out of her senses," Miss Ogilvie said, more sharply than she customarily spoke to Mrs. Halloran.

"A feat," said Mrs. Halloran. "Incredible."

"It was my father," Aunt Fanny said clearly. She sat up, resisting Miss Ogilvie and Maryjane, and looked directly at Mrs. Halloran. "My father was there," she said.

"I hope you gave him my dutiful regards," Mrs. Halloran said.

"By the sundial, waiting for me; he called me and called me." Aunt Fanny began to cry. "You wicked wicked *wicked* girl," she said to Fancy.

"What did *I* do?" Fancy said, staring, and Maryjane put an arm around her daughter and said, "Now you just wait one little damn minute here."

"She ran away," Aunt Fanny said, "and left me all alone and I was lost."

"Lost?" Mrs. Halloran said. "You have lived here for forty years, Aunt Fanny; what part of the place could lose you now?"

"I never ran away," Fancy said. "I did not."

"She did not," Maryjane said.

"She did so," Aunt Fanny said. "There was a gardener on a ladder clipping the hedge and Fancy ran away."

Mrs. Halloran frowned. "When, Fanny?" she asked. "When did all this happen?"

"Just now—this morning. It was just getting light."

"No," Mrs. Halloran said. "There are no gardeners working on the hedges yet. Your brother wants me to speak to them today."

"On a ladder," Aunt Fanny said.

"Quite impossible," Mrs. Halloran said. "You may very well have seen your father; I would not dream of disputing a private apparition. But you could not have seen a gardener trimming a hedge. Not here, not today."

"Fancy saw him," Aunt Fanny said wildly.

"I did not," Fancy said. "I never saw anyone this morning except my mother and my grandmother and Miss Ogilvie and Essex—"

"We went for a walk," Aunt Fanny said.

"I did *not* go for any walk," Fancy said.

"She has been with me since I woke up," Maryjane said with finality.

"The secret garden was changed, and it was dark and the mist—"

"Aunt Fanny," Essex said, bending over her sympathetically, "suppose you tell us just what happened. Slowly, and try not to cry."

"Essex," said Aunt Fanny, crying.

"She is hysterical," said Mrs. Halloran. "Slap her quite firmly in the face."

"Please, Aunt Fanny. Tell us exactly."

Aunt Fanny caught her breath and accepted a handkerchief from Miss Ogilvie to wipe her eyes. Then, although her voice was trembling, she said, "I could not sleep. I thought I would go for a walk. It was very dark, and misty, but I knew the sun was going to rise soon. I met Fancy on the terrace—"

"You did not."

"Fancy, why don't you tell the truth? I'm not blaming you; Aunt Fanny *loves* you."

"But I *did*n't."

"Go on, Aunt Fanny," Essex said. "We'll sort it all out later."

"We walked down the side path, toward the secret garden. Then we saw the gardener and Fancy said he looked funny."

"I *did*n't."

"You *did*, you bad wicked girl. And we came to the garden, but it was changed. Dirty. Horrible. I was lost, and I couldn't find the way out, and Fancy ran away and I called her and called her and there were hundreds and hundreds of statues and they were warm." Aunt Fanny shivered. "And I couldn't find the summer house and I sat on a bench and thought about Essex and how he might help me—"

"I am not sure how much of this nonsense I can hear," Mrs. Halloran said.

"—and then I found the summer house and started to run to the house but it was so dark and the mist was so thick and when I came to the sundial my father was there."

"I saw her running," Miss Ogilvie said. "At the breakfast table, I glanced out and thought, 'There comes Aunt Fanny, running down the lawn.' I confess I was startled. But it was quite light."

"The sun has been shining brightly for two hours," Essex said. "There is not a cloud in the sky."

"It was dark," Aunt Fanny said.

"I saw you quite clearly running down the lawn," Miss Ogilvie said. "The sun was shining and I thought, 'There comes Aunt Fanny, running down the lawn.'"

"What did your father have to say?" Mrs. Halloran inquired curiously. "I hope he sent his best to the rest of us?"

Aunt Fanny sat up suddenly, staring. "I forgot," she said. "I forgot to tell you, all of you, and I was supposed to bring the message right back here." She began to cry again. "He will be angry," she said.

"Well, tell us now," Essex said. He glanced at Mrs. Halloran and said quietly, "I wonder if we should have a doctor?"

"An alienist," Mrs. Halloran said, and snorted. "Gardeners working before breakfast," she said.

"He said to tell you there was danger. He said—" Aunt Fanny, wringing her hands, tried to be exact, "—he said there was danger, but this house was safe. That he would protect us. He said it over and over again, that there was danger but this house was safe. He said we must stay in the house."

"Did he *indeed?*" Mrs. Halloran said, and Essex, looking over his shoulder, laughed at her.

"He said fire would come, and he said it would be black fire. He said there was danger, and he would protect the house, and we are not to leave the house."

"Can you get a message back to him?" Mrs. Halloran inquired. "Because *I* would like you to tell him that, danger or no danger—"

Miss Ogilvie screamed and scrambled up onto a chair. Maryjane clutched at Essex, and even Mrs. Halloran rose. A small brightly-banded snake was watching them from the fireplace, seemingly frozen with attention, and then, turning at once into liquid movement, slipped from the fireplace across the heavy carpet, within a foot of Mrs. Halloran's shoe, and, without hesitation, angled behind a bookcase and disappeared.

"Good God," Mrs. Halloran said. "Merciful God. Essex!"

Essex disengaged himself from Maryjane with some difficulty and said, "Mrs. Halloran?"

"What was that?"

"A snake. It came out of the fireplace and went across the room and behind the bookcase."

"I *know* it was a snake, but—in *my* house?"

"A snake, a snake," cried Miss Ogilvie, clinging precariously to the back of the chair and seemingly determined to climb right on up the wall, "it will bite us; it was a snake, a snake!"

"Blasphemy," Essex said politely to Mrs. Halloran. "Sent, no doubt, by the noble ghost you were mocking. You should pay more attention to what you are saying."

"*You* did it," Maryjane said violently to Mrs. Halloran, "*you* were making fun of Aunt Fanny's father, but *I* think we've had a warning and believe you me I'm not going to need a second one, believe you *me*. I say I am going to stay right here in this house where it's safe and no one, not even you, is going to kick me out of it to face the danger he said was coming, not out into any fire." She clasped Fancy to her and her hands were shaking. "Fancy stays and I stay," she said.

"I will have this room fumigated," Mrs. Halloran said.

"You won't find that snake," Aunt Fanny said dreamily. "It was shining, full of light. You won't ever find it."

"Essex," Mrs. Halloran said.

"Mrs. Halloran?"

"I am bewildered. Come into the library and explain all this to me."

The question of belief is a curious one, partaking of the wonders of childhood and the blind hopefulness of the very old; in all the world there is not someone who does not believe something. It might be suggested, and not easily disproven that anything, no matter how exotic, can be believed by someone. On the other hand, abstract belief is largely impossible; it is the concrete, the actuality of the cup, the candle, the sacrificial stone, which hardens belief; the statue is nothing until it cries, the philosophy is nothing until the philosopher is martyred.

Not one of the people in Mrs. Halloran's house could have answered honestly and without embarrassment the question: "In what is it you believe?" Faith they had in plenty; just as they had food and beds and shelter, they had faith, but it was faith in agreeably concrete things like good food and the best beds and the most weathertight shelter and in themselves as suitable recipients of the world's best. Old Mr. Halloran, for one, would have been considerably more lighthearted in a faith which promised him everlasting life, but in the concept of everlasting life Mr. Halloran could not believe, since he was dying. His own life showed no signs of continuing beyond a hideously limited interval, and the only evidence he ever saw of ever-lasting life was in those luckier ones around him who continued young and would stay so after he was dead. Not-dying from day to day was as much as Mr. Halloran could be fairly expected to believe in; the rest of them believed in what they could—power, perhaps, or the comforting effects of gin, or money.

Fancy was a liar. She had been with Aunt Fanny and dared not admit to running away. She had not been frightened, but she enjoyed teasing people weaker than herself. Not a servant, or an animal, or any child in the village near the house, would willingly go near her.

Being impossible, an abstract belief can only be trusted through its manifestations, the actual shape of the god perceived, how-ever dimly, against the solidity he displaces. Not one of the people around Aunt Fanny believed her father's warning, but they were all afraid of the snake. Miss Ogilvie, indeed, never again sat in that corner of the drawing room near the snake's book-case, although it had formerly been one of her favorite spots.

"It could have been in the firewood," Essex said, pacing the library floor.

"But the gardener could not have been clipping the hedge," Mrs. Halloran said.

"I have no idea what to think. Aunt Fanny has behaved very strangely."

"I will not dispute *that*. Essex, you may stay."

Essex was silent. Then he said, "People can be persuaded to accept almost anything. Last night I thought myself degraded, fouled, rendered contemptible, cringing. Today Aunt Fanny and her snake have enlightened me; two catastrophes cannot make a right, but I think I had never any expectation of leaving. Aunt Fanny has been very kind."

"I genuinely hope she will feel better," Mrs. Halloran said. "Now I will have to let Miss Ogilvie stay, and Maryjane."

But Aunt Fanny continued very odd. Physically, she was well enough to make it unnecessary to call a doctor, but she went about smiling and happy, almost gay. She laughed like a young girl who has found a first lover, she ate hugely of pancakes for her late breakfast, she sang. Mrs. Halloran believed she had gone mad, but Aunt Fanny mad was so much more palatable than Aunt Fanny sane that Mrs. Halloran bit her tongue, averted her eyes, and winced only occasionally.

Immediately after her breakfast, which everyone had stayed to watch her eat, Aunt Fanny fell asleep, her head on the table, a smile on her face. Asleep, she spoke at length, and, although afterward none of them could remember with exactness the words Aunt Fanny used, they sat appalled and frightened, and certainly heard Aunt Fanny speak as she never had before.

Aunt Fanny was listening to her father, repeating to them what he told her. With a happy smile on her face and her eyes shut, she listened with a child's care, and spoke slowly, word for word. Aunt Fanny's father had come to tell these people that the world outside was ending. Neither Aunt Fanny nor her father expressed any apprehension, but the world which had seemed so unassailable to the rest of them, the usual, daily world of houses and cities and people and all the small fragments of living, was to be destroyed in one night of utter disaster. Aunt Fanny smiled, and nodded, and listened, and told them about the end of the world.

At one point she said sadly, "All those poor people, dying at once," and, again, "We must consider ourselves extremely fortunate."

Those few people gathered in Mrs. Halloran's house, which Aunt Fanny now seemed to believe was her father's house, would be safe. The house would be guarded during the night of destruction and at its end they would emerge safe and pure. They were charged with the future of humanity; when they came forth from the house it would be into a world clean and

silent, their inheritance. "And breed a new race of mankind,"
Aunt Fanny said with sweetness.

Immediately following this revelation, Aunt Fanny, waking,
asked for and drank a small glass of brandy, after which she
retired to her room and fell into a deep sleep which lasted until
late afternoon. While Aunt Fanny slept, Fancy played with her
doll house and then went down into the kitchen, where she
was not welcome. Miss Ogilvie washed out the underwear she
had worn the day before, and used a small hand iron to finish
up the underwear already dry. Maryjane lay on the chaise in
her bedroom, reading a true confession magazine brought her
secretly by one of the maids, and eating peanut brittle. Essex
sat in the library under a bust of Seneca and did a crossword
puzzle. Mr. Halloran dozed before the fire in his room, and
wondered that the years had been so short. Mrs. Halloran sat
long alone, her open hand resting on the pages of a Bible she
had not opened, or even remembered, for many years.

When Aunt Fanny awakened she was perfectly aware of
all that had happened, including her own revelations, and—
probably resembling in this all souls who have been the vehicle
of a major supernatural pronouncement—her first reaction of
shivering terror was almost at once replaced by a feeling of
righteous complacence. She did not know why these extraordi-
nary messages had been sent through her own frail self, but
she believed without question that the choice had been good.
She was completely subject to some greater power and, her
own will somewhere buried in that which controlled her, she
could only become autocratic and demanding.

For a few minutes she lay quietly on her bed, wondering, and
then she rose and went to look at herself in the mirror. There
seemed as yet no outward change to her, so she thought to put
on her dead mother's jewels, and, at last, decked in diamonds
never cleaned since they were put away on her mother's death,
Aunt Fanny made her way upstairs to the wing which was occupied by Maryjane and Fancy. She knocked on the door of
their sitting room, and heard Maryjane ask who it was, then
tell Fancy to get up and unlock the door.

"It is Aunt Fanny, my dears," Aunt Fanny said, and the door was opened. Fancy had been putting away her doll house, and Maryjane was lying back, her confession magazine underneath her. "Aunt Fanny," said Maryjane. "It was kind of you to come. My asthma is worse, much worse. Will you tell them downstairs?"

"But now you may give up having asthma, Maryjane," Aunt Fanny said.

"Why?" Maryjane sat up. "Is she dead?"

"You know perfectly well," Aunt Fanny said irritably, "that she is well on her way to being reborn into a new life and joy."

"Reborn?" Maryjane fell back. "That's *all* I need," she said.

"Shall I push her down the stairs?" Fancy asked, as one repeating an incantation rather than as one asking a question; perhaps she had to recite this regularly to her mother.

"Is Fancy subnormal, do you think?" Aunt Fanny asked.

"She's Lionel's own child," Maryjane said.

"Well, tell her to stop saying that. Evil, and jealousy, and fear, are all going to be removed from us. I told you clearly this morning. Humanity, as an experiment, has failed."

"Well, I'm sure I did the best *I* could," Maryjane said.

"Do you understand that this world will be destroyed? Soon?"

"I just couldn't care less," Maryjane said. "Unless they save a special thunderbolt for *her*."

"Everything, Aunt Fanny?" Fancy was pulling at her sleeve. "The whole thing? All the parts I've never seen?"

"All of it, dear. It has been a bad and wicked and selfish place, and the beings who created it have decided that it will never get any better. So they are going to burn it, the way you might burn a toy full of disease germs. Do you remember when you had the measles? Your grandmother took your teddy bear and had it put in the incinerator, because it was full of germs?"

"I remember," Fancy said grimly.

"Well, that is just what they are going to do with this diseased, filthy old world. Right in the incinerator."

"Did your father really tell you all this?" Maryjane asked.

"It is as though something I had known all my life, and believed without ever really knowing what it was—some lovely, precious secret—had suddenly come into the open. When my father spoke to me he only reminded me of what I had always known, and forgotten. I am very happy about it."

"Who is 'they'?" Fancy asked insistently.

Aunt Fanny shook her head. "I am sure we will hear more about it," she said.

"What *I* don't see," Maryjane said petulantly, "is how it is going to help my asthma. Lionel used to rub my ankles."

Aunt Fanny put her hand gently on Maryjane's arm. "Those who survive this catastrophe," she said, "will be free of pain and hurt. They will be . . . a kind of chosen people, as it were."

"The Jews?" Maryjane said indifferently. "Weren't they chosen the last time?"

"I *wish* you would take me seriously," Aunt Fanny said, her voice sharpening. "It's not as though *I* had any choice in all this, I *only* say what I'm told, after *all*. Naturally you are included in any plan for the inhabitants of this house, but I can hardly see what earthly use you will be to us if you persist in saying every silly thing that comes into your head. After all, Maryjane, I am *sure* that there must be a great many people who would be *glad* to be saved when the world is destroyed. After *all*," and she rose and turned to the door.

"You're wearing your mother's diamonds," Maryjane said. "You know by rights they should have come to me. Lionel always said so."

"I'm interested," Fancy said. "Aunt Fanny, I'm *terribly* interested. It ought to be a pretty big fire."

"Dreadful," said Aunt Fanny.

"I'd like to see it," Fancy said.

"Well, I'm sure your Aunt Fanny will let you watch," Maryjane said. "Fanny, if you're going downstairs remind them about my tray, will you?"

Aunt Fanny swept downstairs and into the drawing room where Essex and Miss Ogilvie were drinking martinis with Mrs. Halloran. Essex, moving belatedly to hold the door for Aunt Fanny, was caught helpless, holding his glass aimlessly while Aunt Fanny passed him regally to take her chair unassisted.

"A truly unusual day, Orianna," she said. "Essex."

Essex sat down.

Aunt Fanny gestured to Essex, said "A glass of sherry, if you please," and then, to Mrs. Halloran, "Now that we know what is going to happen, Orianna, I think we had better decide where we stand."

"If I did not detect somewhere in that the air of a prepared speech," Mrs. Halloran said, "I would be afraid of you, Fanny."

"Thank you, Essex." Aunt Fanny noticed Miss Ogilvie nodded, and went on, "There will be no more of *that*, Orianna. You will be civil."

Mrs. Halloran opened her mouth and closed it again.

"Let us not forget that your origins are low," Aunt Fanny said. "There are areas of refinement not possible to one of your background. One area of refinement," she explained with sweet patience, "is—if you will permit me to put a name to it—the supernormal. *There* you must allow *me* superiority, and it is the supernormal which has laid siege to this house, and captured it undefended. A little more, please, Essex?"

"I have never seen this before," Essex observed to the sherry decanter. "Aunt Fanny is possessed."

"Drinking spirits," Miss Ogilvie said, nodding wisely.

"Spirits indeed," Aunt Fanny said. She smiled approvingly at Miss Ogilvie. "We are in a pocket of time, Orianna, a tiny segment of time suddenly pinpointed by a celestial eye."

"Now, you cannot suspect *that* of being a prepared speech," Essex said to Mrs. Halloran.

"I wish Aunt Fanny would stop babbling sacrilegious nonsense," Mrs. Halloran said, and there was an ominous note in her voice.

"Call it nonsense, Orianna, say—as you have before—that Aunt Fanny is running in crazed spirits, but—although I am of course not permitted to threaten—all the regret will be yours."

"I feel it already," Mrs. Halloran said.

"The experiment with humanity is at an end," Aunt Fanny said.

"Splendid," Mrs. Halloran said. "I was getting very tired of all of them."

"The imbalance of the universe is being corrected. Dislocations have been adjusted. Harmony is to be restored, inperfections erased."

"*I* wonder if anything has been done about the hedges," Mrs. Halloran said. "Essex, did you speak to the gardeners?"

"The ways of the gods are inscrutable," Aunt Fanny said, her voice high.

"Inscrutable, indeed," Mrs. Halloran said. "I personally would never have made such a choice. Put it, Aunt Fanny, since you will not be silent, that the first harmony to be established is that between you and myself."

"I cannot be silenced," Aunt Fanny said, shouting, "I cannot be silenced; this is my father's house and I am safe here. No one can drive me away."

"Distasteful," said Mrs. Halloran, shrugging. "Essex, will you fill my glass? And I believe Aunt Fanny will have more sherry. We have time before dinner. Miss Ogilvie?"

"She is doing it again," Essex said later, coming to stand by Mrs. Halloran on the terrace. "Listening. Nodding."

"If anything had been needed to perfect Aunt Fanny's exquisite charm," Mrs. Halloran said, "it would be this prophetic lunacy."

"*I* believe she has lost her mind," Essex said.

Mrs. Halloran turned to move slowly down the wide marble steps, and Essex came soundlessly beside her. "It is a lovely night," Mrs. Halloran said. "Aunt Fanny may be certifiable, certainly. It is not impossible in my husband's family. But it is irrelevant."

"If Aunt Fanny is *not* mad," Essex said. "Had it occurred to you? We may expect a world cataclysm in the very near future. Unless of course it is not impossible that in your husband's family they may be mistaken."

"What concerns me most is her defiance," Mrs. Halloran said. "It is not usual in Aunt Fanny."

"I suppose the destruction of the world will not turn on Aunt Fanny's manners. I would not let her mingle freely with your friends, however, or at least not with strangers."

"Essex," Mrs. Halloran said. She stopped by the sundial and put her hand down gently; under her fingers the letters said WHAT IS THIS WORLD? "Essex, I am not a fool. I have gone for many years disbelieving most of what people told me. But I have never before been requested to take an immediate opinion on the question of the annihilation of civilization. I have never known my sister-in-law to get any message accurately, but I cannot afford to ignore her."

"Does that mean that you find yourself believing Aunt Fanny's claptrap?"

"I have no choice," Mrs. Halloran said. She moved her finger caressingly along WORLD. "Authority is of some importance to me. I will not be left behind when creatures like Aunt Fanny and her brother are introduced into a new world. I must plan to be there. Oh, what madness," she said, her voice agonized, "why could he not have come to *me?*"

After a minute Essex said, "I see. Then I suppose I must withdraw my word claptrap, and substitute something more politic."

"Claptrap will do." Mrs. Halloran laughed. "I am positive of it, but I insist upon being saved along with Aunt Fanny. I have never had any doubt of my own immortality, but put it that never before have I had any open, clear-cut invitation to the Garden of Eden; Aunt Fanny has shown me a gate."

"Then I will have to book a ticket, too. I cannot believe Aunt Fanny, but I will not doubt *you.*"

Mrs. Halloran turned and started back toward the house. "I do wish Aunt Fanny had never thought of it," she said, and sighed.

"At least we are not enjoined to live in celibate poverty," Essex said.

"I agree that I would not be so willing to believe in Aunt

Fanny if her messages dictated that I give away all my earthly possessions. But then, of course, Aunt Fanny would never accept such a message; it could not have been meant for *her*."

"I wonder if there are others. Other places, on the earth. Learning these same unbelievable things, right now."

"That presupposes the existence of other Aunt Fannys. I cannot bear to think of it."

"When we believe," Essex said seriously, "we must do so wholly. I am prepared to follow Aunt Fanny because I agree with you: it is the only positive statement about our futures we have ever heard, but once I have taken her side I will not be shaken. If I can bring myself to believe in Aunt Fanny's golden world, nothing else will ever do for me; I want it too badly."

"I wish I had your faith," Mrs. Halloran said.

3

The weather, of course, continued fair. No one could find the snake behind the bookcase, and the hedges, in particular the hedges along the walk to the secret garden, were clipped to bare bone. Aunt Fanny wore her mother's diamonds every day, even at breakfast, and wore, besides, a look of quiet satisfaction peculiarly irritating to Mrs. Halloran. Maryjane's asthma improved somewhat. Essex, who was skillful in slight arts, carved a tiny totem pole for Fancy's doll house, with a recognizable likeness of Aunt Fanny at the bottom. Mr. Halloran asked that his nurse stop reading him weekly magazines and begin on *Robinson Crusoe*, and during the long afternoons anyone passing the doorway to Mr. Halloran's sunfilled room might hear the flat level voice continuing, "A little after noon I found the sea very calm, and the tide ebbed so far out that I could come within a quarter of a mile of the ship, and here I found a fresh renewing of my grief; for I saw evidently, that if we had kept on board, we had been all safe . . ." Mrs. Halloran sketched out a rough plan for a tiny amphitheatre to be constructed on a little hill beyond the orchard, without announcing any particular design for its possible use, and one morning received word of the imminent arrival of guests.

"I am expecting guests," she said at breakfast, folding the letter carefully and putting it back into its envelope.

"Here?" said Aunt Fanny blankly.

"Where else?" said Mrs. Halloran.

"This is still a house of mourning, Orianna. Had you forgotten?"

"You never remember Lionel, Fanny, except when he might

be an inconvenience to me. I am expecting guests. A Mrs. Willow and her two daughters. Very old friends of mine."

"From another walk of life, I suppose," Aunt Fanny said with a little smile. "If they are such *very* old friends of yours."

"No, Aunt Fanny, they will not please you. How delightful that I should be in a position to entertain them even if they do not please Aunt Fanny."

"Two daughters?" said Miss Ogilvie. "Will they attend my little school for Fancy?"

"I hardly think so. The older of them must be nearly thirty, and I expect there is very little she can learn from you now, Miss Ogilvie."

"At least," said Aunt Fanny, with the same little smile, "we need not expect them to stay for long."

"I have not seen Augusta Willow for nearly fifteen years," Mrs. Halloran said with seeming irrelevancy, "but I cannot believe that she has changed *that* much."

"When are they coming?" Miss Ogilvie asked.

"The sixteenth. That would be Friday, Essex, would it not?"

A car was sent late Friday afternoon to meet Mrs. Willow and her daughters, and Maryjane finding herself unequal to meeting company so late in the day, Mrs. Halloran waited in the drawing room with Mr. Halloran by the fire, and Essex and Miss Ogilvie and Aunt Fanny to receive her very old friend, whose voice was heard from the driveway as she got out of the car, directing the disposition of numerous pieces of luggage. Mrs. Halloran smiled at Aunt Fanny, who seemed to be counting under her breath the severally designated little blue bags and large tan dress cases and hatboxes and jewelcases and overnight bags and dark red heavy cases, and said softly, "Aunt Fanny, how lucky that your father has set an arbitrary end to this visit," and then, still smiling, rose to greet her friend.

Mrs. Willow was a large and overwhelmingly vocal woman, with a great bosom and an indefinable air of having lost some vital possession down the front of it, for she shook and trembled and regarded herself with such enthusiasm, that it was all the casual observer could do at first to keep from offering to help. Whatever she had lost and was hoping to recover, it was not her good humor, for that was unlosable, and seemed, in fact, as much a matter of complete insensitivity as of good spirits; Mrs. Willow was absolutely determined to be affable, and would not be denied.

"And you *have* gotten older, Orianna," she said, entering, "how glad I am! The older we get ourselves the more we like to see it in our friends," and she smiled amply around the room, as though prepared with only the faintest encouragement to gather them all to her bosom, that repository of lost treasures, and cherish them for having grown older every minute since they were born, "and I can't say," she continued happily, "that you've done anything to improve the looks of this old place. *And* I won't say," she went on, "that Richard Halloran looks well." She nodded toward Mr. Halloran, in his wheel chair by the fire.

"This is a house of mourning, ma'am," Aunt Fanny said.

"And *this* is Aunt Fanny. My sister-in-law," Mrs. Halloran said. "I had forgotten what a disturbance you make, Augusta."

"Don't I?" said Mrs. Willow. She turned slowly, to regard with individual speculation each person in the room. "Who's that young man?" she asked, as one going directly to the heart of a problem.

"Essex," Mrs. Halloran said, and Essex bowed, speechless.

"Miss Ogilvie," Mrs. Halloran said; Miss Ogilvie fluttered, looked for help to Richard Halloran, and made a weak smile.

"You remember my gels?" Mrs. Willow asked, gesturing. "That one's Arabella, the pretty one, and the dark one's Julia. Curtsey to your Aunt Orianna, pets."

"Do try to call me Mrs. Halloran," Mrs. Halloran said to the two girls. These, accustomed to the manners of their mother, tended clearly to underestimate the rest of the world; the dark one, who was Julia, nodded gracelessly, said, "Hello," and turned away. Arabella, who was the pretty one, smiled prettily, her eye falling—as perhaps it had not before—upon Essex, behind Mrs. Halloran's chair. "How do you do?" she said.

"Well." Mrs. Willow, having surveyed the room and the people in it, turned back to Mrs. Halloran. "Pretty dull here, are you? You like my gels, Orianna?"

"Not so far," said Mrs. Halloran. "Of course, it is not impossible that they may improve upon further acquaintance."

"Richard," said Mrs. Willow, going to him by the fire, "you remember me? Do you keep well? I can't say you *look* fit."

"My brother is grieving, ma'am," said Aunt Fanny.

"It's Augusta, is it not?" Richard Halloran said, looking up. "They think I am unable to remember, Augusta, but I remember *you* clearly; you wore a red dress and the sun was shining."

Mrs. Willow laughed hugely. "I've come back to cheer you a little, Richard."

"Do *you* remember," Richard Halloran asked, raising his eyes to Mrs. Willow, "when we rang the bells over the carriage house?"

"Do I not," said Mrs. Willow comfortably. "Ah, you used to be a gay one, Richard. Plenty of pranks in *your* time, I'll be bound. But you're too warm here by the fire; you," she gestured to Essex, "come and help me move his chair."

"If you please," Aunt Fanny said, coming forward with dignity, "my brother is perfectly comfortable here. This is my father's house, ma'am, and my brother may sit where he pleases within it."

"Of course he may, dear," Mrs. Willow patted Aunt Fanny on the shoulder. "Just as soon as I have him a little bit away from the fire."

"*This* is what you bring into a house of mourning," Aunt Fanny said bitterly to Mrs. Halloran.

Mrs. Willow was not listening; she had moved Richard's chair enough away from the fire to allow her to stand wholly in front of the fireplace, and she lifted her skirt in back to warm her legs.

"I shall expect you to keep away from the servants, Augusta," Mrs. Halloran said.

"Well, now," and Mrs. Willow laughed, and the chandelier

jingled. "Just because of one time I could tell you about," and she turned to include the room in her confidential smile. "Imagine old Orianna remembering—I'll tell *you*," she added pointedly to Essex, "when my gels aren't around. Now," she said, "why don't we get caught up on old times? Orianna, tell me everything that's happened since I saw you last."

Arabella, who was the pretty one, was already whispering confidentially into the ear of Essex, and Julia, who was the clever one, was listening to Miss Ogilvie's whisper; "Someone to *talk* to around here," Arabella was saying, and "Snake behind the bookcase," Julia was hearing.

"I think you have quite enough company without me," Aunt Fanny said to Mrs. Halloran. "Perhaps I might be permitted to spend the evening privately with my brother?"

"Splendid," Mrs. Willow said heartily. "Poor Richard badly wants cheering. You give him a few good laughs, my dearie, and he'll perk up a wonder."

"Orianna?" said Aunt Fanny remotely.

"Of course, Aunt Fanny." Mrs. Halloran looked without fondness upon Arabella. "Richard," she asked, "shall we take you back to your room now?"

"I will not have eggs again," Richard Halloran said. "Orianna, tell them in the kitchen that I will not have eggs again."

"Certainly you will not. And Aunt Fanny will be with you; I believe that they have made you a chocolate pudding."

"Orianna," said Aunt Fanny in sudden apprehension, "where are you putting Mrs. Willow and her daughters? Naturally, in the left wing with Maryjane?"

"We must not intrude upon Maryjane's grief, Aunt Fanny. They will be at the end of the long hall near the stairway, and on the floor above you. You cannot possibly hear them."

"I *will* hear them, Orianna," Aunt Fanny said tautly. "You know perfectly well. I will hear them; my rest will be constantly disturbed."

"Then don't tell anyone what goes on." Mrs. Willow gave a huge wink and Aunt Fanny put her hand to her throat, and closed her eyes.

"Will you say goodnight, Richard?" Mrs. Halloran asked, turning the wheel chair, and Mr. Halloran bowed his head graciously and said, "Goodnight to all of you."

"Sweet dreams to you," Mrs. Willow said, and Miss Ogilvie said, "Goodnight, Mr. Halloran," and Julia and Arabella glanced up, and down again. Mrs. Halloran took the wheel chair slowly out of the room and across the hall and Aunt Fanny gave one last malevolent glance at Mrs. Willow and followed her.

"*That* was sweet of you," Julia said spitefully to her sister, "hanging around and whispering around her, and that big innocent stare."

"We're supposed to get along," Arabella said, touching her blond curls lazily.

"Trying to cut me out with her the first five minutes we're here."

"We could *see* how she fell in love with *you*."

"Shut up, both of you," Mrs. Willow said. "You're not here to squabble, my pretties. Belle, tomorrow I want you to offer to read to her, or hold her knitting, or some such—just stay around her. Admire the gardens, and get her to show them to you, and you can put in some good work *there*—*you* know, flatter her a little; we all like *that*. Julia, you've got more patience—you take up with—what's the little one's name?" she asked Essex.

"Fancy," said Essex, enchanted.

"Fancy. Julia, you get after the little girl. Play with her. Tell her stories, comb her hair, look at her toys. Romp."

"If you please," Miss Ogilvie said stiffly, "Fancy is my pupil. She will be engaged at her schoolwork for the greater part of the day."

"She will?" Mrs. Willow looked at Miss Ogilvie. "No one's going to cut you out," she said at last. "There's plenty for all of us, honey."

Miss Ogilvie laughed shortly. "Aunt Fanny's father might not think so."

Mrs. Willow frowned. "What have I got to do with Aunt Fanny's father?" she asked. "The old boy's dead fifteen years."

Miss Ogilvie laughed again, glanced at Essex, and then leaned forward. "I suppose *I* had better be the one to tell you," she said.

"Good *morning*, Aunt Fanny," Mrs. Willow said; the sun was shining goldenly on the terrace where Aunt Fanny and Maryjane were sitting after breakfast, "good morning to you. And to *you*," she said, to Maryjane. "Are you the mother of that delightful child? My gels are both in love with her already."

"You won't get any breakfast," Aunt Fanny said with satisfaction. "The table was cleared an hour ago."

"I'll run along down the kitchen in a minute. They will be sure to have something for a starving old woman. How well your brother is looking, Aunt Fanny. I am quite surprised to see how well he looks."

"He has had a blow recently, ma'am; he could scarcely look *very* well."

"A blow indeed," Maryjane said darkly. "Unmotherly monster."

"I?"

"A mother," Maryjane explained, "who pushes her only son down the stairs and leaves his devoted wife a widow."

"Maryjane," Aunt Fanny said. "Not before this lady, please."

"A widow," Maryjane said. "A fatherless orphan."

"I'm very sorry to hear it," Mrs. Willow said inadequately, and then, in a rush to Aunt Fanny, "I think you were away when I visited here long ago; I have always remembered the magnificence of this house, and the kindness of your father."

"My father was an upright, courteous man."

Mrs. Willow's voice was saddened. "You will certainly not believe this, but his passing was a deep personal loss to me. I valued him more than I can say; a truly upright man, as you say."

"You are right," Aunt Fanny said. "I certainly do not believe that."

"Aunt Fanny," said Mrs. Willow, "I do not want to keep on offending you. I have the greatest admiration and fondness for every member of your family, and so do my two daughters."

"And well you should," Aunt Fanny said. "I was not brought up to make friends out of my own class, Mrs. Willow."

"But there are to be no more differing classes, are there?"

"What do you mean?"

"Miss Ogilvie told us last night of the joyful message you had from your father; Aunt Fanny, you have been very much favored."

"Good heavens," said Aunt Fanny. "She actually *told* you?"

"I thought your father instructed specifically that all within the house were among the . . . ah . . . blessed. We have come, my daughters and I, in very good time."

"Good heavens," Aunt Fanny said again. "Good heavens."

"Yes," Maryjane said, "it is quite true. I am to have no more asthma. Aunt Fanny's father said clearly that sickness, like my asthma, would vanish from the earth. I will never have asthma again, after the world has been cleansed."

After a minute Aunt Fanny spoke faintly. "I have never disobeyed my father," she said. "His instructions were quite clear; perhaps I was wrong in not telling you myself. Mrs. Willow, you and your daughters are—" Aunt Fanny gasped, and nearly choked "—welcome here," she finished at last.

"Thank you," Mrs. Willow said gravely. "We will try to deserve your kindness. And now," she said, "I think I will dig up a little breakfast, and then drop in on old Orianna and pass the time of day."

Mrs. Willow settled herself dubiously into a delicate flowered armchair and relaxed slowly, listening for cracks in the wood. "Orianna," she said, "you know perfectly well you ought to do something for me, me and my gels."

"Girls," Mrs. Halloran said. She had been working at the household accounts when Mrs. Willow interrupted her, and she kept one hand protectively on her pen, but without optimism. "Girls, if you please."

"My little affectations," Mrs. Willow said. "You know *perfectly* well you will have to do something for me."

"And your daughters. Gels."

"My big hope is getting rid of them, naturally. I always

thought that bringing up children was a matter of telling them what to do, but they certainly make it hard for me. There's no denying, for instance, that my clever Julia is a fool and my lovely Arabella is a—"

"Flirt," Mrs. Halloran said.

"Well, I was going to say tart, but it's your house, after all. Anyway, it's money we need, as if there was ever anything else. I don't figure there's any way you can come right out and *give* us some, but people as rich as you are must know other people as rich as you are and somewhere along the line there must be someone you can help us get a dime out of. Marriage would be best, of course; we might as well aim high while we're about it. It better be Belle, though; she's prettier and if you tell her anything enough times she'll do it eventually. Besides if Belle married money the chances are good I could ease a little of it out of her; with Julia, I could whistle. Who's this young character with the little kid?"

"She's what my son Lionel married."

"God almighty." Mrs. Willow was wistful. "All his money. Even so, though, I don't think I would have wished it on either of my girls, even Julia. On account of you, I mean; there's no sense taking *you* on just to get our hands on enough money to try and live. I think," Mrs. Willow said, "I'd rather die, actually. No offense intended, of course. She talks a lot, doesn't she?"

"Maryjane?"

"Haven't you heard the kind of things she says?"

Mrs. Halloran laughed, and Mrs. Willow nodded, and sighed. "Now *that*'s no way to go about it," she said sadly, "you imagine *me* in a soft spot like that? What does she think it's going to get her?"

"Perhaps it helps her asthma."

"If it was one of *my* gels," Mrs. Willow said with feeling, "I'd see that she managed it altogether different; she's got the kid, after all, and there's no one else, you've *got* to leave it to the kid unless she fouls it up somehow. She could be talking the kid right out of everything; what she wants to do is keep her mouth shut until it *counts*. Well." She sighed. "You always see other people getting the good chances."

"You might tell your daughter Arabella that Essex is penniless."

"What?" Mrs. Willow glanced up sharply. "Yes? Well, I'll tell her. You know," she went on slowly, "they're not bad girls. That is," she said unwillingly, "they're probably bad girls the way we understood it when you and I were bad girls . . . I mean, *bad*. But they're not dishonest, or unkind. Not bad girls."

"Just *bad*." Mrs. Halloran smiled.

"You remember, do you? Then you see they do deserve some kind of help? After all . . ." Mrs. Willow shrugged, and was silent. After a minute or so, during which Mrs. Halloran regained her pen hopefully, Mrs. Willow went on, "I tell you, Orianna, I've *got* to get rid of those girls; every time some young fellow looks twice at Belle or dances with Julia my hands start to shake and I get so anxious my teeth chatter. I just can't afford them much longer, and you can see as well as I do that they're not up to most of the competition they meet; Belle's past twenty-five and even her hairdresser—"

"I suppose it's too late for them to learn shorthand?"

"It's almost too late for them to learn new dances," Mrs. Willow said sullenly. In a fever of irritation she put out her cigarette and got up to pace furiously up and down the satin room. "For God's sake," she said, "I'd take *any*body. Even somebody penniless. If he had rich friends."

There was a long silence. Mrs. Willow walked back and forth, eyeing the draperies, the jade cigarette box, the fine thin legs of the furniture. Mrs. Halloran stared down at her desk, at her unfinished accounts. Then Mrs. Willow said abruptly, "What a *hell* of a thing to do," and Mrs. Halloran raised her head. "Orianna," Mrs. Willow said, "what is this?"

Mrs. Halloran turned curiously, and Mrs. Willow said, "Look at this thing. It's disgusting. What's the idea?"

"Augusta," Mrs. Halloran said, "I can generally follow your conversation, since it rarely departs from one or two favorite subjects. But I confess that at present—"

"Look, then, damn it. If you don't want people to see it why do you leave it standing there?" Mrs. Willow brought it over; it was a framed photograph of Mrs. Halloran with a hatpin pushed through the tinted throat so that the pin stood out, wickedly behind the photograph and the rhinestone head of the pin sparkled like a huge diamond against the throat of Mrs. Halloran in the photograph.

"Dear me," said Mrs. Halloran. She took the photograph in her hand and looked at it thoughtfully. Then, "No," she said, handing it back, "I have no idea how it got there."

"Hell of a practical joke," said Mrs. Willow, pulling at the hatpin. "Hardly get it out."

"Then leave it in," Mrs. Halloran said indifferently.

"It gives me the creeps. There." Mrs. Willow set the picture down and the hatpin on the low table beside it. "Well," she said, running her finger carefully along the picture frame, "do you think you can?"

"Can what, Augusta?"

"Do a little something for my gels—girls? Not much, just something?"

"I believe there may be an opening here for a housemaid."

"I'm not an idiot," Mrs. Willow said slowly, "at least not idiot enough to threaten you. I didn't go sticking a hatpin through your picture—"

"That was probably Fancy; she's been told not to come in here."

"—and yet it seems to me that you could use a friend or so, and particularly someone who's known you a long time and doesn't have anything to lose by you, only something to gain. But you might as well know that your sister Fanny—"

"Who hasn't a cent."

"—has bidden us welcome to this house; we may stay as long as we like."

Mrs. Halloran turned, staring. "Did she *tell* you?"

"Put it," Mrs. Willow said carefully, "that either we hustle off with a little check in our hands, or we stay, and—" she grinned, "—get born again with all of you."

"I will not pay you to go, certainly." Mrs. Halloran's voice was quiet. "And I will not go against Aunt Fanny, although I believe she is sadly mistaken here. Yet," she said sadly, "you and I have so little else to hope for."

4

Mrs. Halloran, who was a tired and sometimes lonely person, sat by herself in her room before the thin-legged desk; it was late evening, her accounts still undone, and distantly she could hear the voices of the other people in the house, and sometimes laughter. Only human beings and rabid animals turn on their own kind, she was thinking; gratuitous pain is unknown in nature. At what point, she wondered, could I have been brought to deny myself all this? Lose the house? How could I have turned aside? And could I bear to lose it now?

She told them over softly. Richard, Fanny, Maryjane, Fancy, Augusta Willow, Julia, Arabella. Essex. Miss Ogilvie. Could I really die? she wondered, and then, resolute, turned to her accounts. All things must be neat and shipshape at her hands; even if the world outside withered and dissolved Mrs. Halloran would face a new world, herself in order, and balanced, relinquishing nothing of what was her own.

Downstairs, they were in the library. In his room Mr. Halloran slept, his nurse nodding beside him, but in the library, Aunt Fanny and Mrs. Willow were playing bridge against Miss Ogilvie and Julia, while Maryjane told Arabella the plot of a movie she had recently seen, and Essex, constrained by Aunt Fanny, advised the play.

"These are not new cards," Aunt Fanny said, turning her hand over. "There should always be new cards in the card cupboard, Essex."

"I'm afraid I took them out," Miss Ogilvie said. "I took the first I came to."

"We must have new cards for my deal," Aunt Fanny said. "Essex, do you see my cards?"

"Yes, Aunt Fanny."

"My father never touched a soiled card."

"I dealt." Mrs. Willow overrode Aunt Fanny. She looked deeply into her hand, sighed, thought, adjusted a card, sighed again, and put her cards down on the table. "Pass," she said. "Will Orianna be down tonight?"

"I hardly think so," Essex said.

"She is adding up how much we all cost her," Maryjane said. "Every time she goes up to look over the bills I wish I had bought more in the village."

"Who dealt?" Miss Ogilvie asked.

"He was a doctor in *this* movie," Maryjane said to Arabella, "you know, with a white coat and devoted to his profession? And his wife, you know?"

"I guess I pass," Miss Ogilvie said.

"Really, partner!" Julia said; she was prepared to suffer much at Miss Ogilvie's hands.

"Two hearts," Aunt Fanny said, "Essex, come and look at this hand."

"*Two?*" Mrs. Willow said. "*Two* hearts, partner? Essex, does she really mean *two* hearts?"

"Mrs. Willow, I was taught bridge by a professional. My father believed that no expense should be spared on my education. Bridge, dancing, lessons in drawing and on the harp. Italian. Astronomy—"

"Four spades," said Julia in some haste.

"Julia, pet, you interrupt Aunt Fanny."

"What does four spades mean?" Miss Ogilvie asked. "Essex, what does she mean by four spades?"

Aunt Fanny went on. "I was only trying to explain that my education was not, as you sometimes seem to believe, wholly neglected. I was not, perhaps, a diligent student, but that implies no criticism of my father, whose only aim was to see me a cultivated, gracious woman."

"And *she* refused to believe him," Maryjane said to Arabella, "because she had no faith, you know? And of course he *had* lied to her before, about adopting the child. And then the natives got cholera . . . cholera? Essex?"

"Pass," said Mrs. Willow. "I have absolutely nothing at all," she explained to Aunt Fanny.

"Talking across the table," said Miss Ogilvie roguishly. "Now, Mrs. Willow, *you* know better."

"I shall of course withdraw my bid," Aunt Fanny said stiffly.

"Not at all," Miss Ogilvie said. "We wouldn't *dream*—"

"I was taught by a professional, Miss Ogilvie. If my partner reveals her hand, intentionally or unintentionally—"

"Essex," Miss Ogilvie said, "what shall I do? Julia has bid four spades, and Aunt Fanny has withdrawn her bid, so what shall *I* do?"

"—and of course he had to inject the stuff into himself first, to *show* them, and he didn't know his wife had—"

"Five hearts, then, I guess."

"That was Aunt Fanny's suit, Miss Ogilvie."

"Oh, dear." Miss Ogilvie consulted her hand. "I guess I didn't mean hearts, anyway. I'm sorry, everybody. I *did* mean diamonds."

"Five diamonds?" Julia asked.

"I stand corrected," Aunt Fanny said. "I was under the impression that one's first bid was of the suit one intended. I am happy to know that I have been wrong all these years, and so, of course, was the professional teacher from whom I learned. I have not, of course, kept up with the newer rules, so I am now aware of a kind of bid I had always thought illegal."

"—and the chief's little son, the apple of his eye, and really the *cutest* little fellow, even though he was—"

"Essex?" said Miss Ogilvie helplessly.

"Six no trump," Julia said.

Aunt Fanny folded her cards and put them in the center of the table. "If we should ever play bridge again," she said, "will you, Essex, see that we have clean cards? I had not passed, Julia; you had no authority to bid." She turned her chair away from the table and, awkwardly, the others set down their cards. "Essex," said Aunt Fanny, "have our guests been offered drinks? Cigars?"

"Mrs. Willow," said Essex gravely, "will you have a cigar?"

"—and then, of course, all the other natives, and I wish you could have seen it; he was so tall and dignified, and yet he was so happy, too, and in spite of his wife—"

"I *will* have a drink, however," Mrs. Willow said.

"—and *she* died, although actually in real life they are *still* happily—"

Julia gathered up the cards and laid out a game of solitaire; she began to whistle softly.

"Consider," said Essex, "consider—you drink straight Scotch, Mrs. Willow?—consider our several methods of estimating reality. We are, not to put too fine a point on it, gathered here waiting, and yet we have no way to prepare; this is not real, what we are doing now—we have no function, beyond waiting."

"A pleasant way to wait," Mrs. Willow said, looking at the light through her drink.

"Nothing is actually quite concrete," Essex said; the absence of Mrs. Halloran made him a little free and he was, in any case, slightly drunk. "We cannot concern ourselves with anything of this world, and we are far from achieving the next; Aunt Fanny, is there nothing we can do?"

"I am tired of waiting, myself, Essex. But my father said we would be told in time. I think," said Aunt Fanny, with an unusual burst of confidence, "that we are like people at a summer resort, waiting for their vacations to end. We have *never* had anything to *do*, you know, but now we are waiting besides, and it is almost unbearable."

"Reality," Essex said. "Reality. What is real, Aunt Fanny?"

"The truth," said Aunt Fanny at once.

"Mrs. Willow, what is real?"

"Comfort," said Mrs. Willow.

"Miss Ogilvie, what is real?"

"Oh, dear." Miss Ogilvie looked for help to Mrs. Willow, to Julia. "I couldn't really say, not having had that much experience. Well . . . food, I guess."

"Maryjane," said Essex, "what is reality?"

"What?" Maryjane stared with her mouth open. "You mean, something real, like something not in the movies?"

"A dream world," Arabella supplied.

Julia laughed. "Essex," she said, "what is real?"

Essex bowed to her gravely. "*I* am real," he said. "I am not at all sure about the rest of you."

"How could you know about me, for instance?" Julia laughed.

"A few simple tests . . ."

"Do you actually have a *test* for reality?" Miss Ogilvie asked with interest.

"Observation, perhaps," Essex said, wickedly. "Recollection. Intention, desire, mystic perception of the absence of nothingness. I am going to be sorry that I ever named the subject."

"If you are talking about one of my gels I can promise you that you will be sorry, Master Insolence."

"Mrs. Willow, I was talking about yourself."

"Then reality, as you call it, is something I think I *do* know something about. If it's actual real things you mean, and I suppose you wouldn't be talking about it if you didn't, then there's *plenty* I can tell you. Reality!" Mrs. Willow said, as though she might be saying "Superstition!" or "Leprosy!" She sighed deeply. "*We* know, don't we?" she said to Aunt Fanny, and Aunt Fanny jumped. "We're an older school, we've been trained," Mrs. Willow said. "We've been *taught*, not like you younger things, with your schools and what not. You young people never *think*," she observed profoundly, "and that's what I *mean* by reality."

"What *kind* of tests?" Miss Ogilvie could not be stopped. "You mean . . . intelligence tests?" She glanced around, blushing. "I mean," she explained, "the more we know about such things the better able we are . . ." Her voice trailed off, as though even Miss Ogilvie could not contemplate an increase in her own abilities; even a test of intelligence, the silence said clearly, would not appreciably profit Miss Ogilvie.

"Well, reality," Mrs. Willow said finally, "all it means is money. A roof over your head, of course, and a little something three times a day and maybe a drop to drink. But mostly money. Clothes. Looking nice, and feeling a little chipper, and of course," she added, giving Essex a wink—and provoking Arabella into saying "Mother, *dear!*"—"a man in your bed.

Reality!" and now it sounded as though Mrs. Willow might be saying "May wine," or even possibly "tropical moonlight," and she gave a happy little sigh.

"Fortune telling," Essex said to Miss Ogilvie. "Intelligence tests—palmistry—tea reading—projective tests—"

"I *adore* them," Julia said. "*Can* we?"

"Table tipping," Essex said.

"Then," Miss Ogilvie said, trailing a little, "Aunt Fanny's father—"

"—and they found the buried treasure right on that spot," Arabella was saying to Maryjane. "I mean, right where the figure had been beckoning to them. Isn't it *divine?*"

"Now I don't hold with spiritualism," Mrs. Willow said. "Present company excepted, of course," she said to Aunt Fanny. "I've seen many a good woman waste the little bit she had left on nothing but a white shadow with a creepy voice, calling and crying over it and spending her life and even her money wasting away to nothing but a shadow herself. Mediums, you know," Mrs. Willow said in explanation to Miss Ogilvie, who had her mouth open again. "Mediums preying."

"Good heavens," said Miss Ogilvie.

"You surely cannot mean to include *me* with—"

"Well, Aunt Fanny, the way I see it you're a lady, and a lady isn't going to tell lies about her own father. I like to think I've got an open mind on any subject, but I sure as almighty hell wish I'd been there when Daddy came."

"Maybe he'll come again," Julia said.

"I'd really *die*," Arabella said.

Essex said rather sternly, "Aunt Fanny is not a medium or a charlatan, Mrs. Willow."

"Lord, dear, I never said she was. I'm curious, is all; there's a lot more I need to know about all this. And who the devil," she went on, "are *you?*"

"How do you do."

Mrs. Willow's voice had been so level that no one had turned, accustomed by now to her grasshopper speech; when they heard another, a strange voice, answer, all of them were startled and wheeled toward the doorway, all except Miss Ogilvie, who assumed immediately that Mrs. Willow had successfully raised an apparition (perhaps Aunt Fanny's father, come to undertake his own defense, and Miss Ogilvie having showed surprise; even, perhaps . . . skepticism). Miss Ogilvie gasped and covered her eyes.

"How do you do," Mrs. Willow said formally, herself a little shocked by the promptness with which she had summoned a stranger into Mrs. Halloran's library; almost lowering her voice Mrs. Willow went on, "Are you looking for someone?"

"Knock twice for yes, once for no," Essex murmured.

"Mrs. Halloran?"

Thus adequately convinced of either the mortal simplicity of the appearance before her, or—not impossibly—the utter lack of an adequate intelligence system among the inhabitants of another world, Mrs. Willow laughed and said in her normal voice, "Mrs. Halloran has retired. Can I help you?"

"I'm Gloria Desmond."

"Gloria." Mrs. Willow inclined her head regally. "I am Augusta Willow. My daughters, Arabella and Julia. Mr. Essex. Miss Ogilvie. Miss Frances Halloran."

Aunt Fanny came forward; she had, after all, had more ghostly experience than any of them. "I am Miss Halloran," she said. "My brother is resting, and my sister-in-law is engaged; I am afraid you will not be able to see her tonight. If I can—"

"I will be glad to send up a message," Mrs. Willow said, moving in. "What did you want to see her about?"

"I have a letter for her."

"What does it say?" Mrs. Willow inquired.

"It asks if I can stay here with her till my father comes home."

"Who wrote it?"

"My father did. He's Mrs. Halloran's cousin."

"Unusually ladylike for *that* family," Aunt Fanny told Miss Ogilvie, who, somewhat reassured, was staring with her mouth open.

"Where did he go, your father?"

"Africa."

"What for?"

"To shoot lions, of course."

"What on earth *for?*" said Mrs. Willow blankly.

"Some people shoot lions," the girl said pleasantly, "and some people do not shoot lions. My father is one of the people who do."

Aunt Fanny leaned forward. "How old are you?"

"Seventeen."

"Where did you come from?"

"My home. In Massachusetts."

"How did you get *here?*"

"By plane. My father left for Africa yesterday and before he left he wrote this letter to Mrs. Halloran asking if she would put me up until he gets back because the people I was supposed to stay with had a death in the family and so my father put me on the plane and said Mrs. Halloran had written him once asking him to come for a visit and he supposed the invitation was still open and there wasn't time to telegraph or anything because we thought I would be here practically by the time the telegram arrived. We did not know," the girl went on, "that I would get off the plane and have to take a two-hour bus trip and then a taxi from your village and then climb over a locked gate and walk in these shoes up a thousand miles of drive and then bang on the front door till I was tired and finally walk in here and come to this room where I heard voices and then stand here answering a million silly questions before anyone even told me I could put my suitcase down but now I think I will put my suitcase down and take off my shoes and then if you have any more questions—"

"It's because we thought you were a ghost," Arabella explained helpfully.

"A ghost? Why would I be a ghost?"

"We have had a death in this family, too," Aunt Fanny said. "You have come to a house of mourning, child. But I am sure that my brother will welcome you, even in his grief."

"You really climbed over the gate?" Essex asked.

"When I am visiting a place," Gloria said, "I don't like being locked out, even if they don't know I'm coming."

"The least your father could do," Mrs. Halloran said pleasantly to Gloria at the breakfast table, "is bring me back a lion."

"We used to do it when we were girls," Mrs. Willow said. "It's very easy, and very accurate. And of course, needing information the way we do—"

"My father—"

"I'm not saying a word against him, dearie. Only he does seem kind of . . . vague. Inconclusive. What *we* want to know is who, what, where, when, and how. And this is how to do it."

"I am not sure," Aunt Fanny said, "that my father would agree . . ."

"Only trouble is," Mrs. Willow said, "and of course it's not really a trouble, but we need a virgin."

"That is a subject," Mrs. Halloran said with unseemly haste, "which, if pursued, could only develop into low comedy. I suggest we turn our minds to something else at *once*."

"We used to do it when we were girls," Mrs. Willow said in explanation. She pulled a small table away from the wall and set it near the fire, checking earnestly to make sure that there was no glare of reflected light. Next to the table she put a straight, stiff chair, which had perhaps never been sat upon before. It came from a dark corner of the drawing room, and was upholstered in dead green satin. Its legs were carved and gilded; it was clearly uncomfortable and slippery. "The mirror," Mrs. Willow said. "Bring the one on the wall there, Essex." She laughed. "It's reflected all of us so many times it must know our faces by now." Essex brought the mirror, awkwardly; when he took it down from the wall it was unexpectedly heavy, and Mrs. Willow had to leap forward to catch it before it fell. Mrs. Halloran, stony-faced, looked for a minute at the darker spot on the silvered wallpaper which the mirror had left behind.

"Some of these things," Mrs. Halloran said, "have not been moved since the house was built."

"I don't doubt it," Mrs. Willow agreed amiably. "You should have this room done over, dear. It's perfectly impossible." Then, reflecting, she went on, "Although that sounds silly, now, doesn't it? Because even if you wanted to do it over, why bother? For such a short time, probably, I mean, and afterward, of course, there won't be anyone to do it."

"I have always liked it the way it is," Mrs. Halloran said.

Mrs. Willow and Essex put the mirror down onto the table and it reflected dutifully the carved cupids and painted clouds of the ceiling. The heavy frame of the mirror was gilded, and there was an expensive fault in the glass, so that a wave seemingly passed across it, altering the cupid faces and giving a look of sea-depth; Mrs. Willow had taken from the kitchen a small can of imported olive oil, and now she carefully poured a little onto the mirror, and it spread and ran and flattened, and the mirror caught light and shone. "Now," Mrs. Willow said, looking around the room.

"Low comedy," Mrs. Halloran murmured. "Essex, do you volunteer?"

"I have an antipathy to mirrors," Essex said.

"What do I have to do?" Gloria came forward. "Just look in the glass?"

"As though it were a window," Mrs. Willow said, and Gloria sat down gingerly on the green satin chair.

Gloria giggled, and Mrs. Willow put her hand on Gloria's head, protectively, and said in a steady tone, "Rest your arms on the table on either side of the window. Put your face down close to the window and keep your eyes wide. Try not to blink. Try not to think. We will all be very quiet, and in a little while you will see through the window to what is on the other side. When you see something there, just tell us simply what you see."

"Suppose I don't see anything?"

"Then someone else will try. We used to do this all the time, dear, when we were girls. Now, everyone, sit well away from

Gloria, so you will not cast a shadow. And be quiet, if you please."

Mrs. Halloran, with the air of one divorcing herself from a dull parlor trick, although one which had been perfectly acceptable when she was a girl, sat in her usual chair by the fire, and Essex sat near her. Julia and Arabella sat together, prettily, upon a rose-colored sofa near the fire, and Miss Ogilvie took a place in a far corner, as befitted one in a humble station and not expected to be the first to face any danger. Mrs. Willow and Aunt Fanny hovered near Gloria, silently pressing one another to move back. Gloria leaned her head forward, and her long hair fell down along either cheek.

"It hurts your eyes," she said.

"Gloria," Mrs. Willow said hypnotically, "you are looking through a window, a strange window because it looks out onto a world you have never seen before. It is dark there now, perhaps, because on the other side they still have not found the way to the window, but remember, when they know the window is there they will come to speak to us. You are waiting at this window to be given a vital message. Be alert, child, be ready; remember that you are on guard at this window and when they come you must be prepared to see them."

"Please don't breathe on my neck," Gloria said.

"Gloria," Aunt Fanny said, "can you see my father? Tall, very pale?"

"I can see the sundial, I *think*," Gloria said hesitantly. "No, it is not the sundial. It is a white rock. There is water around it—no grass. It is like the sundial because it stands there alone with grass all around it, but it is only a white rock."

"A trysting place," said Mrs. Willow with satisfaction.

"Not on *my* land," Mrs. Halloran said firmly.

"Now the rock is a mountain. And the grass is tops of trees. There is water running down the mountain; it is a waterfall. Like one of those toys—everything shifts and changes, and by the time I see something it is gone. Now it is the sun, very bright. It hurts my eyes. A fire. White. All over, covering everything, even the trees and the waterfall. And colors, red and black. I've got to close my eyes." She put both hands over her eyes and Mrs. Willow sighed.

"It was my father, almost certainly," Aunt Fanny said. "Very bright."

Gloria leaned forward again and said, "It's still there, only getting darker. Circles of color, blacker and blacker. No, no, stop," she said, and she half-rose, her face close to the mirror. "I don't want to watch," she said, staring. "Like eyes, eyes all looking, they are going to get out—they are going to get out—shut the window against them, quick—shut the mirror, before they get out! No, wait," and without looking away she waved Mrs. Willow back, "it's quiet now. They can't get out. The others are there. Standing, in a row. Looking at us. They want something."

"Who do they want?" It was Miss Ogilvie from her corner, straining against her chair as though tied.

"It is the house. They were standing all in a row and now it is the windows of the house; it looks tiny. It looks like a tiny picture, barely colored. The sun is not shining. There is a bird walking down the terrace, even from here I can see how bright he is, red and blue and green, like jewels."

"We have *never* had peacocks on the terrace," Mrs. Halloran said. "My father-in-law thought them feeble-minded."

"It is walking down the terrace and now down the steps onto the lawn. Blue, and green. Tiny, and bright. It is coming straight down the lawn, right at me. I think it sees me and is coming right at me. It has a sharp nose and red eyes and it is smiling, bright and colored and coming faster—make him stop—make him go away—it's hideous—make him go away!"

Gloria wrenched away from the table and covered her eyes. Mrs. Willow patted her shoulder and said, "A little brandy, Essex, please," and looked over Gloria's shoulder into the mirror skimmed with oil, reflecting distorted cupids and dirty clouds.

"I am sure that it was my father," Aunt Fanny said. "I would not look into that mirror, of course, but it is not necessary. I know that it was my father, and he has come to see if we are mindful of his instructions. Don't be afraid," she said to Gloria. "That was my father you saw."

"It was awful," Gloria said.

"He was always a very strict man," Aunt Fanny said, "but good to his children. If I had been in your place, Gloria, I should have said something, or at least made some gesture to show you recognized him. Because of course he has *his* feelings, too."

5

"You are not familiar, I think," Essex said slowly, "with a kind of unholy, unspeakable longing? I mention it to you because I think you may be the only person here who is capable of recognizing such an emotion. It is not a pretty thing to feel."

"Perhaps you might teach me," Arabella said.

"It is a longing so intense that it creates what it desires, it cannot endure any touch of correction; it is, as I say, unspeakable."

"No," said Arabella, "I do not think I can remember that I ever felt anything like that."

"It is unholy because it is heretic. It is foul. It is abominable to need something so badly that you cannot picture living without it. It is a contradiction to the condition of mankind."

"I have always lived very well, you see," Arabella said. "My mother has made a particular point of seeing that I lacked for nothing."

"I dread that it may be only a longing for annihilation. No person who has seen his own face plain can want to live longer."

"Well, I can't understand *that*. I mean, I can understand a person's not liking his own face, but people can't help their faces, after all. I know I always feel very sorry for girls who are not nice-looking. And I'm sure I think you've got a very pleasant face."

"The sight of one's own heart is degrading; people are not *meant* to look inward—that's why they've been given bodies, to hide their souls."

"Of course, I was very lucky, and please don't think I believe it *was* anything but luck; beauty is only an accident, like the way a person is born."

"I am filthy, sickened, beastly. I have seen myself plain."

"My sister Julia, on the other hand—"

"I am rotten; that is why I am so frightened—I am terribly afraid that this hope which Aunt Fanny—"

"Aunt *Fanny*," said Arabella, "you're talking about Aunt *Fanny?* But I thought all your unspeakable thoughts were about *me*."

"Well, *I* don't care what the old biddy says," Julia said, taking the turn by the gates in a wide sweep of the steering wheel, and barely slowing the car, "*I'd* go anywhere *I* pleased."

"It's very difficult," Miss Ogilvie said hesitantly. "That is, she *does* mind, and being dependent, I suppose it's the least we can do, not asking to have the gates unlocked."

"Not *me*," Julia said. "You saw the way *I* take care of things; I just told him it was all right with the old lady, and maybe he thought I was taking you two to church or something, because he wouldn't *dare* to keep *me* inside."

"I merely do not choose, often, to leave my home," Aunt Fanny observed from the back seat. "Your modern automobiles . . . particularly this one; Julia, do you mind moving just a *little* more slowly? Automobiles, and noise and dust and strange people . . . I prefer a somewhat less feverish life, thank you."

"What will she say when she hears you two have been gallivanting around?" Julia asked, peering at them in the rearview mirror.

"I do not gallivant around," Aunt Fanny said, and Miss Ogilvie said, "We didn't think she'd have to know. Unless *you* tell her."

"I keep your secrets," Julia said darkly, "and you keep mine."

Although the fact had probably not influenced the first Mr. Halloran in his choice of a site for his house, the village had been, shortly before his time, very much the subject of sensa-

tional publicity. Young Harriet Stuart, it was generally believed, had one morning arisen unusually early in the Stuart
house just outside the village, and taken up a hammer with
which she murdered her father, her mother, and her two
younger brothers, putting an abrupt end to the Stuart family
tree. Fall River, Massachusetts, was nothing to the villagers
near Mr. Halloran's proposed big house; Harriet Stuart was
their enshrined murderess. During Harriet's arrest and trial,
the villagers met more strangers than had ever come their way
before, and after Harriet's acquittal it was customary for almost daily groups of tourists to get off the bus in front of the
Carriage Stop Inn, and wander, guided by a villager, up the
half mile to the Stuart house, where they were occasionally rewarded by a fleeting glimpse of Harriet's housekeeper and
guardian, an aunt who must sometimes have wondered if Harriet's hammer days were over, working in the garden or taking
in the groceries. Sometimes the most persistent, staying past
the departure of the second bus (and thus making necessary a
night spent in the arms of the Carriage Stop Inn) were able to
catch sight of a tall figure dressed in black, moving past the
upper windows of the house.

The village story, no matter who was lucky enough to capture the tourists, seldom varied: "They couldn't prove it on
her, see, because no one knew *why* she did it, and being fifteen
years old and all, she got off. They said at the time it was a
crazy idea she was even put on trial, because no jury in their
right minds could see her sitting there, quiet and sad and looking like any young kid, and really *believe* she did it. We knew
her around the village—she was born here, after all, and her
two brothers besides, and even *we* couldn't think, sometimes,
she was up to it. Now right here, right along these bushes here
by the road, is where she fell when she said she was running
for help, and here's where they found the hammer later, and
she said it was a tramp chasing her, one got in through the
back cellar window and he must have dropped the hammer
here. She run all the way down the road to Parker's Bakery
yelling for help. Later we'll go round the back and look
through the fence and you can see the window she said the

tramp got in at, even though they said, the prosecution, it hadn't been opened for years, but the defense got an expert said there were clear signs someone had been walking around the cellar near the window. Right there, that window on the second floor third from the end, that was the window of the room where her mother and father slept and they say *she* sleeps in there now—remorse, or something. Or maybe it just has the best bed, though not many people would want to sleep in *that* bed, I guess—it's where she did them in, you know. The two boys were around back, we can see their window when we go around. *Her* room was on the very end, down there, and they say she got up when it was still dark and she had the hammer with her—took it to bed with her the night before, you know—and came right down the hall to her parent's bedroom and *wham!* Then, across the hall to the boys. *Wham* again. Nothing to it, says Harriet. Then, down the stairs, and down the front walk, left the gate open, fell into the bushes back where I showed you, dropped the hammer, and down the road in her nightgown to Parker's Bakery; Bill Parker, *he* didn't believe her at first—she yelled him out of bed and he put his head out of the window and told her to go home. Then she told him again and he got some pants on and got up Straus the butcher and old Watkins and they went up—before you take the bus you go see old Watkins; he'll tell you what it looked like when they got up here. One funny thing—she was barefoot and all cut and scratched from the bushes when Mrs. Parker took her in, but no blood on her. The prosecution, they said she couldn't hardly do such a set of things as *that* without getting blood on her, and they say she did it and then washed herself and put on a clean nightgown. The prosecution said she burned the bloody nightgown in the stove, but the defense, *they* got in an expert said it wasn't nothing but old rags in the stove, even though no one said why anyone wanted to go burning old rags; round here, we mostly take our old junk over to the dump, although you ask my wife, she'll tell you she *wears* our old rags.

"No one ever knew, though. She got off, and she came back here to the house where she was born, and she lives there now.

Goes out for walks at night, they say, although me, *I* wouldn't like to meet her—can't tell what might happen if she come to take a dislike to you. Funny thing, though, Straus—he's the butcher—says they never order meat, though they used to. A vegetarian, Harriet Stuart.

"Come around the side and I'll show you the shed the hammer come from, and then we'll look through the fence and maybe get a look at Auntie and anyway see those other windows. He was a carpenter, Stuart—built most of this place himself, though Harriet had the fence put up, of course, after she come home. Used to be kids throwing rocks through the windows, sometimes, or yelling things from the road. Seems to me people could bring up their kids better, somehow, teach them to respect other people and other people's property."

Harriet Stuart died quietly in her sleep some ten or twelve years after Mr. Halloran had built the big house, her aunt removed to another town and was known to have changed her name, and the Stuart house stayed empty. No one was willing to live in it because of its lack of sanitary accommodations, and the villagers kept it in repair because tourists came to look at it. The fence was taken down, and it was not thought in doubtful taste to tack neatly lettered little signs upon the doors to the significant rooms, and set a small metal standard beside the bush where the hammer was found. The villagers tried valiantly to pretend that the house was haunted, and occasionally Mr. Straus, who had re-taken possession of the property when the Stuart mortgage lapsed, received letters from scholarly folk who wanted to visit the house in order to write gently humorous, cynical articles proving that Harriet Stuart was innocent, or that she was guilty. One such article referred to the village as "a quiet place, untouched by time or progress."

The present Mr. Straus, who owned the butcher shop, was the son of the original Mr. Straus who owned the butcher shop and had gone with Mr. Parker and old Watkins to the Stuart house; the present Mr. Straus had heard the Harriet Stuart story so often from his father that he could repeat it, now, without hesitation, when people came by the shop and asked him; he knew perfectly where the blood had been spilled and how Mrs. Stuart had made it halfway to the door before the hammer caught up with her, and he could re-create, with telling effect, the look in the dead eyes of Mr. Stuart, gazing with horror upon his murderer; his pathetic recital of how the two young boys were found in one another's arms was very apt to move his hearers to tears. The Stuart house was listed in local guide books as a spot of some grisly interest. Mr. Peabody, when he took over the Carriage Stop Inn, had actually debated for some time the wisdom of renaming the Inn the Harriet Stuart Lodge, but had been dissuaded by the sterner heads in town, and particularly the Misses Inverness, who ran the gift shop next to the Inn, and who regarded the entire Harriet Stuart affair as uncouth, and criminally unfilial. No curios or mementos of the Stuart family were to be found in the gift shop run by the Misses Inverness, although several books discussing the murder were in the Inn library, and a rude pamphlet, purporting to be the work of one of the party who visited the house that night, was on sale in several shops in the village; it gave a vivid and gory description of the house, and had sketches of Harriet Stuart, her unfortunate family, and a map of the probable route she had taken from arising that morning to her eventual arrival at Parker's Bakery.

Harriet Stuart lured a small regular stream of tourists to the village; two busses a day stopped in front of the Carriage Stop Inn, and there was time between them for a visit to the Harriet Stuart house, and a country-style dinner at the Inn, with a few minutes for browsing with the Misses Inverness, and a walk down the one street of the village to purchase homemade jelly and preserves in Mrs. Martin's little shop, regard the site of Parker's Bakery, now, with Parker, defunct; look at antiques in the big barn back of the Basses' house, and inspect, with shudders, the Stuart family memorial in the cemetery, which gave no more than the names of the murdered family and, horribly, their one common date of death. Most of the villagers managed to sell a little something to tourists, and keep their own small businesses besides. Miss Bass, sister to the Mr. Bass who kept antiques in his barn, gave lessons in piano and voice. Mrs.

Otis, whom people believed to be a divorced woman living upon alimony, gave dancing lessons and did hair. The village children went to a one-room school, taught for the past seventeen years by a Miss Comstock; her salary was paid, as had been that of her predecessor, by the Halloran family. The first Mr. Halloran had been responsible for the further education, in college, in medical school, in law school, or in art school, of those village children who showed promise; the present Mrs. Halloran had continued this policy, but teachable children were getting fewer every year; those young people sent away to college had, of course, never come back, and the village grew smaller and older, although the Harriet Stuart stories were handed down as faithfully as the several small annuities from the Halloran family. Mr. Halloran had once made an offer to buy the Stuart house and land, but Mr. Straus had firmly refused, and as a result—the first Mr. Halloran disliking not being able to buy something he wanted—the Stuart legends were not discussed by the Hallorans, and naturally tourists were never admitted inside the walls of the big house. The Hallorans made a particular point of bringing as much of their trade as possible to the village; they bought their meat from Mr. Straus, in spite of the coolness which had arisen over the Stuart holding, and had much of their dressmaking and simple sewing done by old Mrs. Martin, who also made the home-made jellies and jams and an occasional pie upon order. Although the Halloran house received regular deliveries from the big stores in the city, nine miles away, they placed a standing order for groceries from Mr. Hawthorne, borrowed their books from the lending library in the gift shop run by the Misses Inverness, sent down for the mail from Mr. Armstrong, the postmaster, took their petty hardware from Atkins Hardware, and bought, as far as possible, fresh eggs and chickens and vegetables and fruit from the farmers who were legitimately part of the village. On one point, however, the first Mr. Halloran had made an unbreakable law: the servants in the big house came, without exception, from the city. Villagers, Mr. Halloran maintained, belonged in the village, and not within the walls of the big house.

Julia parked the car at the main corner of the village, where the Carriage Stop Inn faced the hardware store. "Any place in particular?" she asked. "The nearest subway station, maybe?"

"I plan to visit every shop in the village," Aunt Fanny said stiffly. "Aside from certain preparations which must be made, I feel it incumbent upon me to make one or two last purchases from each shop; a gesture of some importance, as I see it. The villagers must see that we do not break faith with them, even now."

"What about Miss Ogilvie here?" Julia asked. "You don't mean her to come with *me*, I suppose?"

"I will accompany Aunt Fanny," Miss Ogilvie said. "Perhaps I shall drop in at the lending library and browse."

"And you, Julia?" Aunt Fanny asked. "Can you amuse yourself for an hour at least, perhaps even an hour and a half? I hesitate to propose the lending library."

"I'll find something to do," Julia said vaguely. "Don't worry about me. Just getting out of that house is enough."

"Those two young men you are looking at in that field are the Watkins brothers," Aunt Fanny said tartly. "Good for nothing, both of them. They may look as though they are lying in the shade under a tree, but they will tell you that they are actually out shooting rabbit, or picking apples, or some such nonsense. The Halloran family arranged for the older one to drive one of the dairy trucks from the city, but at the end of a month or so he left them, although they could never actually prove that he had made off with the collection money."

"I wouldn't dream of going near them," Julia said. "I'll meet you right here in an hour and a half."

"Perhaps," Miss Ogilvie suggested timidly, "Julia would be interested in seeing—I know *I* have always wanted to—in seeing the Harriet—"

"Miss Ogilvie," Aunt Fanny said, "I would not suppose that even Julia would be guilty of such self-indulgence. Julia, I would recommend the cemetery. There are several old markers, the oldest in this part of the country. The Halloran family vault is particularly well-carved; my father and mother rest there."

"The cemetery," Julia said. "Naturally. Will I have trouble finding it?"

"I hardly think so," Aunt Fanny said. "The last building on your right is the church. The cemetery is just beyond it."

"If I get lost," Julia said, "I will ask a policeman."

She drove off, going slowly, and Aunt Fanny and Miss Ogilvie stood for a minute, looking after her. Then Aunt Fanny settled herself briskly and said, "Miss Ogilvie, as I told you, I have really a good deal to do. I must not lose time. I have already sent off a great many orders to stores in the city, and today I must complete my shopping; small purchases I cannot overlook."

"Why?" said Miss Ogilvie. "I mean—" she blushed "—why do you have to buy things *now*, when . . . when . . ."

"*Dear* Miss Ogilvie. There are *so* many things one is reluctant to leave behind. Even you must perceive that we do not know, yet, what we shall wish, afterward, that we had brought with us, and there will be no coming back, afterward, to collect items we have forgotten."

"Food," said Miss Ogilvie, nodding. "I understand."

"I have absolute faith in my father. But we must try to think of *everything*."

"Perhaps I can help, then," Miss Ogilvie said. "At least, I can help you carry your packages."

"Carry packages? I?"

"Small things . . ." Miss Ogilvie made a helpless gesture.

"Miss Ogilvie, please do try to be more sensible. I cannot stand here in public, in what is after all the very center of the village, trying to teach you the habits of a lady. I have really no time at all to spend reasoning with you." Purposefully, Aunt Fanny crossed the street and went into the hardware store, Miss Ogilvie following wretchedly.

After the hardware store, Aunt Fanny visited the grocery and then the little shop where Mrs. Martin sold her jams and jellies and yard goods and an occasional pie upon order. When they left old Mrs. Martin, Miss Ogilvie hesitated and glanced wistfully across the street. "The lending library," she said apologetically. "Something to pass the time, you know. I don't suppose," she added with a flash at Aunt Fanny, "that I need worry about *returning* it."

"As a matter of fact," Aunt Fanny said, "I believe I also need a book."

The lending library was tucked into one corner of the gift shop run by the Misses Inverness, and relied for trade rather heavily upon the transient souvenir-hunter rendered into a stupor by the home-fried chicken and pecan pie of the Carriage Stop Inn next door. Miss Inverness kept the library and Miss Deborah Inverness sold gifts; some inner integrity had preserved their shop from being a shoppe, but when the Misses Inverness had first decided to go into trade Miss Inverness had taken some of the stigma away from the shop by hiring Mr. Ossian, the carpenter, to put Elizabethan half-timbering across the front, and to set in an inglenook around the fireplace. The gifts were almost without exception made of china, delicately colored, and involving numberless small deer and kittens and scottie dogs. Miss Deborah did the dusting herself, naturally, and her sister kept the books. Miss Inverness wore purple crepe with her mother's garnet brooch, and tended to be brusque, although she knew—none better—that her heart was really of gold; Miss Deborah wore a little locket around her faded neck and had once been in love with a music teacher.

There had been a little tiff between them three summers ago over ashtrays, since the late Mrs. Inverness had not permitted smoking indoors, and the late Mr. Inverness had been accustomed to take his cigar in the lobby of the Carriage Stop Inn. Miss Deborah had insisted with unusual spirit that even proper ladies—Mrs. Halloran up at the big house, for one—used ashtrays nowadays and had as much as accused her sister of not keeping up with the times. Miss Inverness had capitulated, asking her sister irritably how long Mrs. Halloran at the big house had been setting the standards for the Inverness family? and the gift shop now stocked tiny porcelain shell ashtrays. Miss Inverness read a chapter from Henry James aloud every evening, and they drank their tea from fragile, gold-rimmed cups which had been a legacy to their mother from the first, mortal, Mrs. Halloran.

When Aunt Fanny opened the door a little bell rang musically, and Miss Inverness rose from her seat in the inglenook; Miss Deborah, cornered among the china, could only smile most cordially.

"Caroline," Aunt Fanny said; she and Miss Inverness had played together as children. "How nice to see you."

"Miss Halloran," said Miss Inverness, "Deborah, Miss Halloran is here. And Miss Ogilvie," she said. "How nice."

"How nice," said Miss Deborah, coming with caution between the tables. "Miss Halloran. Miss Ogilvie. How very nice."

"How nice," Miss Ogilvie said to Miss Inverness, and to Miss Deborah, "How nice to see you again."

"How well you look," Miss Inverness said. "And Mr. Halloran—is he well?"

"Not well at all," Aunt Fanny said, and Miss Ogilvie nodded sadly. "I am sorry to say that he does not keep well," Aunt Fanny said. "My nephew's death . . ."

"Such a terrible blow," Miss Inverness said, and Miss Deborah murmured, "Tragic."

"It is a very sad thing to lose an only son," Miss Ogilvie confirmed.

"And dear little Fancy?" Miss Inverness turned to her sister with a brightening face. "Dear little Fancy?" she said.

"Such a sweet child," Miss Deborah said. "She was in here with her mother not long ago. Of course, it was before . . ." her voice trailed off, and she moved a hand eloquently.

"Naturally," Miss Inverness said. "She took a great pleasure in our new little china dogs, made in Italy, you know. Such a *careful* child. She was really quite *quite* taken with them."

"You must see them," Miss Deborah said. "Miss Halloran, you positively must see our new little dogs. The Italians do these things so colorfully, I always think. Dear little Fancy was positively enchanted. I think she was particularly taken with a dear little blue poodle, sister?"

"Such an engaging toy," Miss Inverness said.

"Dare I take Fancy a little something?" Miss Ogilvie said to Aunt Fanny. "Do you think it might be . . . perhaps . . . a little consolation to her?"

"Children are so easily comforted," Miss Inverness said, and Miss Deborah said, "Poor child, some small pleasure might mean everything in the world to her right now."

"We'll certainly take it to her," Aunt Fanny said. "And we are interested, Miss Inverness, in books."

"Of course," Miss Inverness said. "Something to read?"

"Light, please," Miss Ogilvie said. "Some cheerful light reading. It's only to pass the time. So difficult, just waiting," she explained to Miss Deborah.

Miss Inverness laughed roguishly. "I know better than to offer Miss Halloran most of the poor things they are publishing today. There are, however, some few really *excellent* books, some I can honestly recommend, I mean. Some I have read myself, and so has my sister."

"We had better take several," Miss Ogilvie said. "We have no idea how long we will have to wait."

"I see," said Miss Inverness. "Then you would naturally need several."

"*I* want," Aunt Fanny said, "at least one book on surviving in the wilds."

"I beg your pardon?" said Miss Inverness, and Miss Deborah said, after a moment, "*Surviving?*"

"A book which would tell how to build a fire and how to catch animals for food. A certain amount of first aid, too, I expect. Such information as that."

"I can hardly begin to think—" Miss Inverness began.

"A Boy Scout Handbook," Miss Ogilvie said unexpectedly. "I used to have a brother," she confided in Miss Deborah.

Miss Inverness breathed again. "For Fancy," she said. "*Naturally.*"

"To comfort her," Miss Deborah said.

"And," said Aunt Fanny, "I would like, if possible, a fairly elementary book on engineering, and chemicals, and perhaps the various uses of herbs. Perhaps an encyclopedia."

"Well, now," said Miss Inverness, "I *know* that we would not have an *encyclopedia*. Perhaps the library in the big house . . ."

"It's fairly old," Aunt Fanny said. "No really *new* information. Physics, you know, and politics. I wonder if we have time to order a new one."

"But what would little Fancy want with an encyclopedia?" Miss Deborah wondered. "Are you going to send her to school?"

"I was not brought up to be evasive, Miss Deborah," Aunt Fanny said. "I have immediate need for a good deal of practical information on primitive living. Survival. I have no way of knowing what we may be called upon to do for ourselves."

"Aunt Fanny," Miss Ogilvie said, "Miss Inverness and Miss Deborah have always been so kind . . . so thoughtful. Would it not be an act of friendship to include them in our future?"

"I confess I had thought of it," Aunt Fanny said. "But I do not think it will offend Caroline or Deborah if I point out, frankly, that our need will be for more sturdy, more *rugged* personalities. Remember, our little group must include builders and workers as well as—" she blushed faintly—"the mothers of future generations."

"I am sure," Miss Inverness said with some stiffness, "that neither my sister nor myself has any desire to be looked upon as a worker, and it is long since we gave up any notion of breeding children. I am astonished, Frances Halloran, to hear you talk so coarsely. I would not have expected it, not in front of my sister."

"I apologize," said Aunt Fanny, who could afford to be mild. She turned to Miss Ogilvie. "You see," she said, "it is not fair to *them*. We need a different kind of person altogether."

"If your needs are what they seem to be," Miss Inverness said, not altogether mollified, "I assure you that my sister and myself must refuse, most firmly, to be included in any way whatsoever."

"Caroline, dear," Miss Deborah said gently.

"I am sorry," Miss Ogilvie said. "I should never have said anything at all. It was only because one so rarely meets congenial persons, really congenial, and I thought it would be a shame to lose Miss Inverness and Miss Deborah as friends. I am sure they have always been *most* respectable, and it will be sad to think of them after they are gone."

"Our mother brought us up to be respectable, I hope, Miss Ogilvie. I will get your Boy Scout Handbook."

Still contrite, Aunt Fanny selected half a dozen novels, the blue poodle for Fancy, and a shell ashtray for Essex. Miss Deborah made everything into a neat package, which was left in the shop for Julia to gather in later when she came back with the car. Miss Inverness was cool in her farewell to Aunt Fanny, and gave Miss Ogilvie only a small bow; Miss Deborah accompanied them to the door of the shop, troubled and civil, and opened the door for them, the faint musical tinkle of the door-bells for a moment overriding her voice before her sister called her sharply.

On the sidewalk outside the shop Miss Ogilvie said, "Well, I'm happy to think that we will probably never go in *there* again. I think Miss Inverness has gotten very crotchety."

"Like her mother," Aunt Fanny said. "Candles," she said, "candles. I forgot candles."

"Then I'll just run in and have a cup of coffee, dear," Miss Ogilvie said. "In the drug store, because they look at you so strangely in the Inn when you only order coffee."

"Don't *talk* to anyone," Aunt Fanny said. "Put out of your mind any ideas except that we have come into the village for a morning's shopping. I will meet you here in fifteen minutes, and I beg of you to be silent about the future."

"Naturally," Miss Ogilvie said placidly. "It's so difficult for me to describe, anyway."

The drug store, like every other store in the village, sold an enormous variety of goods; no storekeeper in the village found himself able to exist on the marketing of any single commodity; the grocer sold light bulbs and paper supplies, the antique shop carried a sideline of homemade candies and jellies, the hardware store sold toys and newspapers, and the drug store sold them all, besides cigarettes, paperback books, and an unending series of chemicals at its soda fountain. Miss Ogilvie, easing herself gracelessly onto a high stool at the soda fountain, found herself alone in the store except for the soda fountain clerk, a young man with poor hair and pimples, leaning listlessly against a sign showing a tempting chicken salad sandwich adorned with pickles and potato chips; "You want something?" the young man said, picking at his cheek.

Miss Ogilvie sighed happily. "Peach pie," she said, "with chocolate ice cream on top." It was only half-past ten, and luncheon at the big house was not served until one. Miss Ogilvie made a series of small wriggling gestures in order to straighten out her skirt under her, and set her pocketbook on the counter next to her and cleared away an obtrusive ashtray and a container of paper napkins. When the young man set the peach pie with chocolate ice cream on top in front of her Miss Ogilvie smiled at it, and then, congratulatingly, at the young man.

"One of the things I *am* going to miss," she said confidentially, "is fancy food."

The young man let his eye rest briefly on the peach pie, and retired to lean once more against the chicken salad sandwich. "Don't care much for pie, myself," he said. "Cake's more my line."

Miss Ogilvie snapped her fingers in sudden irritation. "I forgot," she said, "I completely forgot; I was so sure I was going to remember to tell Aunt Fanny to get lots and *lots* of those prepared cake mixes. They're so much easier, and it's hard to think how we'd get any baking done, otherwise."

"Or cookies," the young man said. "Lots of people like cookies."

"And blueberry muffins," Miss Ogilvie said. "Dear heavens, I hope I remember to remind Aunt Fanny when I see her."

"Working in a place like this," the young man said, "you'd think I'd be crazy about ice cream. Wouldn't you?"

"Well, *that*'s one thing we can't take," Miss Ogilvie said. "It would melt," she explained. "Since I suppose the electricity will all go off, and then the refrigerator won't stay cold."

"The electricity don't go off," the young man said. "This time of year, with no storms, the electricity stays on without any trouble. My brother's on the lines, he'd tell me."

"But of course," Miss Ogilvie said, wide-eyed, "*that* night the buildings will be gone. The places they send the electricity *from*, I mean. And of course the wires."

"What night?" the young man asked idly.

"I'm not supposed to talk about it, but I guess it's all right to tell *you*, so you can tell your brother that it won't be any use." Miss Ogilvie swallowed a piece of peach pie. "Aunt Fanny told us all about it. It's coming very soon. Fire and floods and sidewalks melting away and the earth running with boiling lava and all the poor people trying to get away." She sighed, and looked down at her pie with sympathy. "All over the world," she said, "*everywhere*. And in the morning there will be nothing left. I suppose it's very hard for you to picture it, but there will be simply nothing; we will look out of the windows— that's all of us, in the big house, not *you*, I am afraid, and I am really terribly sorry. But we will all look out the windows and in all the world there will be nothing but drying earth, with the grass beginning to grow. All the houses and people and automobiles and everything will be just melted away." She sighed again. "I just don't know how we're going to make our coffee that first morning," she said. "I suppose we will have to build a little fire somehow. Kindling," she said. "I will tell Aunt Fanny to get kindling."

"You want to be careful, starting fires," the young man said. "It's pretty dry this time of year."

Miss Ogilvie stared. "You don't understand," she said. "There won't be anything left to burn."

The young man thought deeply. "You saying," he asked at last, "that the day of Armageddon is coming? Like that?"

"I think so," Miss Ogilvie said uncertainly.

"Like where it says in the Bible the day of Last Judgment? The final trump?"

"I think that's different," Miss Ogilvie said. "I mean, the *rest* of you—"

"My ma, she talks like that. She's got this club, the True Believers, they call theirselves. They *all* talk like that. Got people coming over from the city to meet with them, *they* talk like that too."

"You mean there are others?" Miss Ogilvie said, barely breathing.

"The True Believers is what they call theirselves. I listen sometimes, me and my brother, the one I was telling you about; he's on the lines. He says to me, 'Don't you believe it, bud, I see enough electricity to know it's scientifically impossible. *Scientifically* impossible. Let them talk,' he says, 'they got nothing else to do. But don't you get taken in, because them scientific fellows have proved that the world didn't start the way they say, and it ain't going to end the way they say either. Protons and neutrons—that's the answer. Electric force.'"

"These True Believers," Miss Ogilvie asked anxiously, "how many of them are there?"

"Ten, maybe. They meet and get messages from the spirit world. Ma's got a control named Liliokawani, used to be a Egyptian queen. Tells her things." He laughed richly. "Liliokawani," he said. "Boy, did they use to live it up, those Egyptian queens."

Miss Ogilvie pushed her peach pie away suddenly. "Ten *more*," she said. "I better go right away and find Aunt Fanny and tell her. I'm not sure she's going to be pleased. We thought," she explained, "that it was just going to be *us*, just our little circle. We really get along quite well together, so congenial and all, and so refined and everything, and now strangers . . ." She slid hastily off the stool.

"I'll tell Ma you was asking," the young man said. "That'll be a quarter for the pie and fifteen more for the ice cream."

"My father," said Aunt Fanny, "was beyond all things a democratic man. He believed in encouraging the villagers in every possible manner, although I do not recall that he ever mingled among them socially. I cannot picture him visiting this young man's mother. She may easily have been deceived."

"The young man himself was quite positive about it," Miss Ogilvie said miserably. "But really—ten extra people, and we had counted *so* on being alone."

"I do not see that we need bother about it further," Aunt Fanny said. "I am quite positive that my father would agree with me." Her voice went vague; she was looking across the street toward the spot where the bus stopped, bringing Harriet Stuart's visitors, or an occasional traveller interested in dining at the Carriage Stop Inn, or an elderly person come to count the number of people still alive in the village. Mr. Devers, the postman, had gotten off the bus today, because as everyone in the village knew he had gone yesterday to the city to see his only son off for the army, and now Mr. Devers was standing on the corner with his suitcase talking to a stranger. Aunt Fanny was looking at the stranger.

Yes, the stranger agreed over tea and sandwiches at the Carriage Stop Inn, yes, he was a stranger. His tone implied that in faraway villages all over the world he was well-known, and a stranger in this village only. He hinted at himself striding recognized down exotic streets, walking in sandals through dust, moving slowly behind an oxcart or a rickshaw or a dog-sled, kicking aside the encumbrance of a cashmere robe, a furred cloak, shading his eyes from the sun, sheltering his head from the snow, regarding unmoved typhoon and flood, seeing with familiarity such scenes as the quiet eye could not envisage, laughing and looking easily and speaking intimately in strange tongues; yes, he agreed, he was a stranger. It was not possible even for Aunt Fanny to ask where he was from, but Aunt Fanny asked where he was going, as if she had not known when she saw him standing by the bus.

He was genuinely surprised when Aunt Fanny asked him to visit the big house, as though the invitation should not have come quite so soon, as though he had been caught unaware with his persuasions and insidious compliments unexpectedly useless; "Don't you even want to know my name?" he asked blankly.

"I suppose I shall have to introduce you to my brother," Aunt Fanny said. "Although I don't believe any name you might give would be important."

He looked from Aunt Fanny to Miss Ogilvie and back again. "How about my references?" he asked.

"I expect they would be forged," Aunt Fanny said agreeably.

"My mother once hired a butler who gave forged references, because he had been a convict."

"I see," said the stranger.

"My father suspected something in the way he walked. Naturally, when I invite you to my house as a guest I would hardly ask for references."

"I hadn't thought of it that way," said the stranger.

Miss Ogilvie, blushing, said to Aunt Fanny, "He seems to me to have something of a military bearing." She spoke as though the stranger, being so very strange indeed, could not hear her.

"Captain Scarabombardon," said Aunt Fanny unexpectedly.

"At your service," said the stranger, who was clearly extremely bewildered.

"In any case," Miss Ogilvie said, "we will all stand as one when the time comes. Cleansed. Pure."

"I do not recall that my father mentioned anything of our standing as one, Miss Ogilvie. You are a very fortunate man, Captain Scarabombardon." She picked up her gloves. "Julia should be coming with the car," she said. "Come along, Captain."

"Well," said Julia, when the stranger handed Aunt Fanny into the car, "and who might *you* be?"

"He is the captain," Miss Ogilvie explained eagerly. "He is coming home with us, Aunt Fanny invited him."

"Captain?" said Julia, who was not at all that bright, "captain of what?"

"I wish I knew," said the captain.

"Captain Scarabombardon?" said Essex, "am I to be an Harlequin now? I had dreamed of something more heroic. Did I ever tell you," he asked Mrs. Halloran, "of my trip to the moon?"

"Captain," Mrs. Halloran said, "will you have wine?"

The True Believers did not delay; perhaps the shortness of their time encouraged haste; at any rate Mrs. Halloran received, at the breakfast table the next morning, a letter written on violet paper with brown ink. The letter was heavily scented with carnation, and Mrs. Halloran read it aloud, holding it at arm's length.

Dear Fellows in Trust and Faith:

It is with the utmost joy that we here in our humble Society of True Believers, being as far as we knew until now the only select group to be chosen to carry the torch of mankind salute you. If we had known there was any other group like ours we could of gotten together sooner, but it is not yet too late. If you are of genuine faith and truly deserve the higher levels and will repent and sincerely follow the path of true teaching and never turn aside. Our leader will give herself the pleasure of calling upon you very soon and she will of course be able to tell right off whether you are on a spiritual level high enough to join our humble little band. In all life there is hope but of course it will not last much longer. Be prepared.

(Mrs.) Hazel Ossman, Secretary.

Mrs. Halloran folded the letter and put it carefully back into its envelope. "I assume," she said at last, "that someone will offer me a rational explanation of this. I am most reluctant to believe that I am going mad."

"It's that boy in the drug store," Miss Ogilvie said helpfully, anxious that Mrs. Halloran should not believe that she was going mad. "We were talking, yesterday, while Aunt Fanny was shopping."

"Aunt Fanny went shopping? I had not heard."

"I believe that I may go into the village, Orianna, without troubling to ask your permission. I have been accustomed to the village since I was a child, and I cannot remember ever having to ask permission to go there."

"How did you get there, Aunt Fanny? Did you walk?"

"Certainly not. Julia took a car from the garages."

Mrs. Halloran turned her eyes on Julia, who flushed and said defiantly, "No one told me not to."

"Besides," Aunt Fanny added maliciously, "how did you think the captain got here? We brought him back with us."

"I had done you the courtesy of assuming, Aunt Fanny, that the captain was another of your ghostly manifestations."

"Now wait a minute," the captain said. "I understood I was welcome here, and if I'm not I certainly know what to do about it," but he made no move to rise from the breakfast table.

"Captain," said Mrs. Halloran, "Aunt Fanny is kind enough to allow me to entertain my friends here; I can hardly refuse her the same civility. Julia, if you ever again touch anything belonging to me I shall send you away from this house. I leave it to your mother to point out to you what you would then forfeit. Aunt Fanny, you are surely right: you have never had to ask anyone's permission to go into the village, and I am sure that the villagers are used to you by now."

"My father took a great interest in the village. I have always tried to carry on his plans."

"Some of your father's activities in the village, Aunt Fanny, were luckily discontinued with his death. But I see no reason why you should be kept away from your subjects; next time please ask me for a car and I will send a reliable driver with you. Miss Ogilvie, I will expect you to receive these people with me, since you clearly know them better than I."

"I don't know them at all," Miss Ogilvie cried, "they are certainly not friends of *mine*."

"They may very well become friends of yours, however, and perhaps even closer than that; perhaps fellow survivors. We must not be overselect, Miss Ogilvie."

"Aunt Fanny," cried Miss Ogilvie pathetically, but she was abandoned; Aunt Fanny was speaking to Essex.

The leader of the True Believers was a lady of indeterminate shape, but vigorous presence, perhaps fortified by the silent support of Liliokawani, queen in Egypt. She swept into Mrs. Halloran's ballroom with the air of one testing the floor for durability; she was wearing a purple dress which presumably fit her, and a fur boa of color and fluff. Behind her came a second, also purple, lady, whose hair was red, and, behind her, a man whose determined majesty was most convincing; he had magnificent hair, which suffered a little by comparison with the leader's fluffy fur, and he wore, perhaps out of deference, a white waistcoat. At the very last came a withered little lady, peering.

"I am Edna," said the leader. "Our committee. Hazel, who is also our secretary. Arthur. Ah . . . Mrs. Peterson."

"Mrs. Peterson," said Mrs. Halloran majestically. She had been wise in her choice of the ballroom; beneath the sweeping carved ceiling and the white and gold candle sconces these four little people looked toylike; not so much out of place as decorative.

"We have come," said Edna, not faltering, "to inquire into your present position with regard to supernatural visitations. Prophecies. The end of the world, in fact. Someone told us, down in the village, and being as we're in much the same line . . ." She spread her hands eloquently.

"Dreadful are the hopes of man," said Mrs. Peterson drearily.

"Naturally," Edna continued, "we thought we might like to get together with you folks, if your ideas go along with ours. We don't take converts, as a rule, but naturally if you folks got to believing by yourselves I guess we got no choice. Anyway," she finished, "we got to get a place to meet."

"Everlasting darkness is the end of mortal life," Mrs. Peterson added.

"I'm the seer in our group," Edna said. "Who's yours?"

"I am not altogether sure," said Mrs. Halloran at last, "that we have a seer. What we do have, of course, is a place to meet. In that respect we are more fortunate."

"Eternal damnation attends us," Essex said helpfully.

"Well, who gets your messages?" Edna asked. "Her?" She gestured toward Miss Ogilvie, who gave a little gasp and took a step backward.

"Miss Ogilvie does not receive messages," Mrs. Halloran said. "Miss Ogilvie is our . . . contact with the outside world." Miss Ogilvie wrung her hands and looked ready to cry.

"When?" Edna demanded.

"When?" Mrs. Halloran was puzzled.

"My sword shall destroy life," said Essex.

"Horrible is the future ahead," said Mrs. Peterson.

"When is your date? Your outside limit?"

"We have not been so far honored . . ." Mrs. Halloran began.

"Jeepers." Edna was surprised. "Ever hear anything like it?" she asked her committee, and the woman with red hair and the man in the white waistcoat nodded and looked mournful.

"You, sir," the man said, addressing Essex. "Do you atone?"

"Daily," said Essex.

"Sin?"

"When I can," said Essex manfully.

"Metal?"

"I beg your pardon?"

"How do you stand on metal? Allow yourselves metal fastenings? Meat? Ills of the flesh?"

"I am heir to all of them," said Essex, inspired.

The man in the white waistcoat looked puzzled and turned to whisper into the ear of Edna.

"The time is near at hand, and vengeance is swift," said Mrs. Peterson.

Edna nodded vigorously at the man in the white waistcoat and came forward to speak earnestly to Mrs. Halloran. "Look," she said, "we're a whole lot further along than you folks, but even so we're willing to take you in with us on condition you try to catch up some, and of course we could meet here only out on your lawn, maybe, because we largely don't believe in roofs over our heads. Now I may as well tell you right off that we got all our messages already, so we just happen to know that the spacemen are coming—"

"Spacemen?" said Mrs. Halloran faintly.

"Spacemen, from Saturn. Why? Do you—"

"Not at all," said Mrs. Halloran.

"Well, we get it they're due along about the end of August, because the skies are clearest then. Early September, maybe, if it takes longer than they figure now to get here. And the saucers could land right out there on your lawn, see? It would be a good clear place. We're all going to be right there, ready and

waiting, with no metal fastenings and what not, and we figure
we go to Saturn where we get translated into a higher state of
being, but I can tell you more about *that* as we go along. Anyway, you got to start now practicing, get rid of all metal, and
no meat and of course no alcoholic beverages and none of
them fancy wines you probably got around here. Mrs. Peterson here is *our* cook."

"All hope is hopeless," Mrs. Peterson pointed out, "all striv-
ing vain."

"The *main* thing," Edna said, "the most important *main*
thing, is we got to be ready when they come. There's no second
trip, remember. You miss the first saucer—you never get a second chance. Once that saucer with your name on it leaves, it's
gone. And remember they won't take you if you're wearing
metal or been indulging in fancy wines. They *know.*"

"What do they drink on Saturn?" Mrs. Halloran asked with
interest.

"Ambrosia," said Edna unhesitatingly. "We got it in a message, because Arthur here was asking that very same thing.
Now suppose we figure out a schedule of meetings with you
folks, and after a couple times you'll get used to our ways, and
then you'll come out on the lawn with us, and—"

"Where have you been meeting until now?" Mrs. Halloran
asked.

Edna sighed. "Right now we've been meeting over to Mrs.
Peterson's, except her husband's kind of nasty about it and
Mrs. Peterson figures we better start going some place else,
particularly to eat."

"I am sorry," Mrs. Halloran said—she was frequently gentle
when she perceived that sharpness would be wasted—"I am
sorry, but I am afraid that we will not be able to qualify for your
space ship. I myself cannot do without my fancy wines, and I
believe that my associates—except possibly Miss Ogilvie—use
entirely metal fastenings. Miss Ogilvie?"

"Zippers," Miss Ogilvie whispered, pale. "Nothing but zippers. Everywhere."

"So you see," Mrs. Halloran continued, "we shall have to
make our own destinies, in addition to which I cannot possi-

bly hope to persuade my little group to leave this planet for another. Perhaps—after you have gone, of course—we may hope to inherit this one. Perhaps we may even come to like it."

"Well, you certainly don't expect—" Edna began, but was silenced when Mrs. Halloran held up one hand, regally.

"We wish you a pleasant journey," Mrs. Halloran said. "We hope that you will be very happy on Saturn, in . . . a higher order of being? Perhaps you will keep us under observation?"

"This earth has no temptations for us," Edna said stiffly, and Mrs. Peterson droned behind her, "A world well lost, and dire be its fate."

"Thank you," Mrs. Halloran said. "Mrs. Peterson, good day."

"Woe, woe," Mrs. Peterson said, and they filed out, Edna leading and Arthur hesitating briefly to investigate an erotic carving near the doorway of the ballroom. Mrs. Halloran gestured to Miss Ogilvie to follow and see them safely down the stairs, and Miss Ogilvie went quickly, half-backing out and half skittering.

"You know," Mrs. Halloran said, leaning back in her chair, "I could *kill* Aunt Fanny."

"Man's life is but a moment run," Essex said.

"Essex, stop it at once. You would make quite a good impression on Saturn, I should think."

Essex made a face. "Ambrosia is not my drink."

"Something must be done, however. I will *not* have space ships landing on my lawn. Those people are perfectly capable of sending their saucers just anywhere, with no respect for private property. I want all the gates in the wall checked, today. You and the captain had better go. Go right around the wall, all the way. Make sure that no one can get in anywhere—there may be spots where it has weakened, or fallen away. Lock all the gates, and see that they are kept locked. You may put on new locks, if it seems necessary to you. No one is to go in or out without my permission, and I mean *particularly* Miss Ogilvie."

"Aunt Fanny?" Essex asked softly.

"Yes." Mrs. Halloran sighed. "What a plague Aunt Fanny is

getting to be. I will not forbid her to visit the village, provided that she only passes through the gates with my permission. I will tell her that it is for her own protection, and trust that she will believe me. Her captain is, after all, a potential asset, and there is surely room enough inside the wall for all of us."

"This is all very well," Essex said, "but I do not see how it will keep out flying saucers."

"I could put up signs," Mrs. Halloran said irritably, "reading 'NO LANDING OF INTERSTELLAR AIRCRAFT PERMITTED HERE UNDER ANY CIRCUMSTANCES.' If any spaceships land on my lawn we will give them Aunt Fanny and Miss Ogilvie. I am really very angry, Essex; Miss Ogilvie, with her wanton chattering, has very nearly sent us all to Saturn."

"Not so long as you indulge in fancy wines," Essex pointed out.

"Furthermore," Mrs. Halloran said, "if any True Believer attempts to enter this house again, Essex, I want you and the captain prepared to inflict the most direct bodily retribution. The one true belief I want firmly implanted in the minds of the True Believers is the unshakable conviction that I am not one of their number."

"Much like Mr. Peterson, in fact."

"Not at all like Mr. Peterson; I find *his* reaction piddling."

"Perhaps," Essex said wickedly, "Aunt Fanny has been wrong all the time; perhaps this house and everyone in it will go with the rest of the world. The True Believers would then have the last laugh, you perceive. Unless," he added, "laughing also is forbidden on Saturn."

6

Aunt Fanny, meanwhile, was lost. She had planned to take her walk no farther than the beginning of the orchard, to admire the blossoms on the apple trees, and had gone aimlessly and without hurry around the side of the house, through the sunken rose garden, and down the orchard path, but there she had somehow, dreaming, lost herself. She had either come out the wrong gate from the rose garden, or turned off on a cross path, because the orchard was not ahead of her at all; it was not for several minutes that she realized that she had somehow gotten herself into the maze.

Now, the maze was not at all frightening to Aunt Fanny, who had grown up knowing its secrets. Like all mazes, it went to a pattern, and the pattern had been, romantically, built around the name of Aunt Fanny's mother, Anna. One turned right, left, left, right, and then left, right, right, left, and so on, alternating, until the center of the maze was attained. When Aunt Fanny had been a child it had been a dear puzzle to her, and she had spent hours trying to lose herself in the maze, but she could never forget her mother's name. Again and again, coming unerringly to the center of the maze, where there was a stone bench and a marble figure tantalizingly named Anna— although of course Aunt Fanny's mother would never have permitted herself to be portrayed from life in that state of un-dress; not, at the very least, without a petticoat—Aunt Fanny had thrown herself down in tears. Was she to be disappointed, always, because she could not forget the answer? Was she never to lose herself, as other people did so easily, could she never escape into the mad labyrinths and run confused?

And yet now, not a child any more, and long forgetting the maze, Aunt Fanny was at last lost. She stood with her back against a hedge, looking right and left at a divided path, and thought: I have not been here for so long, and it has not been kept up as it should. She was not frightened at first, because she had never yet succeeded in losing herself in the maze. The tall hedges grew up past sight on either side, although they should have been cut to just above her height, and they were not trimmed. The hedges had not been trimmed, before, along the walk to the secret garden, and Aunt Fanny sighed irritably; it was because she was the only person who traveled these ways, and it must not be tolerated.

Anna, she thought, Anna. She could at one time have almost drawn a picture of the maze, knowing so well its trickful turns and alleys, could have pictured faithfully the mysteries where she could not lose herself. There was one point where the path seemed to be going in a circle; although it was the right path, there was one false turn where long ago she had found a bird's nest. The finish, the climax, always came suddenly, when you were convinced that you were turned in the wrong direction. She had long ago made a little castle of her own in one dead end path. Now, so much later, she leaned her head back against the solid hedge and said Anna, and turned right. When I get to the center, she thought, I will check to see if the statue of Anna is as I remember; perhaps it has been neglected, or defaced. When I get out I shall tell Orianna Halloran that the hedges are a disgrace, even in the maze where no one ever comes any more. She turned left; I do not believe, she thought, wondering, that many of the others even know that there is a maze at all—there is so much that everyone has forgotten, or never been told in time. The hedges were so overgrown that the turns were indistinct, and once, where she was sure of a turn right, the branches crossed in front of her and kept her out. Irritably, Aunt Fanny went on.

Left, she turned, and then right again. Still not frightened, she stopped for a minute to remember with amusement a long forgotten fury: this, she remembered suddenly, was a turn which had particularly angered her long ago, because she knew so clearly, always, that it led to a dead end, and had never been able to fool herself with it; no matter how optimistically she had tried, telling herself that yes, this was surely the only right path, she could never make herself forget that she was leading herself down a wrong way. I never will forget it, either, I suppose, she thought, turning right, because it is part of my mind now, and has been for so long. I wish they had made it more difficult. Anna, Anna, Anna.

She was caught in a pocket of hedge. For a minute she believed that the hedges were only so overgrown that they hid the alley, and then she was at last aware that she had gone wrong, taken the bad turning somewhere, lost Anna. But then, she thought easily, wherever you are, Anna will bring you out. She turned back, moved right, hesitated, turned again, and was taken by the calculated bewilderments of the maze.

Once, running, she stopped and sank back, against the strength of the hedge and thought Minotaur, Minotaur; somewhere, the strong branches holding her around, tight away from freedom, she cried out "Anna, Anna" and turned and twisted wildly in a frantic escape from the trap of branches holding her helpless. Once she saw the way out clearly, and even reached her hands almost through the hedge into daylight but could not get through. But this is my own maze, she told herself, this is the maze I grew up in; I could not be a prisoner *here*; I know the way so perfectly, and she turned and was further lost.

It was much darker. Overhead the hedges seemed to meet, shading the alleys mortally; ahead there was nothing but a little light between the touching branches. Left, Aunt Fanny turned, right, right, left, and blundered against the taut grasping fingers of the twigs, felt her dress caught, and her hair, felt scratches on her cheeks under the sharply caressing touch; Anna, she said, turning left, Anna, turning right.

Look, she said aloud once—it was much later; it was very dark, and no one knew where she was—look, here is where I buried a doll once, when I was so small, and I buried my doll on a wrong turning so no one would ever find her grave. Right here is where I buried my doll. I could always find my way out, from here; I used to try to lose myself on this very path—this is where I used to come and hide when I was unhappy, and just beyond this turn is the spot where I cut my hand on a sharp branch and my brother bandaged it for me, because my mother was dead. We both cried, I remember; I used to come along this path pretending I was lost and could never go home again—no longer, she thought in despair; these ways are wrong now.

Then, before she would accept it, she was in the center of the maze. The hedges on either side separated and broadened, and her feet went from the gravel path onto lawn. There, in the gloom, was the marble bench, and, leaning over it pathetically, the statue named Anna, friendless now since no one ever came into the maze, leaning down with love to caress an empty place. Here was the center of the maze where no one could ever be lost who had a memory of her name. Aunt Fanny came unwillingly to the bench and fell against it. There were dried leaves blowing against the marble, and the figure leaned down overhead, holding out bare arms of tenderness and love. Aunt Fanny put her face down among the dried leaves and thought, well I am here, I am at the heart, I have come through the maze—where is the secret I am to learn from my many agonies? Here I am, here I am, where is my reward? What have I earned, learned, spurned? Mother, mother, she thought, and felt the marble warm under her cheek.

FRANCES. FRANCES HALLORAN.

Aunt Fanny found her way out of the maze without fault; she had no time to mistake the paths, running insanely (Anna, Anna) and if she was screaming there was no one to hear her or find her; FRANCES HALLORAN FRANCES FRANCES HALLORAN and Aunt Fanny pushed through twigs and leaves; FRANCES HALLORAN and she was out of the maze, onto the path to the rose garden FRANCES FRANCES FRANCES and there was Essex standing alone; "Essex," she called, "please help me, please—take me home"; FRANCES HALLORAN, and it was not Essex at all.

Aunt Fanny's second revelation was duly recorded by Mrs. Willow on four pages torn from the pad by the telephone in the main hall. Aunt Fanny's words were clearly and carefully spoken, and Mrs. Willow was able to take them down almost exactly, although her hand shook as she wrote. "It is coming," Mrs. Willow copied, "it is coming and my brother will be saved. There will be a night of horror, a night of terror and the father will watch over his children. The children must not be afraid. The children must wait. There will be screaming and imploring but the children may not go outside, the children must wait. It is coming, the father guards his children. Let the children wait."

"Why are you writing it down?" Miss Ogilvie asked. "It's almost the same as before."

"Shh," Mrs. Willow said, writing.

"My brother is not to be afraid." Aunt Fanny, turning wildly on the couch in the drawing room, tried to sit up, fell back, and threw her arms wildly. "My brother is not to be afraid," she said, urgently. "He will take us in his arms, he will shield us, he will cherish us and hide us, my brother is not to be afraid; even if it is all gone my brother will be safe. There is nothing to be afraid of, nothing to be afraid of, we are safe and warm, we are safe and warm, everything is all right, everything is all right, don't be afraid. I am right here, nothing can hurt you, nothing can get in. Brother, go back to sleep. Brother," she cried, striking at the air, "I am here, I am coming, we are safe." Then, very softly, "There will be a night of murder and a night of bloodshed but we will be saved. And now I lay me down to sleep, I pray the Lord my soul to keep—"

"Why are you taking *this* down?" Miss Ogilvie asked. "Everyone knows it by heart."

Aunt Fanny was quiet, and Mrs. Willow leaned over her and asked pressingly, "Tell us quickly, what must we *do?* Are we *all* safe in this house? Are we supposed to stay here? When will it *happen?*"

"Brother," Aunt Fanny said, and Mrs. Halloran said, "Essex, take care of her."

Essex leaned over Aunt Fanny and said gently, "Fanny? Can you tell us what we should do?"

"Essex," said Aunt Fanny, holding out her hand, and Essex, glancing over his shoulder at Mrs. Halloran, took Aunt Fanny's hand and said, "Fanny, tell us what we must do."

"We are absolutely safe here," Aunt Fanny said firmly. "We must cover the windows and doors lest the screams of the dying reach our ears and touch us with compassion; or the sight of the horror send us running mad into its midst. Wrong is wrong and right is right and Father knows best." And Aunt Fanny turned her head against Essex' arm.

"Well?" Essex said, glancing again at Mrs. Halloran, and Mrs. Halloran said, "Just find out how long; I like to know things well in advance. I detest being hurried."

"Aunt Fanny," Essex was saying, "can you tell us *when* this is going to happen? When? How long do we have?"

"You ask too many questions," Mrs. Willow objected. "Even *I* know that the medium can only answer one question at a time. For heaven's sake, with you clamoring at her like that—"

"When, Aunt Fanny?"

"After the snake," said Aunt Fanny. "After the dance. After the snake. After the day the night. After the thief the flight."

"Poetry," said Mrs. Willow disgustedly. She threw down her pencil. "When they start saying poetry they're no good anymore," she explained. "It takes their mind off it somehow."

"Miss Ogilvie," Mrs. Halloran said, "please take Aunt Fanny upstairs and put her to bed. She is no longer of any use to Mrs. Willow."

She had hardly finished speaking when the glass of the great picture window, which filled one short wall of the drawing room, and looked out over the sundial, shattered soundlessly from top to bottom.

7

A place of my own, Mrs. Halloran thought, turning restlessly and dreaming in the great rosy bed with silk sheets, a place all my own, a house where I can live alone and put everything I love, a little small house of my own. The woods around are dark, but the fire inside is bright, and dances in moving colors over the painted walls, and the books and the one chair; over the fireplace are the things I put there. I will sit in the one chair or I will lie on the soft rug by the fire, and no one will talk to me, and no one will hear me; there will be only one of everything—one cup, one plate, one spoon, one knife. Deep in the forest I am living in my little house and no one can ever find me.

"See, sister?"—and Mrs. Halloran dreamed the voice. "I told you we would find *some* place here in the forest."

She turned and saw two children, a boy leading a girl, and the boy wore the face of Essex and the girl was Gloria. For a minute she hesitated, watching from her doorway to see if they were coming toward her and when she saw that they were she fled into her house and shut and locked the door.

"I am so tired," said the girl.

"We can rest here if we want to, in this little house."

"Do you suppose anyone lives here?"

"If they do, they will be glad to give shelter to a lost girl and boy. In such a little house we won't find much, of course, but it will be good to stop and rest for a while. We can have them give us something to eat, and tell them we will sleep here tonight, and then tomorrow we can find our way home."

"Suppose they don't want us?"

"Don't be silly. We're lost, aren't we? And besides, we're only children."

"Brother—the house! It's made of candy!"

"Are you sure?"

"Of *course* I'm sure—come and taste it; look, the roof is sugar, and the walls are gingerbread, and the flowers are all hard and sweet and the dust is sugar dust. And taste the window frame—it's flavored with cinnamon, and the chimney is chocolate; you must climb up and get me a piece."

"And the tree here," said the boy, nibbling, "the tree is mint."

Feeling the roof being eaten away over her head, Mrs. Halloran opened the door carefully and looked out. For a minute, not knowing what to say, she only watched the boy and girl tearing great pieces away from her house and then, frightened, she shouted, "Stop it at once! This is *my* house!"

"Don't be silly, old woman," said the boy, his mouth full, "it's made of candy, isn't it?"

"I built this little house for myself and not for children to come and destroy; both of you get away at once, do you hear? This is *my* house where I live all alone."

"Shan't," said the girl and the boy paused in his eating to stare. "Old lady witch," he said at last.

"I am *not*."

"You are so, you are so." The boy shouted with his mouth full and Mrs. Halloran saw with terror that half the roof of her safe little house was gone, and worse, not eaten but crumbled and thrown on the ground where the children had pulled at it wildly. "You're an old witch," the boy chanted, and the girl took it up, throwing handfuls of dust, "You're an oooooooold witch."

"This is *my* house," Mrs. Halloran said, and the boy threw a piece of chocolate at her; when it struck close to the doorway where she stood he shouted with laughter and came running over to pull away half the doorway with one great tug, and he fell to munching at it while he said, giggling, "Old witch, old witch."

Mrs. Halloran thought clearly in her dream: if I could get them to come inside, she thought, where I live all alone, I might shut them up somewhere until they promise to spare my house; I might put them into cages until they promise to go away. "Will you come inside?" she said softly, and then, thinking, "There is even more candy inside."

"Did you hear?" said the boy to his sister, "*She* says there's more candy inside, come *on*."

They pushed her rudely away, forcing themselves through the broken doorway into the house, and she said, smiling but not turning, "Son, look into that little closet beside the door; you'll find licorice in there." Then she almost laughed, and said, "Daughter, go into the kitchen and search the cupboards; there is peppermint, and little cream cakes."

As the little house shook and strained with the eager burrowing of the children inside, she turned slowly and with pleasure followed them in; she closed the closet door on the boy and slammed the cupboard shut on the girl, and then came outside again to sit on the grass before her door and enjoy the evening sunlight, hearing them call pitifully to her from inside.

While she was sitting in the sunlight a woman, frantic, burst through the trees screaming, "My children—what have you done with my boy and my little gel; where are my children?" and when Mrs. Halloran looked up and laughed, the woman brushed her aside and hurried into the house, stopping as she went to break a piece of gingerbread off the roof. In a minute she returned, guarding the boy with one arm and the girl with the other, and the boy was saying "—and she was going to cook us and eat us because she's a witch, and she offered us pieces of her house and said there was licorice in the closet and there wasn't because all she wanted to do was get us inside and then she locked us in and she said she was going to cook us and eat us and we could hear her building the fire under the oven to roast us for her dinner."

The little girl added, "And she's a witch because she said there were cream cakes in the cupboard and she made me go inside and she was laughing all the time," and the little girl snatched away a fragment of the window frame and stuffed it into her mouth. "And I never got any chocolate from the chimney," she said, sulkily.

"Witch, witch," said the woman, turning to scowl viciously, "and don't *you* worry—we'll be back, with the others, and we'll show you what we do to witches who eat children, don't you worry." Shouting, "Witch! Witch!" they hurried off through the forest, and Mrs. Halloran, turning miserably in her sleep, looked hopelessly at her little house where she had lived alone, with one cup and one plate and one spoon, her little house which was not made of candy at all.

"There is something on the sundial," Maryjane said. "I can see it from here."

"A bird, most likely." Arabella, intending to walk slowly down the long lovely lawn, found herself turning toward the sundial in order to follow Maryjane. "I hate that thing," Arabella said. "The sundial."

"It's not a bird. It's something. But what *is* it?" as they came closer.

"My God." Arabella shuddered, and drew back. "Don't *touch* it."

"Of course I'll touch it; don't be silly. It's only one of the dolls from Fancy's doll house. But how *disgusting.*"

"Stuck full of pins," said Arabella.

"Disgusting. Someone's taken one of Fancy's dolls and put pins all through it. How *can* people treat a child like that, even around here?"

"It's an old lady doll," said Arabella, peering.

"Of course, it's Fancy's grandmother doll. The last I saw it was safely in the doll house, sitting at the little table. And now someone's taken it and ruined it."

"Is it really spoiled?"

"I don't care whether it's spoiled or not, it's just the *idea* of the thing. Fancy *loves* those dolls."

"Can you take the pins out?"

Maryjane pulled, tugging out one pin after another and dropping them into the grass. "Sometimes people make me so *mad,*" she said.

"I don't think it's hurt the doll. Those little dolls are only made out of wire and padding; that's how they can bend to sit down, you know, and look like they're walking."

"It *seems* all right," Maryjane said. "I'll take it back and put it in the doll house again and maybe Fancy won't ever know it's been gone."

"Or if she does notice you can just say you don't know what happened to it. Because you *don't,* after all."

On a very bright clear morning, the gates having been unlocked for the occasion, the first of Aunt Fanny's preparations arrived, the result of her shopping in the village and her orders sent to the city. Over the next few weeks, more of Aunt Fanny's orders kept coming, from mail order houses and supply houses in farther cities, in answer to Aunt Fanny's letters and telegrams.

The first truck, arriving on that bright clear morning, drove up to the service entrance of the big house, but it was almost immediately clear that there was not going to be room enough in the storage basements for the truck's contents, let alone for Aunt Fanny's further orders. In addition, there was some furtive conviction in Aunt Fanny's mind that the contents of the various cartons, and the exceedingly odd assortments of material she had gathered, ought to be kept as much as possible away from the servants in the big house, perhaps to avoid gossip; Mrs. Halloran, who was content to have the servants and villagers believe, as indeed they did, that Aunt Fanny's fine aristocratic mind was slipping rapidly into imbecility, directed, with some amusement, that Aunt Fanny's supplies be stored in the library, where the books lay against the walls, and the great tables and chairs in the center of the room could be pushed back to make space.

A series of mystified deliverymen carried the boxes and packages, some inadequately wrapped, through the service entrance, down the long hall into the formal portion of the house—the door between propped open by Essex with the bust of Seneca—and into the library, where everything was stored away. It was a scene not unlike the original provisioning of the library by the first Mr. Halloran, and the room of books, well dusted but not catalogued, looked down with an air of unbelieving surprise. Essex did not attempt to catalogue Aunt Fanny's purchases, but Mrs. Halloran, looking in some surprise on a carton of cans of peaches, asked Aunt Fanny, "Surely we are entering a land of milk and honey? Must we take our own lunch?"

"Sh," said Aunt Fanny, as a deliveryman entered, carrying a case of canned spaghetti. "Those cartons will fit into the bookshelves," she said, "lift some of the books out; it will give us more space for the cartons." The deliveryman set the carton down, unloaded half a shelf of books onto the floor, and put the carton into the bookshelf. He gave Aunt Fanny a puzzled look and went out. "I don't really think we'll need to supply our own food," Aunt Fanny said, with a trace of embarrassment. "It only seemed that perhaps, at first—while things are growing back, you know, and before we are quite *used* to the new ways—of course, there *will* be a period of adjustment. Put it in the bookshelf," she directed.

Mrs. Halloran regarded the little bundle of umbrellas the deliveryman was stuffing into the bookshelf.

"For the sun," Aunt Fanny explained eagerly. "We will have to build shelters eventually, of course."

"But surely . . . the house . . ."

"Sh," said Aunt Fanny. "Put it on the bookshelf, please."

Before the first truckload was delivered completely, it was quite apparent that the library was not going to hold everything, even though many of the books now sat in untidy piles on the floor and the shelves were filling up. Essex, inspired by some obscure compulsion he did not care to analyse, went to the back of the house where the orchard supplies were kept, and brought back half a dozen bushel baskets, and Aunt Fanny and Miss Ogilvie and Julia and Arabella tumbled the books into the bushel baskets. Aunt Fanny instructed the deliverymen returning to the truck to carry out bushel baskets of books and Mrs. Halloran, perhaps inspired by Essex, directed that the bushel baskets of books be carried to the barbecue pit and dumped there. While Essex industriously arranged cartons of canned milk and canned olives and canned soup on the shelves of the library, the captain and Mrs. Willow soaked the books with kerosene and watched them burn in the barbecue pit. As the first reluctant smoke rose and drifted past the library windows, Essex for a minute hesitated, moved a hand protestingly, and turned to Mrs. Halloran, who said, "They were none of them of any great value, Essex. Not a first edition among them, I should think," and added, obscurely, "and not made of candy."

"I suppose I should be pleased that my cataloguing days are at an end," Essex said, and turned to set a carton of paper cups on the bookshelf.

The work of unloading the truck and loading the library shelves, carrying out and burning the books, went on swiftly. It was only noon when the enormous van backed heavily away from the service door, and the library had an odd air of not having been changed in any very fundamental manner; half the shelves were packed with cartons, but they were neat, and when Essex brought back the bust of Seneca he remarked, "A library is really a very good place to store things. I had never realized it before."

"There is room for a good deal more," Aunt Fanny said, looking with anticipation at the two sides of the room still holding books. "I think we shall do very nicely. Larger items, such as the bicycles, for instance, can go into the cellar."

"I am still not clear," Mrs. Halloran said, "on these quantities of supplies. Surely it was expressly stated that a world of plenty—"

"Even in a world of plenty," Aunt Fanny said sharply, "you could hardly imagine that we would process our own olives, Orianna. Certain small luxuries . . ."

"What has happened to the old-fashioned silkworm?" Mrs. Halloran asked, fingering a bolt of scarlet synthetic fabric. "Do you expect us to dress like madwomen, Fanny?"

"I hope," said Aunt Fanny stiffly, "that even in a better world I shall still continue a lady."

"Aunt Fanny," Essex said, "you understand that my belief in you is in no way failing?"

"Well?" said Aunt Fanny; she sat down in one of the great library armchairs and fanned herself lightly.

"Aunt Fanny," Essex said, "it is not possible that you might be wrong?"

"Wrong about what, Essex?"

Essex fumbled. "Wrong . . . about your father?"

"How could I be wrong about my father? He was a man of complete integrity. Tall, and with a good presence. Bred well," and Aunt Fanny glanced, fleetingly, at Mrs. Halloran.

"Aunt Fanny," Essex said, "I am not doubting your father's word."

"Hardly, Essex."

"But please do not laugh at me, because I am actually very much frightened. All these things you have brought here—"

"Acting under my father's instructions, I need hardly explain."

"It seems so remote," Essex said wildly.

"Not remote, I assure you; not remote at all. I should try to understand, if I were you, that when my father takes the trouble to come so far, the business must be very serious indeed. And I am persuaded that the end may come sooner than we realize, although of course my father has engaged to let us know in enough time."

"And you believe him?"

"Believe my father, Essex? My *father?*"

"Aunt Fanny," Essex said, "tell us about it again. What will it be like, afterwards?"

"Much as it is now, I expect. I foresee a period of adjustment; it will take some time, for instance, for the earth to recommence its cycle of reproduction, and such things as trees may take a while to grow to the point where they produce fruit. And we will have to find food somewhere. I can only suppose that we will come out, that first morning, into a world wiped clean and bare, with no sign that it has ever harbored anything living except ourselves. It will be lovely, with the loveliness of all fresh beginnings, but I cannot see how, those first few days, we can expect to live off the land. Soon it will be quite a Garden of Eden, of course. Although as I recall the

Garden of Eden, it was not so well managed; I mean," said
Aunt Fanny, blushing, "for all we know, there may have been
hundreds of prohibitions. Not only just that one tree, for instance."

"But no prohibitions for us?" Essex asked tensely.

"None, I should think. We will of course learn a good deal
more about it as time goes on. But not, I should think about
things we may *not* do; I would really believe that, humanity
being for all practical purposes at an end, the kind of moral
disapproval which has been so necessary up until now will be
wholly unnecessary; *we,* after all, will not need to learn to behave ourselves."

"You talk of our living among green meadows and flowers
and trees," Essex went on insistently; "What—" and he held
his breath "—what about this house? It will be here, full of
valuables in this world and that."

"I have been thinking about that, too," said Aunt Fanny,
and gave a kind of little laugh. "It has seemed to me that this
house will become a kind of shrine, for our children and for
their children. Living in the fields and woods as they do, living
under a kindly sun and a gentle moon, with all their wants
supplied from nature, they will have no thought of houses, and
a roof will become to them synonymous with an altar; we may
yet live to see our grandchildren worshipping in this house."

"I should hope so," Mrs. Halloran said.

"I am—instructed, as I said, by my father—arranging to accumulate in this house all those items of practical value we
might otherwise leave behind. There are things which may be
useful to the innocents of that other world, and they will find
them here, in the shrine of their gods. Tools, for instance. Jewels, which may seem almost magical to them. The lovely lines
of the stairway; we must not let a sense of beauty vanish from
the world."

"My silver service," Mrs. Halloran said drily.

"Possessions of the gods," Aunt Fanny said. "My father
would like that."

"Not in *my* lifetime," Mrs. Halloran said. "They are legally
willed to me."

"I think," Gloria said unexpectedly from a dark corner of the room, and her tone silenced them, "I think they will come, those far-off people, moving fearfully into this house and not daring to touch anything, looking at the furniture and walls and floors the way we look at cave paintings or catacombs or ancient palaces; I think they will come on a kind of pilgrimage. They will come in little groups, walking on carefully designated paths so that they will not touch anything or brush against the walls or jar any furniture, and they will walk very softly the way people do when they are walking in the footsteps of many many dead people and are afraid of wakening them or angering them; I think they will not understand much of what they find in this house, but they will tell stories about it, and about us. I think it will be a sacred and terrible and mysterious place for them."

"I forbid all this," Mrs. Halloran said loudly and suddenly. "I will *not* leave this house in my lifetime. The rest of you may live in trees with my blessing."

"Your blessing will count for so little," Aunt Fanny murmured, "afterward."

8

"'I had, as I hinted before,'" the nurse read, going slowly in her flat voice, "'a parcel of money, as well gold as silver, about thirty-six pounds sterling; alas! there the nasty, sorry, useless stuff lay; I had no manner of business for it, and I often thought with myself, that I would have given a handful of it for a gross of tobacco-pipes, or for a hand-mill to grind my corn; nay, I would have given it all for six-penny worth of turnip and carrot seed out of England, or for a handful of pease and beans, and a bottle of ink.'"

Daily Julia and Arabella and Maryjane brought in armfuls of heavy, rich roses for the silver bowls in the drawing room and the dining room. The sundial stood out more whitely against the deep green of the lawn; there were apricots on the breakfast table. Aunt Fanny, in her mother's diamonds, listened always, and late one night Mrs. Willow, aroused by what she thought was someone after the silver, found Aunt Fanny at the head of the great stairway in her nightgown, rapt and still and smiling; "The time is drawing closer," she said, when Mrs. Willow roused her.

Although Gloria was most unwilling, Mrs. Willow was not a patient woman, and disliked the vagueness of Aunt Fanny's appointments; she insisted that Gloria look into the mirror again. "You're *used* to it," Mrs. Willow explained, "you know it by now. We don't want to keep starting new people at it. Besides, no one but you will do it."

Reluctantly, Gloria sat again before the mirror where the oil ran and shivered, and leaned her face down to look. "I hope I see something pleasanter this time, that's all," she said. "If I see any more of those terrible things you can just get someone else to look, and I don't care whether they get mixed up or not on the other side."

"I wonder what nonsense we would be engaged in, if we were not doing this," Mrs. Halloran remarked.

"We are the gods," Essex said, "sitting on the front porch of Olympus, regarding the doings of men. It is probably just as well that we have some nonsense to occupy us; think of the harm we could do if we were bored."

"Well, don't all keep watching *me*," Gloria said. "You make me nervous."

Mrs. Willow and Aunt Fanny moved back a little, eyeing one another.

"We'll just wait," Mrs. Willow said comfortably. "You let us know when you see something."

"I hate it when it starts to move," Gloria said. She stirred uneasily in her chair. "It's like being seasick—everything kind of churns around, and you think you can't last another minute, because you're sinking into this horrid moving whirling twirling curling—I see a country. It's clear. I see a country, a nice country."

"What country, dear?" Mrs. Willow was making notes, in a notebook she had bought for the purpose and into which she had copied all of her previous records of Aunt Fanny's statements.

"Just a countryside. Trees, and grass, and flowers. Blue sky. Nice birds."

"People?"

"No people. No houses. No fences or roads or television aerials or wires or billboards. No people. There's a hill, with trees on it, and . . . it's like a meadow. Soft." She hesitated. "There aren't any . . . separations in it, that's what I'm trying to say. Nothing like walls or fences, just soft green countryside going off in all directions. Perhaps that's a river over there."

"Presumably every prospect pleases," Essex said.

"Wait . . . I can see someone coming, over the hill; Essex, it looks like you, only you aren't dressed . . . you haven't got any . . ." Gloria turned scarlet and put her hands against her cheeks, but she did not sit back.

"Go ahead, dear," Mrs. Willow said. "We're not squeamish."

"You might try to get me into a lion skin or a pair of bathing trunks," Essex said. "I probably don't know there are peeping toms around."

"You are . . . could you be hunting?"

"Hunting for what, in God's name?" said Mrs. Halloran.

"Almost certainly for a pair of bathing trunks," Essex said. "Couldn't I please stand behind a bush?"

"Be quiet," Mrs. Willow said. "This is quite serious."

"It's so lovely," Gloria said.

Essex opened his mouth to speak, but Mrs. Willow gestured violently at him and he was quiet.

"It's such a *beautiful* country. Essex is gone; there are just soft hills and trees and that blue blue sky."

"Thank God I am out of sight," Essex said irrepressibly. "I was beginning to have that feeling of being stared at."

"Look," Gloria said, "oh, look," and she laughed. "It's changing," she said, "it's like a little painting of a landscape, and it's changing so I can see over the hill and through the trees and now there are people, very far away. They're . . . dancing, I think; the sun is so bright. Yes, dancing."

"Dressed?" asked Essex, who was enjoying himself enormously.

"I can't tell, it doesn't matter anyway. They're very far away, and so tiny, and the trees are so tall around them; I really think they *are* dancing. And I can see the flowers and grass moving a little, as though there were just the smallest breeze, and now I see a . . . is it a deer? And birds. And a rabbit."

"Our ark has landed," Mrs. Halloran said to Essex.

"Tell me, dear," Mrs. Willow said, "if we ask you questions do you think you can see the answers?"

Gloria closed her eyes. "I'll try," she said, sitting back. "That was pretty."

"It really gives me quite an odd feeling," Essex said. "I shall probably never hunt again."

"It seems to me," Mrs. Willow said, "that Gloria really sees in the mirror what we want her to. Be quiet, Essex. What I mean is that before, when she saw all horrible things, it was because we were all frightened and confused. Now that we know pretty well what to expect, it seems to me that they are showing her more of what we want to see. Maybe I'm not making myself clear." She looked over at Miss Ogilvie, who nodded mutely. Mrs. Willow sighed. "Gloria, dear," she said, "we don't want you to dwell on destruction and fear. We like your pretty pictures much much better. Now I have a good idea here; I'm going to ask you to look into the mirror and try to see the people in this house, just one month from today. That would be the end of June. Now think about the people in this house, and look into the window and see a picture of what we will be doing one month from today." She turned to the others. "Trying to find out how much time we have left," she explained. "Go along, Gloria."

Gloria leaned forward, her elbows on the table and her chin between her hands. She looked steadily into the mirror, and her long hair fell on either side of her face, almost touching the table. "Roses," she said at last. "Roses on the table in the dining room. Pink."

"That would be the rambler," Aunt Fanny said. "My mother's favorite. They planted six bushes for her, and it's true, they come into bloom about the last of June."

"All of us are there," Gloria said, and giggled. "It's funny," she said, "I'm there, too. It's like a little picture, only the people are moving. We're tiny. We're having breakfast. Essex . . ."

"What am I wearing?" Essex asked prudently.

"A white shirt, I think. You're telling a story, and we're all laughing. I'm wearing my blue and white cotton dress; it must be very warm."

"Then I believe that we can assume that nothing will have happened before the end of June," Mrs. Willow said. "Gloria, think now. Try the end of July. Try to see all of us near the end of July. The end of July, Gloria."

"We're playing tennis," Gloria said almost at once. "We're

all at the tennis courts. Julia and the captain are playing against Arabella and me."

"I might have known," Arabella said, with a cross look at her sister.

"All the rest of you are sitting out on white chairs and benches and there is a green and orange and yellow umbrella and a little table; you're drinking; it must be terribly hot because we're wearing light dresses and shorts. I'm wearing a pair of blue-striped shorts and it's funny, because I don't own such a thing."

"I'll lend you mine," Julia said helpfully.

"We use that same umbrella by the tennis courts every summer," Mrs. Halloran said, "but how does Gloria know about it, or its colors? It is packed away in the carriage house, and has been since long before she came here."

"I can see it," Gloria said.

"The important thing is that what she sees shows us that nothing has happened yet," Mrs. Willow said. "Naturally there will not be tennis courts or colored umbrellas *afterwards*." She leaned forward and put her hand again on Gloria's head. "Look again, dear. Look and see what we are doing at the end of another month. What are we doing, in the mirror, around the last of August?"

Gloria frowned, leaning closer to the mirror. "It's hard," she said, "because it's so dark. All the windows are closed. I don't know who's there, they're all like shadows. The sun is gone."

"What are they doing?"

"I think . . ." Gloria said hesitatingly, "I think they're trying to push something . . . maybe the big hall chest. Maybe a big sofa or something like that. They're going to push it against the door. The candles are lighted, but it's still very dark. They're in the big hall, I can see the tiles on the floor. They're . . ." she shivered ". . . barricading themselves in, I think. It's very dark."

"Can you see any faces?"

"I can see Fancy, I think. Maybe it only looks like Fancy because it's smaller . . . no, it *is* Fancy, she just came near a lighted candle. She's . . . laughing."

"Laughing? While we barricade the doors?"

Essex spoke softly to Mrs. Halloran. "Edna's True Believers said the end of August, you know."

"If that crackpot has the date right I will eat a Martian," Mrs. Halloran said.

"Try to move a little farther, Gloria," Mrs. Willow said. "Try to see the end of that night; try to see the next morning."

"I can't," Gloria said. "It's going away." She sat back and looked at the mirror, which showed the faulted reflections of the cupids on the ceiling. "It scares me," she said.

"Aunt Fanny proposes, Gloria disposes," Mrs. Halloran said. She touched the sundial gently. "We will not count many more hours *here*," she said.

"It still does not surprise you to know how easily we all capitulated?" Essex asked.

"I am not wholly convinced yet, Essex."

"You let the library go."

Mrs. Halloran laughed. "Perhaps I am an instinctive book-burner."

"I think you had a reason for encouraging Aunt Fanny to burn the books."

"Surely, Essex, Aunt Fanny is not so young as she was; I can hardly refuse her these small pleasures. In any case, opposition to Aunt Fanny is not part of my general plan; in our better, cleaner world I will come to grips with Aunt Fanny."

"The captain and Julia have been whispering together in corners," Essex said. "Mrs. Willow is always watching them."

"We cannot afford to lose the captain," Mrs. Halloran said. "If Aunt Fanny is right, Essex, your own tasks would without the captain approach the superhuman."

"You forget," Essex said. "I am to be the huntsman."

After a minute Mrs. Halloran said, "That did not please me. I am beginning to dislike that girl, Gloria. And I suspect her visions."

"You can easily assure yourself of her truthfulness, however; I have a small scar on my left thigh."

––––––––––

"Does the old lady keep much cash around the house?" The captain's voice was soft, and Julia only nodded. They were sitting in the summer house, from which they could see into the secret garden behind and down the long lawn ahead of them; far away Mrs. Halloran and Essex bent over the sundial.

"I don't know how much longer I can stand it," the captain said.

"My mother keeps watching us," Julia said.

The captain laughed. "I don't mind your mother," he said. "She's not as bad as the rest; even the old party in the corner . . ."

"Miss Ogilvie."

"Miss Ogilvie. She's not too bad. But the crazy one . . . Aunt Fanny, I mean . . . she was around knocking on my door last night when everyone was asleep; 'Captain,' she says, 'let me in, let me in, I'm only forty-eight years old.' God." He shivered. "I was going to shove all the furniture in the room against the door and lean on it."

Julia laughed. "One of these nights you'll forget to lock your door."

"Not *me;* catch me taking a chance like that. How can we get away? The gates are locked, and she sent me and Essex to make sure no one could climb over the wall."

"Worse than that, we'd have to have some kind of a car. We can't walk all the way to the village and even if we get to the village there's only two fool busses each day. They'd catch us in half an hour."

"What makes you so sure they *want* to catch us?"

Julia grinned wickedly. "Not *me,*" she said. "It's not *me* they want. They'd let me go and gladly, even my mother. *I* am not the father of future generations."

"My God," the captain said. "Can we try for it today?"

"We're not in prison," Julia said, "and I'm not going to be treated as though we were . . . you know, trying to sneak out in a delivery truck or something like that. I wonder if we could just *tell* her we want to leave?"

"Not *me,*" said the captain. "I personally wouldn't be surprised if they had a dungeon in the cellar."

"Mother?"

"What is it, Belle?"

"Julia's out in the summer house with the captain again."

"I know it."

"You know what I bet they're doing?"

"Yes, I know what you bet they're doing. But they're not. It's *my* guess they're planning to run for it."

"You mean Julia's going to leave this house? With the captain?"

"I think so."

"That's not *fair*. There are *only* two men in the house, after *all*, and the other one is Essex. You *can't* let him leave."

"I don't know how I could stop them."

"Well, it's not *fair*. You've *always* liked her better than me."

"Aunt Fanny, they're there again. Out in the summer house. Whispering in each other's faces."

Aunt Fanny smiled obscurely. Miss Ogilvie peered through the curtains of the little sitting room where she and Aunt Fanny spent their mornings sewing. "Sitting close together," Miss Ogilvie said.

"I hope they will not be too disappointed," Aunt Fanny murmured.

"Well, they certainly don't *look* like they might be disappointed. I think Mrs. Halloran ought to put a stop to it. It's not healthy for Fancy, having things like that going on right in public."

"I believe their paths will not always run side by side," Aunt Fanny said. "For the present, perhaps, but the briefest consideration of the future, Miss Ogilvie, should point out to you their differing roles."

"Well, of course I know what the captain is for," said Miss Ogilvie, and blushed. "That is," she explained, "I never really thought about it particularly, not for *myself*, that is. But I mean, why can't Julia . . ."

"Miss Ogilvie, in this finer world of ours you do not suppose that we, you and I, will work with our hands? Surely you appreciate the need for a . . . what shall I call it? . . . a servant class? Who, after all, are to be the hewers of wood and the fetchers of water?"

"How nice," said Miss Ogilvie, and blushed again.

"My instructions from my father," said Aunt Fanny mysteriously, "have been far more detailed than many of you realize."

"Fancy, bring Mama her chocolates, will you?"

"I can't, I'm busy."

"Do you want your poor sick Mama to have to get up and get them herself?"

"I'll do it in a minute."

"You're a sweet baby, Fancy. Maybe in a little while you'll run and ask the captain to come and read to me."

"He's out in the summer house with that Julia, talking and talking."

"I'm sure he won't mind leaving *her* to comfort me a little when I'm not well."

"I'll ask him. But I bet he doesn't come."

"You better tell your granny about how the captain and Julia are always hanging together."

"'It happened one day about noon,'" the nurse read flatly, "'going towards my boat, I was exceedingly surprised with the print of a man's naked foot on the shore, which was very plain to be seen in the sand. I stood like one thunderstruck, or as if I had seen an apparition. I listened, I looked round me; I could hear nothing, nor see anything; I went up to a rising ground to look farther. I went up the shore, and down the shore, but it was all one, I could see no other impression but that one.'"

9

"My dear Julia," said Mrs. Halloran, deeply shocked, "is it your impression that you are being kept here as a prisoner?"

"I just want to leave, is all," Julia said sullenly. "The captain and I . . . we want to get the hell out of here."

"By all means." Mrs. Halloran shook her head. "I could hardly condemn you to stay. My own opinions would not, certainly, encourage *me* to leave, but I have no reason to suspect that you take your opinions from mine. That is, I feel that you are miserably mistaken, but since you do not share my belief, any attempt on my part to prevent you from leaving would be ridiculous, and, I suspect, wholly wasted."

"I just want to get out of here," Julia said. "*With* the captain."

"Yes. *With* the captain. Since you have taken on the burden of announcing your joint intentions I conclude that the captain does not possess quite the dashing military bravado Aunt Fanny found in him; do not be alarmed, child . . . you may leave, and your captain may leave, any time you choose. I am only disturbed that there should have been any question in your mind . . . beyond, of course, the great final question which occupies the rest of us so entirely."

Julia stared. "You're not going to try to stop us?"

"Am I an ogre? Is this castle of mine guarded? Patrolled by dragons or leopards? Do we live under a spell, as in the City of Brass, or an evil enchantment, as madmen flung down upon their faces when they step outside their gates; can you believe that . . ."

"I'll tell the captain," Julia said. "And, Mrs. Halloran . . . thanks."

"Not at all, child. Remember that you will require your mother's consent as well as mine."

"She won't care if I go or stay."

"Transportation to the city may be a difficulty for you. I regret that I have at present no one whom I can spare to drive you there, but I know of a fellow from the village who may be available. I will arrange it, of course. I suppose you are anxious to be on your way as quickly as possible?"

"We certainly are."

"Then I will not trouble you to wait until tomorrow. The car will be waiting at the main gates, at nine this evening."

"That will be fine," Julia said, her eyes shining. "We can be in the city tonight."

"Considering the short, the painfully short, amount of time left you to enjoy the pleasures of the world, I cannot criticize your haste."

"Look," Julia said, "one reason I'm leaving, and the captain too . . . we don't believe that crap, any of it."

"I said earlier that I did not ask you to believe anything. I am only wishing you godspeed, into the world and out of it."

"Well," Julia said uncertainly, "you've been nicer about it than I expected. I will say that for you. I never thought we'd be able to talk you into it. Anyway, thanks."

"If you will now send the captain to me, I should like to say goodbye to him. I see the question on your face, Julia, and I will answer it: yes, I do intend to give him money, because I feel indebted to you both . . . not choosing to share our new world, you have been thoughtful enough to withdraw from it without attempting to jeopardize the chances of the rest of us. Now run along and pack all your prettiest clothes; it is already after seven, so I will have a dinner tray sent to your room, in order not to interrupt your preparations."

"Mrs. Halloran," Julia said, hesitating in the doorway, "look . . . thanks again."

"You are certainly welcome, child, for anything I may have done."

"Julia said you wanted me, Mrs. Halloran."

Mrs. Halloran turned from her desk, smiling. "Captain," she said, amused, "what are you so afraid of? I have invited you to come here to say goodbye."

"We thought, Julia and I, that you were going to be sore at us."

"Not at all. I explained to Julia that there was nothing in any of our plans which justified keeping people here against their wills. You *do* want to leave?"

"I sure do." The captain sat, awkwardly, and stared at his feet. "I wouldn't go, you know—you've been pretty nice to me, after all—if I really figured I was . . . well . . . leaving you in the lurch, as it was. I mean, in all this stuff about being the only people left in the world, and so on, what Julia thought was . . ." he stopped, red. "I mean," he went on in a rush, "if you need *men*."

Mrs. Halloran laughed. "Any Utopian community has need of both sexes, surely," she agreed. "And I believe the Shakers, who live together as brother and sister only, are dying out with all the rapidity one would expect; a basic regard for reproduction of the species—and how could such a regard *not* be basic, I wonder?—cannot be excluded from any of our plans, even Aunt Fanny's. That does not mean, Captain, that we must capture our men, like a pack of lunatic priestesses feeding on their mates. I have every hope, in short, of replacing you amiably and very likely without even the use of force."

"Mrs. Halloran," the captain said, looking up earnestly and speaking with great care, "you *do* believe this, don't you? That is, you do honestly and in your heart believe that everything is going to go and you people here in the house will be the only ones left?"

"Worse still," Mrs. Halloran said gently, "I believe that you and Julia are going willfully out into a dying world and that you will have perhaps only a few weeks of life before you are . . . persuaded . . . that my beliefs are correct. I am sickened to think of your state of mind when you learn, at last, that you were mistaken."

"I don't get it." The captain shook his head. "I don't figure you're crazy or anything," he said, reassuringly, "I don't for a minute want you to think I'm criticizing you. But I just don't see how any person with any sense can go for that stuff. How can the world end? There's no sense to it. Besides," he went on ruefully, "one thing I know—nothing like that happens in my lifetime. I mean, why should I figure I'm so special, the world is going to end while I'm around?"

"I am sure you will be around," Mrs. Halloran said, "and certainly a number of amazing things have already happened during your lifetime, and not the least of them is that you should be alive at all. But this is a time-wasting debate. I know that you and Julia are eager to be off, and I feel poignantly that you have so little time that I am unwilling to diminish it by so much as an hour. I have arranged with Julia that a car from the village will be waiting by the main gate at nine tonight, and by eleven you should be in the city, drinking deeply, I hope, of its gaieties."

"Yes," the captain said. "The sooner the better."

Mrs. Halloran turned to her desk and her checkbook. "I will not stop to put this gracefully," she said. "I have explained to Julia that I am eager to smooth your remaining path; I suspect that you are both expensive people, and so I have made out a check for you." She tore the check from the checkbook and handed it to the captain, who hesitated, tried to seem indifferent, and then looked at the check.

"Listen," the captain said, pale, "this is a damn nasty joke."

"Not at all," Mrs. Halloran said. "I am not above spiteful gestures, surely, but at least this time my intentions are perfectly aboveboard. I spoke to the president of the bank in the city not half an hour ago; poor man, I took him away from a dinner party, and he will not enjoy dinner parties for long. The check will be freely honored."

"But—" said the captain. He waved the check helplessly. "You did make a mistake," he said at last.

"No mistake," Mrs. Halloran said gently. "That is the maximum sum I am able to command on short notice. The president of the bank was easily as astonished as yourself, but he is accustomed to doing what I tell him. That check—which, I agree with you, is enormous—will be honored upon your presentation of it."

"But *why?*"

"We are not going to need it," Mrs. Halloran said. "Please try to understand, Captain—we are not going to need it any more."

The captain sat down abruptly. "You *mean* this?" he demanded. "You are really going to sit there and nod at me and hand me more money than I ever dreamed of in all my life, just for nothing? Why, I've only been here three weeks—I couldn't *steal* this much." He waved his hands wildly. "This kind of money is something I never even *heard* of, they don't make that much, it isn't *real,* and you just sit there and *give* it to me—lady, maybe I was wrong about you not being crazy."

Mrs. Halloran laughed again. "Maybe you were," she said. "My own belief is that there will not be time for even you to spend it all."

"It'll take some spending, I admit," the captain said, looking at the check again. "Now look, I'm not aiming to quarrel with someone who just handed me a lousy fortune, but I'm *not* crazy, and I got to figure there's some string attached. Something's going to happen to me."

"Please believe that I am crazy, if you like, but not that I am dishonest."

"I ought to grab this thing and get up and run and not stop running till I get to that bank and I make sure it's true. But I don't like not understanding what goes on, and I like to make sure that young Harry—Harry's my real name," he explained.

"Indeed? I shall continue to call you Captain."

"Anyway, that young Harry doesn't get left out in the cold. You really believe—now let me get this absolutely straight one last time—you really believe that you can give me this money because it's not going to be any more good to you? Right now this check is worth exactly what it says but in a few weeks it's not going to matter what money I have because I won't be there and the bank won't be there and the money won't be there and there won't be any place to spend it anyway?"

"Exactly as I would have put it," Mrs. Halloran said.

"Then take it back," said the captain. He rose and set the check down softly on Mrs. Halloran's desk. "I never took odds like that in my life," the captain said. "I know a lot about you by now, and if you're ready to put that kind of money on the line, I figure Harry goes along with you. I stay."

"Think carefully, Captain. We have so little time; you may not have another opportunity of changing your mind."

"I don't have to think," the captain said. "I know when I'm beat."

"Then you had best get right down to dinner. I will see that Julia is notified, and will join you shortly at the table."

After dinner Mrs. Halloran hesitated at the table for a minute, after the others were gone, to speak to Mrs. Willow. "I imagine that Julia is well on her way," Mrs. Halloran said.

"I just hope she is," Mrs. Willow said viciously. "Damn selfish unnatural child."

"You will be more pleased with her, perhaps," Mrs. Halloran said, "when I tell you that before she left she took the liberty of helping herself to the money on my dressing table."

"How much?" said Mrs. Willow, and then: "I suppose you left it there accidentally?"

"Not at all. I hardly liked seeing Julia go off with no adequate financial resources."

"How much?"

"I am embarrassed," Mrs. Halloran said. "I feel like Aunt Norris. I could not put my hands onto more than about seventy dollars. Seventy-four dollars, to be exact, and eighty-nine cents. She took the silver, naturally."

"Julia is not above carrying small change," Mrs. Willow said.

"We will miss her," Mrs. Halloran said vaguely, and continued on into the drawing room, and her shawl, and her evening walk with Essex.

Julia, her suitcase on the ground beside her, stood in the warm dark evening by the main gates of the house. There was only a single light over the gates, and it showed more than anything else the elaborate scrolled H which centered each half of the gates; far away, beyond the long reaches of the drive, she could see an occasional dim flicker which must be the lights from the house, and she smiled. She felt almost pity for her mother and sister, trapped in the monumental lunatic asylum, and a growing excitement at the thought of being, tonight, in the city with the captain, with money and laughter and noise. She was pleased at having slipped soundlessly into Mrs. Halloran's room, to take the money the careless old woman had left lying around, she was deeply amused at the thought of herself and the captain, wandering luxuriously—perhaps to the Orient, perhaps to Spain—while her mother and her sister waited cruelly in the big house for a magnificent destruction which never came about; she was even glad that she had said thank-you to Mrs. Halloran, since some day she might choose to come back here, furred and jewelled, to smile pityingly upon her older sister, grown weak and silly waiting for a new world.

When a car pulled up beside her she was startled for a minute, and then, looking more closely, annoyed. Mrs. Halloran had not been above a petty revenge: the car was old and shabby, and the driver looked like a ruffian.

"You the party going to the city?" he asked, leaning forward over the steering wheel to peer at her.

"I'm going to the city, yes. Did Mrs. Halloran send for you?"

"Right. Pick up a lady at the gates, nine o'clock."

"There's a gentleman coming, too."

"Not now, there ain't." The driver laughed richly. "No gentleman coming *this* trip, lessen you mean *me*."

"You are mistaken. I am waiting for a gentleman who is going to the city with me."

"Not the way *I* hear it. Mrs. Halloran, she says to me on the telephone, you go at nine o'clock tonight to the main gates, you get a lady there, take her to the city. She will be going quite alone, Mrs. Halloran she says, quite *quite* alone."

"I am sure that Mrs. Halloran could not have said anything of the sort. We are going back to the house, right now, and make sure about this. And when Mrs. Halloran hears—"

"'We are going back to the house right now and make sure about this,'" he said in a high false voice. And then, "How?"

"Why . . ." Julia turned; the gates behind her were locked. One of the gardeners had met her at the gates, unlocked them for her, and seen her out, and she had supposed vaguely that the man was still around, prepared to unlock the gates again for the captain. When she called, however, and shook at the gates, there was silence, and no movement, beyond the faint reflection of the one light onto the scrolled H on either half of the gates.

"Whyn't you climb over?" said the driver, and snickered.

"I want you to take me directly into the village to a telephone. She can't treat me like this."

"Well, now, I guess I couldn't rightly do *that*. Mrs. Halloran, *she* said take you to the city."

"But *I* say—"

"Now, *you* know Mrs. Halloran," he said, in a horrid wheedling voice, "what you think happens to *me* if she says take you to the city and then I turn around and take you somewheres else? Dearie," he said, "it's the city or nothing, see? And it's going to rain, and the way *I* see it, if you was really to ask *my* opinion, either you get in the car with me and we go along to the city like she said, or *I* go home and you stay right here until Mrs. Halloran makes up her mind you should go somewheres else. And *if* you stay here," he went on, still in that disagreeable, almost triumphant voice, "and it's going to rain, and you're going to get wet, it'll be a mighty long time before morning when someone comes along to open these here gates. So now why don't you be a nice reasonable girl and come get in the car with me?"

Julia, who did not often cry, was only prevented now by a black determination to hide from this creature, and so from Mrs. Halloran, that she was frightened, and bewildered, and lonely. "I'll go to the city," she said. "I can telephone Mrs. Halloran from the hotel, anyway, and when I do," she said, putting her hand on the doorhandle of the car, "do not suppose that I am going to praise the way you have behaved. I intend to tell her everything you have said."

"What'd *I* say?" he demanded, whining. "All I said was I got to do what Mrs. Halloran *tells* me. Where'd I get if I didn't do what Mrs. Halloran tells me? Now you get in like a good girl and we let bygones be bygones."

There was only one place in the car for Julia to sit, and that was in front next to the driver. The back of the car, seatless, seemed to be filled with old bottles and pieces of chain, which rattled and clanked disturbingly as the car began a slow crawl away from the main gates of the house.

"Better tell you right off," the driver said, "this is going to cost you twelve dollars." He had clearly started to say "ten" and then changed his mind, and the sharp break in the word seemed to amuse him, as though he had no need for dissimulation. "Twelve," he repeated enjoyably. "Don't go into the city this time of night for *nothing,* you know."

"Mrs. Halloran will pay you."

The man sneaked a sideways look at her. "Mrs. Halloran, she said something funny about that. She said she had left money for you, and you would pick it up and be the one paying me."

"Oh." The car picked up speed reluctantly, shaking itself as though ready to balk and throw its riders, but the big man held it down firmly and after a moment they went more evenly along the road. Julia intended that there should be no further conversation between herself and the unattractive driver, but he spoke chattily, raising his big voice without effort over the clatter of the motor, "What you going to the city for?"

"Because I choose to," Julia said childishly. She turned pointedly as though she were going to look out of the window, although there was no window on her side at all, and the wind came disagreeably in on to her face; she could feel the first stinging raindrops. She turned her jacket collar up and hunched her shoulders around her ears, in a feeble defense against the rain on one side and the conversation on the other. "Going to take the money I get from you," the big man said placidly—he smelled musty, Julia thought, and foul—"and buy me some chickens. Got a little place for them out back of my house. I live in the village, of course." He waited for some comment from Julia, and then went on, "Going to sell the eggs, maybe bring 'em up to the big house, sell 'em to old lady Halloran." They were moving steadily upward, and Julia remembered the soft lines of hills visible from the windows of the big house; not long ago, while she was in her room packing, she had seen the hills from her window and told herself joyfully that beyond them lay the city; "Tonight I will be there myself," she had thought, hugging herself ecstatically.

Peering through the rain, Julia thought she could distinguish a cleft in the line of the hills and although she did not want to speak she finally asked, "Is that where we're going? Through that sort of pass?"

"That's right," said the driver. "City's on the other side. Funny thing about that pass," he continued affably, "always full of fog. Down here, rain or hot or sunshine, but up there it's always fog. Something to do with the hills."

"Is it far?"

"Another five miles, maybe. Then another seven, eight, miles to the city. They call it Fog Pass," he added, as one explaining something uniquely reasonable. When Julia was silent again he went on. "Caught a rabbit up there once. It got so mixed up in the fog it didn't even see me coming. Stood right there on the road watching me like it didn't know what I was. Ran smack over it with the car."

Julia turned slightly and let the wind drive the rain against her face. "Funny thing about rabbits," he said. "Most people think they're lucky. *That* one wasn't lucky," and he laughed. He had clearly reached a subject very dear to his heart, because he went on contentedly, "Killed some kittens once, my old lady had a cat always having kittens and this time I told her I'd get rid of the things for her. Cut off their heads with my pocket knife."

Julia, thinking: I will go to the biggest lightest hotel and telephone my mother, was silent.

"Got rid of some puppies by pouring kerosene on them and lighting—"

"Please don't," Julia said violently, and he laughed.

"Didn't know *you*'d be bothered," he said. "Folks do things like that all the time. Why, I knew an old man once lived up in these hills about a mile and *he* used to catch rats and—"

"Please," Julia said.

"I could tell you things I saw in the army," he said. "*Everybody* knows about *them,* pretty funny, too, sometimes. You just touchy or something?"

"I don't like to hear about it," Julia said.

"Well, if you don't have to *watch,* I wouldn't guess you'd mind." He seemed to be puzzled. "Why," he said, "my old lady was right there when I cut up them kittens. She didn't mind."

"How much further is it to the pass?"

"Mile or so. You're anxious to get to the city, I guess?"

"I certainly am."

"What you going there *for?*"

"I have an appointment," Julia said wantonly.

"Who with?"

"A friend."

"That so? What about that feller you thought was coming with you? The one Mrs. Halloran told me not to take? Where's *he* come in?"

"Look," Julia said, turning to look at him, "I'm sick and tired of answering your questions and listening to your dirty talk. You just leave me alone."

"Did I touch you?" he asked, indignant. "I'll leave you alone all right, dearie, Mrs. Halloran she didn't say nothing to me about *not* leaving you alone, I wouldn't touch you with a ten foot pole. Or maybe," he went on slyly, "you was asking? Because I got no *reason* to be coming back tonight. I kind of like the city." He thought, grinning to himself. "Oh, it wouldn't *cost* you any more," he assured her. "I might even buy you a beer or maybe two." Turning her back to him coldly, Julia put her face into the rain from the window. "Once I get that twenty bucks from you—" he said.

"You told me twelve," said Julia, startled into speech.

"Must of misunderstood me," he said calmly. "Happen to know it's a twenty dollar fare to the city. Might even be twenty-five before we get there," he said, and laughed. "You want to stop for a little while?"

"No," Julia said.

He laughed again. "You'd maybe rather walk?" he asked.

They turned a curve, still going uphill and came suddenly into fog; it was not fog like any Julia had ever seen, but rather an impenetrable, almost tangible, weight of darkness pressing down upon them. She could smell its faint smoky atmosphere, even over the odors of filth and decay coming from the man next to her, and he slowed the car down until it was barely moving. "Got to take it easy along here," he said. "Hills on one side, downhill on the other. Go off the road *that* way, you run into a hill, go off the road *that* way, you'll likely hit a tree or something, and just end up in the river way down below."

"Are you sure you know the road?"

"Do it blindfold." He chuckled. "*Doing* it blindfold," he said. "Right here's where I run over the rabbit. Fog lifted a minute and there he was." He laughed again. "Did you say you'd rather get out and walk?" he asked.

When Julia did not answer, he suddenly put his foot down and the car stopped. "Now," he said, and his voice was still friendly, "now you give me the money or we don't go no further. We maybe don't go no further *any*way," and he touched her on the back with his great dirty hand.

Julia caught her breath. "Don't be silly," she said sharply. "Do you think I'm going to let you get away with anything?"

"Fierce," he said approvingly. "Ever tell you what I done with a dog bit me once?"

"Mrs. Halloran—" Julia began.

"What she don't know won't hurt *her*. And anyway, *you* don't matter to *her*. She won't care, don't worry."

"When I tell Mrs. Halloran—"

"Now who's being silly?" He reached across her and opened the car door on her side. "You don't want to pay for your ride?" he asked, "you don't get no ride. And *I*'ll tell the old lady all about it."

Julia hesitated, looked at him, saw him grinning dimly in the fog, and, terror-stricken, slid out of the car on her side. When she turned back to look at him she thought that the look on his face was one of dismay that she had called his bluff, and, standing on the road, she said, "I'll just walk along the road until some other car comes by. You've just lost yourself some money, mister."

"You get back in the car," he said. "Pay me my money and there won't be no trouble."

"Find someone else to steal from," Julia said. "Go home and tell Mrs. Halloran you didn't get the money. Go home and torture your cats and dogs and leave decent people alone." She slammed the car door and turned away from the car. For a minute she thought he was going to get out of the car and follow her, but he leaned forward and said anxiously, "Listen, miss, you better get back in the car."

He's frightened, Julia thought. She smiled and said, "I will give you exactly one dollar to drive me to the city."

"Now you *know* you're asking for trouble," he said, and this time he opened the door of the car as though prepared to get out. Thoughts of the rabbit and the kittens were vivid in Julia's mind, and she backed up and moved away from the car. Clinging to her pocketbook, stumbling a little, she ran, thinking as she did so that it was ludicrous for someone who had been not an hour ago in the big house to be so taken in, to be running in frantic terror down a lonely, foggy road. Behind her she heard him calling "Miss?" and she stood still, afraid to make another sound.

It came to her then with a pang of elementary fear that it was only necessary to step a few feet in any direction to disappear completely into the fog. She turned, almost ready to make a compromise somehow with the driver, and found that the road and the car had gone into the fog and that although she knew precisely in which direction she had moved, her faulty feet and blind eyes would not lead her back. She called carefully, "Mister?" and then thought, the fog muffling her voice and coming into her mouth, that perhaps he might yet find her by her voice, come silently up behind her in the fog and never give her a chance to tell him that he might have all her money if he wanted. She stood perfectly still, listening, and then turned to see if he was behind her. When she saw nothing she began to move cautiously. Better to take a chance on another car coming by, she thought, sooner or later someone will come along. She tripped over a rock and hurt her ankle and the noise held her motionless until she was sure that he had not heard her, was not moving softly through the silent fog.

A vague idea of her surroundings stayed with her; in back of her, approximately, was the road and on it the car; she was perhaps ten feet to the side of the road—too close, perhaps, to the sharp drop down to the river, but only just far enough from the driver for safety. There should be about fifteen feet on the side of the road before the slope down to the river became really steep, and on the other side—she hoped suddenly and fervently that it *was* the other side—there was a fairly wide space before the sharp rise of the hills.

Her shoes, which were destined for the soft levels of a dance floor in a nightclub in the city, twisted and turned and hurt her feet brutally over these unseen stones, and her silk skirt was fouled with burrs. Wait, she told herself with her teeth set, wait till I get somehow into the city and to a telephone; my mother will let Mrs. Halloran know what *we* think of this kind of treatment; what a rotten way to treat a guest. Wait until I wander into the city from the hills, bedraggled and tattered, telling of having been abandoned and robbed on the road; wait, she said over and over again through her teeth, wait till I can get even with all of them.

An abrupt sound startled her, the sound of wheels upon the road, and she turned toward it. The noise was bewilderingly loud for a minute, and then began to fade away. Although she had moved involuntarily away from the sound she realized in that minute that it had been *much* farther away than it should have been; had come, in fact, from the left of her instead of the right—or *should* it have been on the right? Was she then on the wrong side of the road and going perhaps steadily away from it? She turned and started sharply left, and almost immediately felt the ground begin to slope away under her feet; have I turned around in the fog? she wondered, and saw ahead of her a tree shape blurred in the fog. The trees, she thought, the trees were on our left as we came—toward the river? Moss grows on the north side of the trees, the drop down to the river is slow at first and then sharp, but, by the time she had thought, she had lost the tree and had no idea whether she was going toward it or not.

A small feeling of genuine apprehension came slowly upon her. This was not, could not possibly be, a small unimportant delay in her getting to the city; no matter how she stumbled and struggled along, she was lost; it was very possible that she would not get to the city tonight at all, would not reach a telephone, would not sleep in a hotel; she might even find herself, with embarrassment and relief, embracing the first of the search party to reach her; it might be that she would be sought for generally, over the hills, with men calling to one another and listening for her voice in reply, led by the intrepid driver of the car, perhaps even laughing when they found her, asking her if she'd ever do *that* again, telling their wives when they got home that yes, they'd found the fool woman, scared to death and half-crazy . . . if, indeed, it occurred to the driver to send anyone to look for her?

She shook her head violently to rid her mind of this cloudy nonsense, and caught her foot on a rock or a root and fell heavily. In the fog there was no one to see if there were tears in her eyes, and for a minute she lay on the ground saying "Oh, damn, damn *damn*" over and over again to herself, and almost aloud. No, she thought, it was really too much; she had not deserved this of anyone, it *was* too much. It occurred to her that she might just lie here without moving until someone found her and the thought brought her to her feet again hurriedly. For heaven's sake, she informed herself, imagine lying on the ground with a circle of men looking down with flashlights and dogs nosing at your shoes and probably they'd want to carry you back, and what would you look like *then*? It seemed that she had probably sprained her ankle and it hurt just enough for her to lose some perspective on her position. I shall *not* be lost, she said grimly, perhaps again aloud, and stamped on, putting her weight down firmly on her hurting ankle. If I hear one dog baying or one man shouting I will climb into a tree and hide, if I can find a tree, and she laughed wildly.

The sound of her own laughter in the fog startled her and for a minute she stood still. What on earth? she thought, and, is this possible? for *me?*

In order to find out more clearly where she was she brought both hands to her face and first rubbed her eyes and then bit sharply on her fingers, without knowing why. Then she said, still aloud, "*Now,* my girl, *now,* Julia, my fine creature, suppose you just get a goddam hold of yourself. What would they say if they saw you now? That bastard captain? Or even Arabella? They're all laughing at me now," she assured herself wisely, "Arabella's got the captain, and they're sitting in the light and laughing at me, but they can't, they *can't.*" Blaze a trail, she thought, pile rocks together in a signal of distress, write messages and set them afloat in bottles . . .

"Now listen here," she said. She was moving slowly, almost aimlessly; her hand brushed against a large rock and she did not lose her balance, but leaned peacefully against the rock and looked out blindly into the solid fog. "*Now* we're getting somewhere," she said to the rock, "*now* we're making some progress. Just got to be a little careful not to fall down the hillside into the river, *that's* all. Only thing we need to worry about— otherwise everything is fine, fine, fine, fine, fine, fine . . ." I got out of the car and turned right, she thought, or left, went uphill or down, and hurt my ankle and walked. "Close your eyes, my sweet baby," she said aloud, "you can see better with your eyes closed, close your eyes and take my hand and I will show you the way home."

She closed her eyes and with one hand resting against the rock began to walk; it was more than a rock, although she did not actually care, it was a wall, and she went awkwardly and clinging along beside it, following the line of the wall through weeds and rocks and falling through ditches. There now, she thought, as the ground under her feet seemed to be going a little uphill, there now, all I needed to do was sit down and think it out. I *do* hope that man is frightened because he lost me; see, I am thinking clearly because I can remember how I got here; I was not always walking in this fog, not at all.

She hit her foot against another rock and stumbled, and

twisted against a tree; this is really too much, she thought, tears in her eyes, and stepped ahead and knew as she put her foot down that it was a mistake; she was over the edge into the river because her foot went down and down and never found the ground and she fell and rolled wildly downhill; this is really more than I can endure, she thought deliberately, and fell unendingly, wracked and bruised, lying against the great iron gates with the elaborate H worked into the scrollwork on either side.

"Good morning, Julia," said Mrs. Halloran at the breakfast table. "I heard that you had come back to us. I am only sorry that you had such miserable weather. We had a singularly clear, bright night."

"Go to hell," Julia said distinctly through her cut mouth.

"Julia, behave yourself," Mrs. Willow said.

"If I had been there," the captain said, helping himself to elderberry jelly, "I would have given that fellow a bad time."

"You're really *terribly* bruised," Arabella said. "After breakfast will you tell me what he *really* did to you?"

"All of you go to hell," Julia said.

"Odd that the gardeners should have been out so early," Mrs. Halloran said. "Of course, you were there quite a while, as it was. But I would not have expected the gardeners to find you so early." She nodded to the captain. "Coffee, Captain? When you go upstairs," she continued to Julia, "be sure to put the money back on my dressing table, since you had no chance to spend it. Strange, is it not, how one can manage to cling to some unimportant trifle at a time of strain? Julia kept her pocketbook as someone, running from a burning house, might carry out a worthless vase, or an old newspaper."

"Go, go, go to hell," Julia said.

"My dear," Mrs. Halloran said, "if you continue uncooperative I shall not let you go to the city again."

10

On the morning of Sunday, June thirtieth, Gloria, in the middle of her breakfast, suddenly stood up, spilling Miss Ogilvie's coffee, and stood, her hands over her face. "It's true," she said faintly, "it's all true."

"Gloria, you have upset Miss Ogilvie's coffee," Mrs. Halloran said.

"Look," Gloria said. She took her hands down from her face and pointed. "The pink roses," she said, "we're having breakfast."

"The pink roses are from the rambler," Aunt Fanny said. "It was my mother's favorite, and there were six bushes planted for her in the rose garden. Not one of them, I am pleased to say, has died; I have made a particular point of looking after them, and—"

"Don't you see?" Gloria said. "There are the pink roses on the breakfast table, and I'm wearing my blue and white dress and a minute ago we were all laughing at something Essex said—don't you see? It's all exactly the way I saw it, before, when I was looking into the mirror."

"Well, of course," Mrs. Willow said comfortably, "it had to happen sometime, didn't it?"

Twice during the month of June large trucks had delivered further shipments for Aunt Fanny, which had been stored in the library. Only one wall of books still stood and because the ashes of books—unlike the ashes of cloth, flesh, or even tea leaves and coffee grounds—are not healthy for growing things the gardeners had twice emptied the barbecue pit and taken

the ashes to the village dump, which was just beyond the cemetery. Most of the property now stored in the library was in
cartons, items purchased by Aunt Fanny in quantity and neatly
packed. There was a carton of anti-histamine preparations, in
addition to the carton of first-aid kits. There were cartons of
plastic overshoes and rubbers, in assorted sizes, of instant coffee, of cleansing tissue and sunglasses. Suntan lotion, salted
nuts in cans, paper napkins, soap, both bar and flaked, toilet
paper (four cartons). Two complete tool boxes, with a keg of
nails, since the bags of nails which Robinson Crusoe brought
from the ship had proved so comforting; mindful of Robinson
Crusoe, Aunt Fanny had added a grindstone, and, with some
embarrassment, several shotguns and an assortment of hunting knives. At Miss Ogilvie's suggestion the library stock also
included a small portable cooking stove, with several cans of
fuel, and an entire carton of folders of matches. Maryjane proposed the citronella for mosquitoes—there was a great roll of
mosquito netting standing in a corner—and several remedies
for bee stings, sunburn, and snake bite. Essex and Mrs. Halloran added as many cartons of cigarettes as Aunt Fanny
would allow them room, and from the cellars of the house
Mrs. Halloran brought up a representative selection of wines,
although she confessed that she was puzzled by her own gesture. Foreseeing the day when their cigarettes would run out,
Essex bought a pamphlet on the growing of tobacco, and
thoughtfully laid in a gross of corncob pipes. Arabella suggested needles, thread, pins, hair curlers, deodorants, per-
fumes, bath salts, and lipsticks. Mrs. Willow, naming herself
as the only really practical person in the house, insisted upon
blankets, a wheelbarrow, reels of nylon rope, axes, shovels,
rakes, and a barometer. It was Gloria's conceit to begin a file
of daily newspapers, which she planned to continue until their
last publication. The captain supervised the storage of eight bicycles in the cellar, but voted against the addition of a motor
bike, since a motor bike would require gasoline and he felt that
in anticipation of a general holocaust the storage of gasoline in
the cellar would be unwise. Julia, who continued sullen, asked
for and was granted the inclusion of a carton of knitting nee-

dles and several cartons of variously colored yarns. "So I will have something to do with my time," she explained disagreeably.

The only books to be included were Aunt Fanny's Boy Scout Handbook, the encyclopedia, Fancy's French grammar—so that Miss Ogilvie could keep Fancy from forgetting the little she had gained—and a World Almanac. No writing materials of any kind were included, and gradually these books came to be called "unburnables" in order to differentiate them from the rest of the books in the library, which were absolutely burnable.

"In Tibet," Essex remarked idly one morning, while moving over a carton of canned tunafish in order to make room for a carton of tennis balls, "in Tibet, arsenic is used in the preparation of paper pulp. In Tibet, the paper is highly poisonous, and lingering in a Tibetan library is consequently a matter of considerable danger. As a matter of fact, in Tibet curling up with a good book is frequently fatal."

Early in July Miss Ogilvie found one of Mrs. Halloran's handkerchiefs near the summer house. It had been tied around the neck of a dead garter snake, and the snake had been draped over a branch of a cypress tree. Miss Ogilvie, concerned, told the captain, who told Mrs. Halloran, who told him to dispose of it, and the captain dug a hole at the farther end of the rose garden and buried the snake and the handkerchief.

According to the notes carefully kept by Mrs. Willow, it was on July tenth that Gloria again looked into the mirror. She reported then that she saw fruit trees, heavy with fruit, small figures, at some distance, bathing along the edge of a stream, and a pack of horses running in a glorious wild freedom. When pressed, she saw that on August twenty-seventh the people in the big house were gathered in the dining room for dinner as usual. On August twenty-eighth they sat, talking, in the drawing room. On August twenty-ninth they were dancing, she thought, on the lawn. On August thirtieth there was nothing; the mirror was dark. Pressed further, for August thirty-first, for September first, for September second, Gloria caught again one glimpse of the soft untouched green world she had seen before, asked to return to August thirtieth, she first saw only darkness and then fell back, screaming that her eyes were burned, and had to be put to bed with a damp cloth over her face and one of Maryjane's sleeping pills.

"Thus it seems," Mrs. Willow wrote in her notes, "that August thirtieth is to be the day, the last this world will ever know." And then—quite out of character, actually, and in a shaken hand, she added, "God help us all."

"But I insist that the house *must* be barricaded," Aunt Fanny said, adding, with a kind of inspiration, "It is like a child hiding its head under a blanket. We have absolute faith in my father, of course, but even though his protection applies to the house and to everyone in it, I can see strong reasons for covering the windows and blocking the doors."

"As *I* see it," the captain said, "it sounds like we're hoping no one will notice us. With absolute faith in your father, of course," he told Aunt Fanny.

"I am not happy about barricading the house," Mrs. Willow said slowly. "Seems to me it sounds like *not* believing in Aunt Fanny's father, sort of. I mean, either he protects us or he doesn't."

"He *told* us to barricade the house," Aunt Fanny said, nettled. "I think of it as cooperating with him—showing him, as it were, that we are willing to go halfway to ensure our own survival, rather than wait passively for *him* to do it all."

"Well, a blanket over the window is really not much protection," Mrs. Willow said bluntly.

"Perhaps," Essex said, "it was planned to give us something to do while we are waiting."

"The human animal burrows instinctively in times of danger," Mrs. Halloran said. "I find Aunt Fanny's picture of the child under the blankets not an inept one."

"We would *feel* safer, I'm sure," Essex said.

"Perhaps," Gloria said softly, "the blankets over the windows *are* just to keep us from looking out?"

"I am a rake," Essex said. "I should have been born into a time when it was easier for a young man to borrow money. Or, of course, I should not have been born at all."

"Silly," Gloria said. "The sun is shining, and the sky is blue, and here we are, sitting quite close together on a bench all alone, and of all the things in the world to talk about you choose yourself."

"We are more intelligent than Julia and the captain," Essex said. "We could leave here. We could go into the village—I assume that having climbed over the gate once you could do so again—and walk, if need be, to the city. Or we could wait for the bus, sitting in the lobby of the Carriage Stop Inn. If we did not choose to stay in the city—and I do you the credit of assuming that you would want to get farther away than that—we could go on, as far as we could manage, and then settle down temporarily in another hotel, or inn, or rooming house; at any rate, some kind of a furnished room to live in. All the furnished rooms I have ever seen had wicker furniture, and a painting of the Bridge of Sighs on the wall. We would have to find money somehow. One of us, in short, would have to work."

"That's not hard," Gloria said. "I can work."

"I expect it would have to be you, anyway. I would sit in the furnished room and pretend I was a writer, perhaps. When you came home in the evening after a long day ushering in the movie theatre—"

"—selling jewelry in the five and ten—"

"—I would expect to be asked at once how the writing went today. I ought to get some paper and a pencil, so I would look authentic."

"And how did the writing go today, dear?"

"Very poorly, my love. One ballade, three villanelles, a kind of triolet thing, and an outline for a learned article on Freud. Gloria," Essex said, turning to look at her; "I have never loved anyone in my life until now."

"I know," Gloria said. "I know perfectly."

"I want to mate with you in a brave new world, all clean and shining, and yet I want to be your husband in this world, and live along in the kind of grimy squalor married people live in. I want a furnished room and jobs and dirty diapers in the corners and poor food—can you cook?"

"Admirably."

"You would have to cook poorly, to meet my ideal. I want the kind of dismal future only possible in *this* world. I could put up with your long hours at the five and ten—"

"—ushering at the movie theatre—"

"I could put up with your inferior cooking—"

"I am an excellent cook."

"And your poor housekeeping—"

"I keep a lovely house."

"And your squalling children—"

"They are lovely, clean children, and all in bed asleep."

"—but I would always be afraid. Or at least for as long as always lasted."

"Afraid of Aunt Fanny, you mean?"

"Afraid of Aunt Fanny."

Gloria was silent.

"If Aunt Fanny is right," Essex went on after a minute, "and I ask your pardon for profaning this bright summer morning with Aunt Fanny's name; if Aunt Fanny is right, we shall, putting it into the baldest of terms, find ourselves in a situation of strong comic possibilities. Imagine, if you can, Aunt Fanny's new world."

"I have been trying to imagine it for quite a while," Gloria said.

"Fresh, untouched, green, lovely. Untrammeled, except by ourselves. A lifetime of warmth and beauty and fertility. The kind of life and world people have been dreaming about ever since they first began fouling this one. I can sometimes catch glimpses of what it will be like, and they are tantalizing—"

"I have seen it, you forget," Gloria said. "In the mirror. It is more beautiful than you can believe."

"I am afraid so. Aunt Fanny must *not* be wrong. That world *must* exist." He sat forward, anxious, holding his hands tightly together and scowling with earnestness. "It *must*; we cannot be promised such a thing, like children, and see it withdrawn. Oh, Gloria," he said, "I couldn't *stand* not being there."

"*I* could," Gloria said, "and I have seen it."

He sighed, and relaxed. "Put it, then," he said, "that if I have one I cannot have the other. I want to live with you in a room furnished in wicker, with a picture of the Bridge of Sighs, and your bad cooking—"

"Superlative cooking."

"—and your job at the five and ten—"

"—the movie theatre—"

"—and the children, and the struggles and the cheapness and all the things we can get for ourselves in this world; I never *dreamed* of wanting these things. But I want the green and gold world more."

"You haven't tried either one."

Essex shivered. "I have tried one," he said. "How do you suppose I have been captured by Aunt Fanny?"

"I wouldn't care, you see," Gloria said. "I can believe in either one, for myself. I would be happy enough if the end of the world caught me sitting in our wicker chair looking at the Bridge of Sighs. Unless, of course, I should happen to be still at work at the five and ten. A miserable way to go."

"But then we would lose everything," Essex said. He looked at her curiously. "You see," he went on, as one explaining glibly something better left unexplained, "you see, in Aunt Fanny's new world, we will at least be . . . alive . . . together. We could not possibly, of course, be . . . well, living in our own room with the wicker furniture; we would not be . . ."

"Dying romantically, in one another's arms?"

Essex shivered again. "I don't want to die," he said, and Gloria laughed. "But I *don't*," Essex said, and Gloria laughed again. "I should have *expected* you'd never understand," Essex said.

"But I'm afraid I do," Gloria said.

"*None* of you is serious about this," Essex said, and then added, making his voice light, "Poor Gloria—had we but world enough."

"Essex," she said, but he was standing.

"I must go and find Aunt Fanny," he said. "We are burning another ten shelves of books this afternoon."

Gloria sat on alone for a minute or so, thinking that the sun was warm and the sky blue, and wondering if the sky would be bluer if Aunt Fanny had never been born. The end of the world, Gloria thought concretely, the whole world, all of it, my father, our house, our friends, gone in one bad night, and here I am among strangers, and willing to dare it all for one more strange than the rest; but I wouldn't, she thought, I am intoxicated by the tradition of romantic love. Assume myself and Essex, with suitcases, endeavoring to climb over the gate secretly; *I* could only do it when I wanted to get *in*. When I came here, she thought, when I came here I would have laughed at such ideas as these. When I left home and came here I would have thought that these people were lunatic, and the gates locked to keep them from getting out; I wish I had a chance to say goodbye to my father.

"He's gone to tell my grandmother," Fancy said suddenly from behind her.

Gloria, startled, was annoyed. "You little sneak," she said.

"He's gone to tell every word both of you said. She makes him."

Fancy came around the end of the bench and sat down where Essex had been.

"Who told her he was here?" It occurred to Gloria that with Fancy everyone found themselves saying things they would rather not have said; perhaps it was because Fancy looked at one so directly, and spoke so clearly herself. "Did you tell?"

"The captain. She's had him following you two around. Like she had Essex following the captain and Julia."

"Why?"

"So she can make Essex tell her what you were saying. She likes to hear things like that."

"She's a terrible old woman."

Fancy laughed. "You sound like my mother. *I* like her."

"Spying on people."

"*She* doesn't spy, the *rest* of you spy, on each other," Fancy said flatly. "Did you make it up, what you saw on the mirror?"

"No."

"I think you did."

"I did not."

"You did."

"How can anyone know what they are really seeing?"

"*I* know. Essex wouldn't run away, anyway, because he's scared of my grandmother."

"She can't hurt him. He can't stand the thought that he might die."

"He talks more about dying than Aunt Fanny, even. The captain's been in danger of his life and reason a hundred times and more and *he* doesn't talk about dying. Only Essex and Aunt Fanny."

"I think the captain tells lies."

"So does Essex."

"He does not."

"He does so."

Gloria laughed again and after a minute Fancy laughed with her. "I like everything," Fancy said.

"And if Aunt Fanny—"

"I heard so much already about Aunt Fanny and her lousy dreams I think I'm going to throw up," Fancy said. "I wish she'd only shut up for a while. It used to be bad enough, Aunt Fanny snuffling all the time, but now that people listen to her it's awful."

"We can't afford *not* to listen."

"Well, I just don't get it myself." Fancy thought, and gestured at the garden which lay before them. "Look," she said, "don't any of you just plain *like* things? Always worrying about the world? Look. Aunt Fanny keeps saying that there is going to be a lovely world, all green and still and perfect and we are all going to live there and be peaceful and happy. That would be perfectly fine for me, except right here I live in a lovely world, all green and still and perfect, even though no one around here seems to be very peaceful or happy, but when I think about it this new world is going to have Aunt Fanny and my grandmother and you and Essex and the rest of these crazy people and my mother and what makes anyone think you're going to be more happy or peaceful just because you're the only ones left?"

"That's because you're not very grown up yet," Gloria said, sedately. "When you get older you'll understand."

"Will I?" asked Fancy innocently. "Right now I'm not allowed to play with the children in the village because my grandmother says we are too good a family for me to play with the children in the village and so later on I won't be allowed to play with the children in the village because there won't *be* any village, and we'll certainly be too good a family because we'll be the *only* family. And what will there be left for me to understand when I grow up?"

"You make it all sound foolish. Fancy, tell me. What *is* going to happen? Do you know?"

"Well," Fancy said slowly, "you all want the whole world to be changed so *you* will be different. But I don't suppose people get changed any by just a new world. And anyway that world isn't any more real than this one."

"It is, though. You forget that I saw it in the mirror."

"Maybe you'll get onto the other side of that mirror in the new clean world. Maybe you'll look through from the other side and see this world again and go around crying that you wish some big thing would happen and wipe out *that* one and send you back *here*. Like I keep trying to tell you, it doesn't matter which world you're in."

"Essex—"

"I'm sick and tired of Essex." Fancy tumbled off the bench and rolled like a puppy in the grass. "You want to come and play with my doll house?"

At four-thirty on the afternoon of July thirtieth, Julia and the captain defeated Gloria and Arabella at tennis, Gloria wearing blue-striped shorts borrowed from Julia, and Mrs. Halloran, Aunt Fanny, Miss Ogilvie, Mrs. Willow, and Essex watching from under the beach umbrella set up near the court. Maryjane, who thought the hot sun beneficial to her asthma, lay on a rug on the grass, and Fancy played at some random game, singing to herself and smiling.

In the shaded porch outside his room, where Richard Halloran spent the late afternoons when the sun was cooling, the nurse read levelly, "'I cannot express the confusion I was in, though the joy of seeing a ship, and one which I had reason to believe was manned by my own countrymen, and consequently friends, was such as I cannot describe; but yet I had some secret doubts hanging about me, I cannot tell from whence they came, bidding me to be on my guard.'"

After dinner Mrs. Halloran walked with Essex, going toward the sundial with her arm against his, relishing his even strength and sympathetic deference; "Tell me again," she said, standing over the sundial.

"'What is this world?'" Essex said obediently, "'What asketh man to have? Now with his love, now in his colde grave, Allone, with-outen any companye.'"

"I do not care for it," Mrs. Halloran said, caressing the W in WORLD.

"Orianna," Essex said. "Do you think that we will be happy there?"

"No," Mrs. Halloran said. "But then, we are not happy here."

"Aunt Fanny specifically promised us happiness."

"Aunt Fanny will promise anything to get her own way. How would she know what happiness is, say, to me?"

"How could anyone know?" asked Essex politely.

"Least of all my dearest and closest friends. Well," Mrs. Halloran said, "we have not long to wait, and I think I will begin to plan my personal future."

The fire in the drawing room was still lighted of an evening because Richard Halloran felt the chill of the drawing dark in his old bones. When Mrs. Halloran had come in with Essex and given him her shawl to put away, she went directly to stand by her husband's wheel chair and face the room. Looking around at them, at Aunt Fanny and the captain, at Mrs. Willow and Julia and Arabella, at Miss Ogilvie and Essex and Maryjane, Mrs. Halloran said, "I want to speak to all of you. You will be astonished, I think: I want to ask your assistance. No, be still; do not reassure me—I think I know what I may count on from any of you. I require only your willing presence."

"Certainly," Aunt Fanny said softly, "what you require, *we*—"

"Be still, Aunt Fanny. I want to speak to *all* of you. The books burning away in the barbecue pit have put me in mind of it; it has come to me that we must—I say advisedly, we *must*—give a celebration for the village; you may call it a farewell party, if you like, Aunt Fanny; it will certainly be the last gesture they will ever see from the big house."

"A farewell party is a pretty idea," said Miss Ogilvie. "It becomes Mrs. Halloran to have thought of it."

Mrs. Halloran lifted one hand and set it on the shoulder of her husband, who stirred. "It may be in order to choose some occasion for this party," she said, "since clearly we cannot publicly announce it as a farewell; I thought of a golden wedding anniversary."

"Who for?" Maryjane demanded, and Aunt Fanny echoed, "Not Richard's?"

"The village," Mrs. Halloran said, "will not care particularly how many years Richard and I have been married—beyond marvelling at my youthful appearance—and I am sure that my good friends will not quarrel with my desire to do honor, one last time, to the husband of my choice and . . ." she hesitated, ". . . the joy of my life. In other words, I choose to hold a celebration, and I do not care how it may be justified; the burning of the books in the barbecue pit has put me in mind of a public barbecue—"

"A witch-burning?" said Gloria, but no one heard her.

"And it is my pleasure that the populace be invited for the afternoon and early evening of August twenty-ninth, for a barbecue, dance, celebration, and farewell."

"Well, now," Mrs. Willow said, moving in heavily, "You're two years older than I am, Orianna, and if you've been married to that Richard of yours any more than twenty-eight years I'll be hogtied and thrown in the fishpond. Willow never lasted till our tenth year, but I guess *I* know how long I would have been married by now, as if I cared."

Mrs. Halloran touched her husband's shoulder caressingly, and said, "In any case, *I* have decided that August twenty-ninth will be the occasion of the celebration of our golden nuptials; let me be sentimental, Augusta, before I have no time left."

"If Willow had lasted—"

"You would be as eager as I to celebrate any anniversary of your union."

"Richard," said Aunt Fanny darkly, "ought to celebrate in sackcloth and ashes. It was the blackest day of my life."

"No doubt," said Mrs. Halloran, "and I count on *you*, Aunt Fanny, to enhance the general joy on the occasion. I thought that—since there is really no purpose in trying to preserve the grounds of the house from the people of the village, when they are to be so wholly revised on the night of August thirtieth—we might throw all the grounds open to our visitors; let them wander in the secret garden and lose themselves in the maze; let them fall into the pool and pick fruit from the orchard. So long as not one of them comes into the house."

"It would be most unfortunate if anyone should stray into the library," Mrs. Willow agreed.

"We will set up a barbecue around by the kitchen garden, although, as I say, we will burn charcoal in it this once. Captain, I will ask you to take charge of the barbecue and supervise the cooking. Essex, you will arrange for a pavilion of some sort, where other refreshments will be served. Julia, Arabella, Maryjane, I have a particular fancy for japanese lanterns; will you see to them, please? Assorted colors, and I think in festoons. Miss Ogilvie, you will of course make the salad dressing, as always. Aunt Fanny and Mrs. Willow, you will oblige me by making a careful examination of the gardens and lawns, to determine what improvements or additions need be made by the gardeners; this is, after all, the last formal entertainment ever to be held here, and I should like to think that everything was looking its best."

"When is this . . . farewell party . . . to take place?" Mrs. Willow asked.

"Since we have only until August thirtieth, as I say, I believe that August twenty-ninth would be the most proper day. We will invite the entire village—subject, of course, to certain unavoidable omissions—to come at five. They will dine upon barbecued beef, and whatever else we plan to offer, and should leave us, I imagine, by eleven in the evening, after having properly admired the japanese lanterns. We will then be able to retire early, in anticipation of a busy day on August thirtieth, and very likely, I should think, a sleepless night. I have, by the way, promised the servants that they will have an unexpected holiday; after the labor and confusion of the garden party, I have told them, they will have the next afternoon and evening off. In the late afternoon of August thirtieth, two of the cars will take the entire staff into the city, planning to return here the next morning."

"As I supposed," said Miss Ogilvie, nodding. "I *thought* we should have to make our own breakfast that morning."

"Several more unimportant items," Mrs. Halloran continued. "Essex can hint to the villagers that a country dance of some kind, celebrating our fifty years of happy marriage, would be supremely appropriate."

"By the villagers," Essex said, "I assume you mean the twenty-odd assorted young ladies who attend Mrs. Otis's dancing classes? I daresay they could do a tap dance on the terrace."

"Suppose I leave that in *your* hands, Essex. I had also thought of some testimonial from the younger children—a pretty little girl, perhaps, tendering me an armful of flowers? You will see that flowers are provided, Essex, and perhaps a short, badly-scanned poem in honor of the occasion."

"Bad scansion I will *not* descend to," Essex said. "I will find some little girl to give you flowers, and see that her face is washed."

"We can ring the bells over the carriage house," Richard Halloran said, inspired.

"Richard," Aunt Fanny said, "you know that you have not been married to Orianna for fifty years."

"I have been married to Orianna for a very long time," Richard Halloran said to the fire.

"I have no objection to your mingling with the villagers, any of you; Miss Ogilvie, you may mingle freely with the villagers. I have also given some considerable thought to my own costume for the occasion; it is going to be in shocking bad taste, but of course it is for my last public appearance. I think to sit on the terrace under a gold canopy."

"Disgraceful," Aunt Fanny said.

"I want my people to have their last remembrance of me—if they have time to give me a thought at all—as truly regal, Aunt Fanny; I plan to wear a crown."

"Orianna, you old fool," Mrs. Willow said.

"A crown," Mrs. Halloran said firmly. "In shocking bad taste, as I said, and probably no more than a small tiara, but it will be in my mind a crown. I have always fancied myself wearing cloth of gold, and bowing."

"Seems to me," Arabella said suddenly, "you ought to be giving *us* pretty dresses, too. Not crowns if you don't want to, but some kind of pretty dress."

"Oddly enough, Arabella, I find the idea entirely suitable. I think we should all go, that last day, newly clothed and fresh."

"Well, not gold for *me,* please. I'm much better in blue, with my eyes. Julia wears the red tones."

"I do not." Julia scowled at her sister. "She wants me to look hideous," she said, "just because she thinks it makes *her* look prettier. I want green, *if* you don't mind."

"I like a flowered chiffon, myself," Mrs. Willow said. "Something bright; *my* size, it doesn't matter anyway. The gels should be in light colors, Orianna, a bevy of beauty around you, if I do say it myself. I can run into the city and if I can't find what I've got in mind I can buy the material and we can put them together here. At least my gels and I are handy with our needles, for so many years of making things do and patching things together."

"*I* wore the patches," Julia said spitefully. "Arabella never had any trouble in just making do with any old thing so long as it was brand new and cost twice what we could afford."

"You—" Arabella began, but Mrs. Willow interrupted smoothly. "No squabbling, girls; at least *this* time we don't have to worry about what it costs; what about you, Miss Ogilvie?"

"I *always* worry about what things cost, thank you, Mrs. Willow; I formed an early habit—"

"No, no, dear; what will you wear to Orianna's party?"

"Oh, dear." Miss Ogilvie looked anxiously at Richard Halloran. "Pink?" she suggested hopefully.

"I should think a nice dove grey," Maryjane said.

"I'd *like* pink," Miss Ogilvie said.

"If anyone cares, I shall wear black," Aunt Fanny said. "To mark my sense of the occasion."

"It sounds like I shall have to do a *lot* of shopping," Mrs. Willow said happily. "I'll go into the city one day next week, and that will give us plenty of time to take things back if we don't like them. What about you, Orianna—shall I look for your golden gown for you?"

"I have already ordered my dress, thank you. And my crown."

"I can't help feeling," Mrs. Willow said, "that you will look like something of a fool, you know. Wearing a crown."

"You have not perceived, then, Augusta, that I wear a crown on August twenty-ninth to emphasize my position after August thirtieth." Mrs. Halloran smiled obscurely. "I shall probably never remove the crown," she said, "until I hand it on to Fancy."

On the third floor of the big house, near the end of the right wing, was a great room which Mrs. Halloran had never visited, although she surely knew of its existence. It occupied almost all of the top floor of the right wing, sharing it only with the little room which the first Mr. Halloran had wanted to make into an observatory from which he could watch the stars. Because the big house was so extremely big the great room on the third floor was rarely remembered, and visited only by Aunt Fanny; in it were the worldly possessions of the first Mrs. Halloran—not the diamonds which Aunt Fanny wore, nor the satin sheets and tiny golden chairs from the bedroom where she died, but the solid, well-chosen, and real possessions which the first Mrs. Halloran had known she owned, and had meant when, dying, she whispered, "Take care of my things," to her husband.

When the first Mr. Halloran brought his wife and his two small children to live in the big house he had built for them, he brought them from a bleak and uncomfortable top-floor apartment in a two-family house, and he made the change for them without a very adequate preparation. The first Mrs. Halloran died without ever seeing the greater part of the furnishings in the big house, and during the long days of her illness took great consolation from the knowledge that her real possessions were safely stored away in an attic room somewhere above her head.

Aunt Fanny, who loved the big house, had always known somehow that the core of it was in the big attic room. Over a period of years she had, quite by herself, reestablished the four-room apartment where she had been born; the attic room was easily large enough for the furniture to be set in order, and Aunt Fanny had been astonished at her own memories, which set furniture and even ornaments into a pattern almost agonizing in its growing familiarity.

The great ugly living room suite, patterned in dark red and blue brocade, which had been a source of such enormous pride to the first Mrs. Halloran, Aunt Fanny had set up first, the heavy couch facing the two deep armchairs. This furniture had been built to endure, and endure it would. Between the couch and the armchairs was crammed an imitation-mahogany bric-a-brac table, and on that—Aunt Fanny had gone into carefully packed cartons, dislodging mothballs—were a dark blue imitation velvet fringed tablecover, a small music box which had been a candy dish, and played the first phrases of "Barcarolle," a model of the Statue of Liberty, since the first Mrs. Halloran had come to New York on her honeymoon, and a photograph album bound in blue imitation leather. Aunt Fanny had turned the pages of the photograph album, looking in some bewilderment at the yellowed snapshots of the first Mrs. Halloran as a girl, somehow ludicrously innocent, in middy blouse and spreading tie; as a bride, looking up at an unrecognizable tall man; as a mother, holding a pig-faced creature which might have been either her son Richard or her daughter Frances; in company with friends who had by now very likely forgotten even her name. In these pictures Aunt Fanny could not find her mother, who was dead, but only a girl in a book, whose story was tragically swift, from girl to wife to mother, and dull, since nothing had ever happened to her from the day she had her picture taken laughing and long-haired in the middy blouse, to the day when, photographed for the last time before the high steps of the two-family house, she smiled uneasily into the camera, her face barely discernible under the odd hat. Aunt Fanny sometimes wondered, turning the pages of the photograph album, how much her mother had ever realized of that life which went by so quickly; had she known, standing for her picture in front of the house where she had lived with her husband, had she known that it was for the last time, that no furniture record of her would exist? Had she known earlier, then, in the middy blouse, that she was going to die? Equally, then, did the faces which looked out from the other pages of the album, the faces of small Franceses and Richards, hold also that sweet indefinable reassuring knowledge? Did the Richard in wide collar and velvet trousers know that *he* was going to die?—he knew it now. Could the truth be read in the tiny Frances who sat, toothless, on a blanket in the sun? "Some day I will be with my mother," Aunt Fanny would think, turning the pages, "I am with her in this book, no one can separate us *here*. Some day we will all be together again." The last pages of the book were empty, because the album had been packed carefully away years ago with everything else in the small apartment and had been stored in the attic of the big house; "Is my furniture all right?" the first Mrs. Halloran had asked the maids, "are you taking good care of my furniture? Are all my boxes of things in a safe place?" Nothing from the attic room had ever been permitted out into the big house; the four-room apartment was intact.

The living room of the apartment also held a small bookcase, in which the first Mr. Halloran had kept the books he used in his mail order education; Aunt Fanny had put them back. They had been in a carton labelled, in her mother's straight handwriting, "Michael's books." There was even among them a book on etiquette, with the passages on the uses of table silver underlined by her father, who memorized laboriously and slowly, and never forgot what he had once learned.

On top of the bookcase Aunt Fanny, with unerring, almost supernatural memory, had put the framed photographs of her grandparents. In those first proud years the Hallorans had bought themselves a victrola, paying for it month by month, and it had stood, polished and handsome, with an imitation mahogany finish, in one corner of their living room. Aunt Fanny had never played it in the big house, and had been too small to be trusted with it in the apartment; the records were carefully preserved in a compartment at the bottom of the machines, which opened to receive them in grooved individual sections. Aunt Fanny recognized the indefinable smell of the phonograph, of oil and mothballs and furniture polish, more clearly than she remembered the Caruso record, or Madame Schumann-Heink, or Chaliapin, singing "The Song of the Flea."

The four rooms in the apartment, which Aunt Fanny had so carefully put back together, included the living room, the kitchen, the parental bedroom, and the bedroom which small Frances and Richard had shared. In the kitchen the stove was cold, the icebox warm, but Aunt Fanny scrubbed regularly the oilcloth on the kitchen table where she had sat for meals with her mother and father and brother—the high chair used by Richard and then Frances stood still in a corner, where Mrs. Halloran had kept it because she never threw anything away, and never let anything decay; there were four chairs around the kitchen table and Aunt Fanny had washed her mother's everyday dishes and put them into the shelves of the dish cabinet and washed her mother's company china and put it into the shelves of the glass-fronted imitation mahogany breakfront which had been meant to go into the living room but had been crowded back into the kitchen. There were two extra chairs in the kitchen, so solidly built that they still stood steady, there was a second cabinet, painted blue like the first, and matching the oilcloth table cover, which had once held food, in cans and boxes; it had a flour bin and a built-in sifter, and, below, a bin for potatoes and onions. Aunt Fanny had washed her mother's silverware, which had been a wedding present, and put it into the drawers of the kitchen table, and in the cabinet where the food had been kept Aunt Fanny had unpacked and stored away the neat piles of dish towels, dish cloths, pot holders, and table napkins.

The beds were set up in the bedrooms, and Aunt Fanny had made them—the big mahogany double bed in her parents' bedroom had a neat, intricately crocheted spread which her mother had made when she was not much older than the girl in the middy blouse and long hair, and had stored in her cedar hope chest; there was her father's dresser, plain and stiff, matching the imitation mahogany bed and the dressing table, which had always seemed unlike her mother to Aunt Fanny, but of course it had come with the bedroom set and had to be used.

Aunt Fanny had placed a picture of her father, stern and uncomfortable, on her mother's dressing table, and a picture of her mother, cloudy-haired and idealized, on her father's dresser. The upholstery of the little bench before the dressing table was rose brocade, and Aunt Fanny had found the carton which held the little pink pebbled-glass pin tray, and the matching powder jar, and her mother's ivory-backed brush and comb and mirror, and had set these things, in correct order, on the dressing table. Her father's twin silver hairbrushes were on the dresser. The two pink hooked rugs were on the floor on either side of the bed. In the cedar hope chest were spare sheets and blankets; in the drawers of the dressing table and the dresser were the contents of three cartons, one labelled "My clothes," one "Michael's clothes," and one, "Michael's work clothes."

In the other bedroom—there had once been a door between the two bedrooms, left open in case a child cried in the night—were the small bed on which Richard had slept, and the crib in which Frances had slept until she was five; the first Mrs. Halloran had been planning and saving to re-furnish the children's bedroom when her husband cancelled all her plans by deciding on the big house. Aunt Fanny could remember the wallpaper in here—it had had a design of dancing bears—and the rest of the room was intact. She and Richard could have moved back here if they would. The little pink dresser had belonged to Frances, and in it Aunt Fanny had put the contents of the carton labelled "Frances, baby clothes." The little blue dresser had belonged to Richard, and it held "Richard, baby clothes," and "Richard, clothes," since Richard had been older when they left. There was a little bookcase, and from it Aunt Fanny had read "Alice in Wonderland," with an odd sense of distortion, since she could only remember her mother's voice reading it to her. There were two toyboxes, one labelled "RICHARD" and one "FRANCES," and in them Aunt Fanny had put, dividing with scrupulous fairness, the contents of the cartons labelled "Richard, toys," and "Frances, toys," and "Children, blocks, chalk, etc." Some day, Aunt Fanny thought foolishly, I must bring Richard up here and see if he wants to play.

There were two cartons Aunt Fanny had not unpacked.
One, labelled "Wedding presents" she had not unpacked because it had never been unpacked. Inside it were the silver tea
service, the silver cake servers, the handsome clock, which her
mother and father had received as wedding presents and put
away safely, planning to take them out to use some day when
they had a nicer apartment, with more space for cake servers
and handsome mantel clocks, but when Mr. Halloran brought
his wife and children to the big house the carton was put away
in the attic room with the other furniture because Mr. Halloran had insisted arrogantly that the big house be complete
down to every slightest detail before he brought his wife there.
In the big house there was no need for any further cake servers; the silver tea service was inferior to the graceful modern
set Mr. Halloran put into the big house, and the handsome
clock would only have looked vulgar on the mantel of Mrs.
Halloran's bedroom, where she wanted it, next to the dainty
porcelain clock Mr. Halloran had put there.

If Aunt Fanny had cared to, she might have lived entirely
in the apartment inside the house, cooking her meals on her
mother's stove, sleeping in her parents' bed, putting records on
the victrola.

The second carton Aunt Fanny never unpacked she had set
away in a corner of her parents' bedroom. It was labelled
"Souvenirs," and Aunt Fanny, knowing that it held a curl—
wrapped in a linen handkerchief—from her head, and one
from Richard's, and the ill-colored, straggling cards they had
given her mother on Mother's Day and Christmas, and perhaps letters from Michael Halloran, was afraid of what further she might find, what autograph albums, valentines, dance
programs that might have belonged to the strange girl with the
long hair among the photographs.

If Aunt Fanny had cared to, she might have dropped from
sight altogether into this apartment in the big house, might
have left the others behind and gone into the apartment and
closed the door, and stayed.

————

"Come along," Aunt Fanny said to Fancy; she had been looking for Fancy and had finally called her from the gardens to
come upstairs; Aunt Fanny met her on the great staircase and
took her hand. "I want to show you something," Aunt Fanny
said. "Just so you will know how well Aunt Fanny loves you, I
want to show you something no one has seen for many years."

"Where?" said Fancy, but came obediently with Aunt Fanny
along the hall and to the stairway which led to the third floor,
"Where, Aunt Fanny?"

"I'll show you," Aunt Fanny said mysteriously; she had no
idea of why she was suddenly so anxious to show Fancy the
big room upstairs, but told herself vaguely that it was a kind of
continuity, a way of establishing one strong direct line from
the first Mrs. Halloran to Fancy; "It's my doll house," Aunt
Fanny said happily, and opened the door with a flourish, as
though she were her mother welcoming a guest.

"What *is* it?" Fancy asked, peering from the doorway.

"My mother's house," Aunt Fanny said. "Where your grandfather and I were born."

"It's funny," Fancy said.

"Funny?"

"Strange," Fancy said hastily. "A big doll house, but no dolls."

"The dolls are here," Aunt Fanny said. "I remember them.
My mother sat here," she said, sitting down on the blue upholstered chair. "Sit on the footstool, Fancy; that other big chair
was my father's. I am the mother, wearing a yellow dress. You
must be me, little Frances. We will pretend that little Richard
is in the other room, studying his lessons."

"Can I touch anything?" Fancy asked, turning uncomfort-
ably on the footstool.

"Little Frances is not allowed to touch things in this room.
When Richard has finished his lessons you may go into the
other room and play with your toys. My father is sitting there
in his chair and he is studying too, one of his important books.
He has a pencil to underline anything that he thinks might be
useful for him to remember. I am my mother and I am always
thinking about my darling children. The dinner dishes have

been washed and perhaps later your father will put a record on the victrola."

"I want to play with the toys now."

"Later, dear. We are a very happy family and we love each other dearly. Don't we?"

"I guess so," Fancy said uncertainly.

"We love each other very *very* dearly. We are always thinking of ways to make each other happy, aren't we? Right now your father is working hard because he is dreaming of someday taking his family to live in a lovely house he will build for them, and I am your mother and I am thinking of how strong and happy and handsome my children are. Aren't I always thinking of you?"

"I guess so."

"My darling little Frances will grow up to be a lovely woman, tall and fair, and someday she will find a man who is as good as her father, and she will marry him and they will have strong and happy and handsome children of their own. But my son Richard will never marry; he will stay with his mother always, standing by his father, so I will always have a strong wise man on either side of me—"

Fancy stood up. "I think I hear my mother calling me," she said, moving toward the door.

Aunt Fanny looked at her mournfully. "Do you know that they are dead now?" she asked. "They were your great grandparents."

"Yes, Aunt Fanny. May I go now?"

"Run along, Frances," Aunt Fanny said remotely. When the door closed behind Fancy she sat quietly in her mother's chair, wondering at the quiet in her mother's rooms. When she closed the door behind her at last, and locked it, she thought: someday someone will come again, and wonder who lived here.

"Here comes Aunt Fanny now," said Mrs. Willow as Aunt Fanny came down the great stairway, "Aunt Fanny, come and decide something for us. We can't make up our minds about breakfast that first morning—would you think ham and eggs?"

"No," Fancy said, as though continuing a conversation begun long before, "I'm the one with the worst problems. You've been lucky."

"So have you." Gloria took up a little doll from the doll house and examined him curiously. "You've always lived *here*, for one thing."

"People growing up . . ." Fancy's voice faded; she seemed to be trying very hard to phrase something only very imperfectly perceived; she laughed timidly, and reached out to touch Gloria's arm. "It's *easier*, being young and growing up," she said haltingly, "when there are other people around doing it *with* you. *You* know, when you can think that all over the world there are children your age, growing up, and all of them somehow *feeling* the same. But suppose . . . suppose you were the *only* child growing up." She shook her head. "You were lucky," she said.

"I haven't altogether grown up yet."

"Gloria, won't you miss things like dancing, and boys, and going to parties, and pretty dresses, and movies, and football games? I've been waiting a long time for all the things like that, and now . . ."

"I can only think we'll have other things as good. Anyway, we'll be safe."

"Who wants to be *safe*, for heaven's sakes?" Fancy was scornful. "I'd rather live in a world full of other people, even dangerous people. I've been *safe* all my life. I've never even played with anyone, except my dolls." Once again she was thoughtful, moving her hand along the corner of the doll house in a gesture oddly reminiscent of her grandmother. "If I could," she said at last, "I would make it stop, all of this."

"Maybe they all feel the same way, really," Gloria said; she too, speaking of something not quite understood, spoke awkwardly. "I think they want the same things you do, only you would . . . inherit them, so to speak, just by growing up. Things like excitement, and new experiences, and all kinds of strange and wonderful things happening; you get them anyway, just by the process of growing older, but for them . . . they've already outgrown all they know and they want to try it all over again. Even at *my* age, you keep thinking you've missed so much, and you get older all the time."

"But what is there left that people like Aunt Fanny and Mrs. Willow are waiting for? What do they think can possibly happen nice to them *now?*"

"I can't answer *all* your questions, silly. I don't know myself. All I know is that being safe is more important than anything else."

"No," Fancy said. "No, it can't be."

"I'm only seventeen years old," Gloria said, "and I know this much—the world out there, Fancy, that world which is all around on the other side of the wall, it isn't real. It's real inside here, *we're* real, but what is outside is like it's made of cardboard, or plastic, or something. *Nothing* out there is real. Everything is made out of something else, and everything is made to look like something else, and it all comes apart in your hands. The people aren't real, they're nothing but endless copies of each other, all looking just alike, like paper dolls, and they live in houses full of artificial things and eat imitation food—"

"My doll house," Fancy said, amused.

"Your dolls have little cakes and roasts made of wood and painted. Well, the people out there have cakes and bread and cookies made out of pretend flour, with all kinds of things taken out of it to make it prettier for them to eat, and all kinds of things put in to make it easier for them to eat, and they eat meat which has been cooked for them already so they won't have to bother to do anything except heat it up and they read newspapers full of nonsense and lies and one day they hear that some truth is being kept from them for their own good and the next day they hear that the truth is being kept from them because it was really a lie and the next day they hear—"

Fancy laughed. "You sound like you hate everything."

"I wouldn't like being a doll in a doll house, I can tell you. I'm only seventeen years old, but I've learned a lot. All those people out there know about things like love and tenderness is what they hear in songs or read in books—that's one reason

I'm glad we burned all the books *here*. People shouldn't be able to read them and remember nothing but lies. And you talk about dances and parties—I can tell you there's no heart to anything any more; when you dance with a boy he's only looking over your shoulder at some other boy, and the only real people left any more are the shadows on the television screens."

"If I believed you," Fancy said, "I would still mind never trying things for myself. But I won't ever believe you until I've gone out there and seen it."

"There's nothing there," Gloria said with finality. "It's a make-believe world, with nothing in it but cardboard and trouble." She thought for a minute, and then said, "If you were a liar, or a pervert, or a thief, or even just sick, there wouldn't be anything out there you couldn't have."

Fancy bent over the doll house. "Anyway," she said, "I don't care how shabby it is. I'm not afraid of bad people, and of not being safe."

"But there aren't any *good* people," Gloria said helplessly. "No one is *any*thing but tired and ugly and mean. I *know*."

The first Mr. Halloran had been accustomed to chart and direct his busy life with suitable maxims; "The more haste, the less speed," he was fond of remarking, "There's always room at the top; you can't take it with you." His battery of architects and landscape technicians had declined, as one man, to adorn Mr. Halloran's home with elaborately painted and carved and engraved statements that Mr. Halloran could not take it with him, but had in many cases compromised with Mr. Halloran's passion for the reassuring presence of a line of good advice. Mr. Halloran—who kept on his desk a framed copy of Kipling's "If"—felt that every human soul was the better for the nudging presence of sound words, and it was only the tactful intervention of a young man—the nephew of the principal architect, in fact—who had taken a master's degree in English literature at Columbia University, that prevented a final rupture between Mr. Halloran and the principal architect, the one declaring that he would go to his death rather than see a wall of his creation scribbled over with things like "A man is always the better for a friend," and the other, with a tenaciousness basic to his personality, stubbornly leafing through a volume of familiar quotations and asking whose money was paying for this house? The young fellow, who had taken a master's degree in English literature at Columbia University, had suggested that Mr. Halloran could have his maxims without doing extreme violence to the feelings of the architect, by favoring a more learned and poetic use of words; in any case, the student pointed out, the difference of meaning and intention between one maxim and another was almost non-existent, and there was no more vital change in conduct suggested by "You can't take it with you" than "When shall we live if not now?"

Thus the gilded and elegantly presented suggestions on many of the walls of Mr. Halloran's house; ineffectual, certainly—in spite of the framed copy of Kipling's "If," Mr. Halloran continued all his days to accumulate nothing except money—but to the people living in the big house it had become a matter of indifference that they dined, exhorted to "Let none save good companions grace this festive board" or slept, assured "Get up, get up for shame, the blooming morn Upon her wings presents the god unshorn," or even "Hated by fools, and fools to hate, Be that my motto and my fate," or mounted the stairs reading, "When shall we live if not now?"

When the student, carried away in a kind of Strawberry Hill intoxication, suggested that Mr. Halloran cause a grotto to be constructed on the grounds of the big house, Mr. Halloran's first anxiety—before even making any definite attempt to determine what a grotto might be, or might be for, or might require in the way of furnishings, since if it existed he meant to have it—was to ensure that proper and suitable mottos would be charmingly placed upon its walls. Mr. Halloran's dim notion of a grotto held that a grotto was enticingly cool in the oppressive warm weather, and his determination upon a grotto-motto followed eagerly; "Fear no more the heat of the sun," the grotto was to say in some manner, and upon this Mr. Halloran was firm.

The student maintained, maligning Horry Walpole mercilessly, that a grotto was no grotto at all unless it overlooked a lake, and Mr. Halloran, who had already an ornamental pool on the garden front of his house, set his builders doggedly to work to construct a lake at the far end of the grounds; at two points, in fact, it touched the wall. The grotto was built of rock near the lake, earth heaped over it, and grass and flowers trained to grow on top in sweet wild profusion, and on the rock wall of the grotto inside was written, in letters of blue touched with gilt, "Fear no more the heat of the sun." The entire air of the grotto was faintly that of a Strawberry Hill confection, and it would have been vastly improved by the presence of a party of ladies, resting there after their saunter through the shrubbery ("La, what a love of a wilderness we have covered," the air just breathed; "hark; are the gentlemen back from their riding?"); or at the very least a dainty repast of fruits and ices, with vine leaves for plates and the entire chorus from the King's Theatre to float, fairylike and singing, in pleasure boats over the small waves.

Perhaps not all of this was apparent to Mr. Halloran. He did not care for his grotto, after all, because it was damp, and the lake was an irritation to him, reminding him always of how messy it had been to construct, and he had never been able to bring his wife there and write her name among the rocks. Worst of all, after the swans which originally swam in the ornamental pool had bitten young Richard and two housemaids they were sent to endure a lonely disgrace on the grotto-lake, where they bred and quarrelled, and were an unending annoyance and menace to the gardeners.

As a child, Aunt Fanny, who had wandered unceasingly and with deep incoherent love over every part of the grounds enclosed by the wall, had spent some amount of time in the grotto, watching the water of the lake move under the soft wind, hiding from the swans, and catching any number of head-colds. Now, older and more susceptible to influenzas and grippes, she came to the grotto less often, and yet every now and then she was irresistibly moved to walk in that direction. During the later days of July, in fact, Aunt Fanny made a kind of pilgrimage to all of her favorite haunts, to admire once more her father's handiwork and hope, somehow, to engrave upon her memory the well-loved spots which were so soon to dissolve utterly.

It should perhaps be recorded that the young master from Columbia University, who had hoped for so much from Mr. Halloran's grotto and had even led himself to believe that Mr. Halloran would be of some use to him in return, in furthering his chosen career, the writing of plays in blank verse, did succeed in reading half of one scene of one play to Mr. Halloran and was rewarded by the offer of a position as file clerk in Mr. Halloran's organization, from which he subsequently rose to the position of chief clerk, and got married.

Aunt Fanny came to the grotto in late July; it had been perhaps six months since she had last seen it, and she was struck at once with its air of mournful neglect; the roses still grew on its head, and the lake still moved gently under the soft wind, but the walls inside, which had been painted blue and green and gold, were faded, and the paint had chipped. A rock had cracked away from the entrance; "Fear no more the heat of the sun," had almost gone. The little rustic benches and tables which had been in the grotto were broken and rotted. Far out over the lake the swans, wholly wild now, moved in distant patterns and Aunt Fanny, hoping that they would not notice her moving, ducked quietly into the grotto and—as had been her custom long ago—set two or three of the rustic chairs and tables across the entrance so that the swans, if they pursued her, could not get in.

Aunt Fanny was really quite angry, angrier than she had ever been before in her life. She was angry at her sister-in-law for planning to wear a crown, and angry at her brother for not preventing it and for letting his wife look like a fool before the villagers. She was angry at Miss Ogilvie and Maryjane and Essex for their passivity and their humble subjection to Mrs. Halloran's every whim. She was most particularly angry, far and beyond any anger she had ever known before, at Mrs. Halloran, for having that morning given Aunt Fanny a carbon—and a carbon, Aunt Fanny thought furiously, not even the *first* copy—

of a typewritten page headed INSTRUCTIONS and composed by Mrs. Halloran herself, with no reference to Aunt Fanny.

Sitting in the grotto, Aunt Fanny took out the paper and read it again.

Instructions

We all know what is going to happen on the night of August thirtieth. Certain measures must be taken for the general good, and each of us must preserve carefully this page of instructions as a constant reference. ANY DEVIATION FROM THESE RULES WILL BE SUBJECT TO PUNISHMENT.

1. No person is to leave the big house, *for any reason whatsoever*, after four o'clock in the afternoon on August thirtieth.
2. Under no circumstances is any person from outside to *enter* the house after that time.
3. Since the servants and staff will be leaving the house by noontime, it is expected that no special demands will be made for their services, after midnight on August twenty-ninth.
4. Due to the unusual conditions which will be existing outside the house on the night of August thirtieth, it has been decided that precautions must be taken to protect windows, etc. All persons remaining in the house will begin work immediately after the departure of the servants at noon to board up, cover with blankets, and in all possible fashions barricade all windows and doors. Mrs. Halloran will make herself responsible for explaining this action to Mr. Halloran.
5. The entire assembly will gather in the drawing room at four o'clock on the afternoon of August thirtieth, for a light meal, and last-minute instructions from Mrs. Halloran.
6. No one is to leave the drawing room during the night of August thirtieth.
7. It is expected that all persons remaining in the big house will so attire themselves as to greet the morning suitably, although a certain consideration of the probable fluctuations in temperature, etc., must be observed. No one except Mrs. Halloran may wear a crown.

8. When the morning arrives, Mrs. Halloran will lead the way to the door, everyone following in sober procession. Mrs. Halloran will be the first to step outside.

9. Since, for all practical purposes, the present calendar will lose all significance after the night of August thirtieth, the following morning will be referred to, from this time on, as The First Day.

10. On The First Day, depending entirely upon circumstances at present only imperfectly understood (the state of vegetation, for instance, or the availability of water) tasks will be assigned by Mrs. Halloran as necessary.

11. No one is to leave the general vicinity of the house on The First Day, and no one is to alter, pick, eat, or in any way deface existing conditions, until the various prohibitions have been determined.

12. Mates will be assigned by Mrs. Halloran. Indiscriminate coupling will be subject to severe punishment.

13. On The First Day, and thereafter, wanton running, racing, swimming, play of various kinds, and such manifestations of irresponsibility will of course not be permitted. It is expected that all members of the party will keep in mind their positions as inheritors of the world, and conduct themselves accordingly. A proud dignity is recommended, and extreme care lest offense be given to supernatural overseers who may perhaps be endeavoring to determine the fitness of their choice of survivors.

"Father," Aunt Fanny said into the cool dim underwater light of the grotto, "Father, what have you done to me?"
FRANCES, FRANCES HALLORAN.
Aunt Fanny, moving in fear, pressed herself back against the painted wall of the grotto; the blue and green and gold swam and curled around her, and she knew at once who was standing in the doorway.

"But I don't *want* to see anything," Gloria insisted crossly. "You can just get someone else to try, that's all. I'm simply not interested in gawking into that silly mirror any more."

"Dear," Mrs. Willow said soothingly, "try to be calm. Naturally you can't see anything anyway when you're so excited; try to relax and think of the rest of us."

"Perhaps the lovely countries of the future have lost their savor for Gloria," Mrs. Halloran said. "Perhaps Gloria is dreaming still of a world of wicker furniture and a job ushering in a movie theatre; perhaps Gloria longs to repudiate all of us."

Gloria turned, astonished, to stare at Essex, and he smiled a little, and shrugged.

"That *was* nasty," Fancy said to Gloria, "but I *told* you he would."

"Essex is primarily a politician," Mrs. Halloran said smoothly, smiling at Gloria. "His interest is thus in the good of the community as a whole; individual whims cannot be allowed to interfere, I think, with our general future."

"Essex is a pig," Fancy said, and put her hand into Gloria's. "Didn't I tell you, Gloria?"

"Essex," Mrs. Halloran said, "tell Gloria that she must look into the mirror, or risk my displeasure."

"Gloria?" said Essex, looking aside.

"There's nothing in there," Gloria said sullenly. "It's just a dirty old mirror covered with oil."

"Orianna, we will all see this country soon enough," Aunt Fanny put in. "It is not necessary to force Gloria to look again."

"I insist," Mrs. Halloran said, "that Gloria look into the

mirror. I will not abide childish temperament, and I can hardly be expected to plan for all of us without adequate information. Gloria *must* see."

"I'm sick and tired of hearing you bully everybody," Fancy said flatly to her grandmother, and there was a long, waiting moment of silence. Then Maryjane spoke, weakly but stubbornly, "Fancy's right," she said. "You can just stop bossing *me* around, for one."

"Always so difficult to know what to do," Aunt Fanny murmured.

"Family quarrels," Miss Ogilvie agreed.

"Well, the way *I* see it," Mrs. Willow swept nobly into the fray, "everyone's gotten kind of on everyone else's nerves, and pretty soon if we don't look out we're *all* going to be sniping at each other—what I used to say to my gels, when they were young things pulling hair over some toy—what *I* used to say, birds in their little nests agree, and what *I*'d like to know—are we or are we not a pack of goddamned little birds stuck in the fanciest nest in town?"

"Such a gift for the apt phrase," Mrs. Halloran said. "I personally deplore this evidence of frayed nerves; we do not have much longer to wait, after all, and perhaps if we cannot contain ourselves we had better remain decently apart." She looked at Gloria. "I will only point out once more that I have undertaken a tremendous responsibility in arranging to lead you all into this new world, and I expect complete cooperation; Maryjane, I do not think you can rightly call it bossing you around when I ask that you exert your dubious talents to the utmost to ensure our mutual safety?"

"Just don't try *always* bossing me, is all," Maryjane said sullenly.

"Well, I guess we all know where we stand now," the captain said heartily. "Mrs. Halloran, we all know the little lady didn't mean to disobey you by not looking into the mirror for you; got to make allowances for a little female jealousy," and he winked at Arabella, who giggled and said *"Honestly!"*

"I am satisfied," Mrs. Halloran said. "In consideration of

the captain's sensible explanation of your motives, Gloria, we will excuse you for tonight."

Gloria stood up and crossed the room to face Essex, who leaned against the back of Mrs. Halloran's chair. "Essex," she said, "I want to ask you once more, in front of everybody. There's still time. They couldn't stop us if we really wanted to go. We would have two weeks at least."

"Don't be silly, Gloria." Essex stared down at his hands on the back of Mrs. Halloran's chair. "I wouldn't leave for anything in the world," he said.

"I think you have been fairly answered, Gloria," Mrs. Halloran said amiably. "Goodnight."

"I think you must be really *crazy*," Fancy said. She was sitting on the foot of Gloria's bed, looking like a small demon in red pajamas. "I never saw my grandmother so close to *really* mad."

"She's a terrible old woman. But you were nice to speak up for me, Fancy."

"And what do you think of Essex now?" Fancy giggled. "He's a kind of a poor fish," she said. "And I *told* you so."

"Poor Essex," said Gloria unreasonably.

"What I can't figure," Fancy said, pulling at a tuft in the blanket, "is why you tell me it's so terrible outside and then make such a fool out of yourself asking Essex to come away with you, right in front of everybody."

"Maybe I didn't really want him to leave. Maybe I only wanted him to *say* he would."

"Well, you know now," Fancy said unsympathetically. "She wouldn't let him go any more than she let the captain go."

"I've been wondering." Gloria sat up in bed and leaned forward to speak to Fancy earnestly. "All the time your grandmother keeps telling us how hard and how serious and how tremendous it is, our waiting here till it all happens, and how careful we've got to be, and how much responsibility she's got for seeing that we don't get ourselves into trouble and how we only have her to direct us and we have to do what she says

and how we can't run and play and be happy in that nice
country—"

"Well? We don't any of us know what it's going to be like,
do we?"

"I do," Gloria said. "I've seen it in the mirror. And in the
mirror it wasn't like that at all. In the mirror, your grandmother hasn't ever even *been* there."

Essex spoke boldly. "I believe, Orianna," he said, "that you
have made a very grave mistake. I would never have believed
that you could be so much in error."

"Are you positive that I am in error? Might you not have
mistaken my motives?"

"I doubt it," Essex said with some irony. "You have seriously
compromised your authority."

"By suppressing that girl's insolence? You had your choice,
Essex; you had only to agree to accompany her."

"You tried to turn me out of the house once, I recall. Perhaps, having stayed then, I lost the ability to go."

Mrs. Halloran smiled, almost wistfully in the dusk of the
garden. "It has already begun," she said. "Some months ago I
told you that, once committed to the belief in Aunt Fanny's
bright world, I was committed absolutely, but I would not go
second to Aunt Fanny or to anyone else."

"Where will you be when you can no longer turn us out of
your house?"

"It is my house now, and it will be my house then. I will not
relinquish one stone of it in this world or any other. Everyone
must be made to remember that, and to remember that I will
not relinquish, either, one fraction of my authority. Perhaps,"
she added drily, "just as you have lost the ability to leave, I
have lost the ability to serve."

"I assume then, that you have no real faith in the fondness
any of the rest of us may feel for you?"

"None," said Mrs. Halloran.

Mrs. Halloran breakfasted with her husband the next morning, in order to explain to him the plans for the last day and

night. When Gloria came into the breakfast room where the others were sitting, she was flushed, and bright-eyed, and almost running. "Listen," she began, as she came through the door, "I've got to *tell* you right away; I never expected anything *like* it. I was combing my hair just now—and I never even finished—look," and, laughing a little, she pushed her hands through her tangled hair, "I was combing my hair and looking in the mirror, naturally, and looking at myself and then without any kind of warning my own reflection just vanished from the glass and I was looking through again, and this time I was walking. I was right *inside*, you see; I was at the top of a little hill and down below I could see great fields of flowers, the red flowers I saw before, I think, and bluebells, and what must have been the same little stream, sparkling and bright and clean—"

"Any people?" It was Mrs. Willow, softly.

"No, only me. I started to run down through the grass and when I came to the foot of the hill I jumped right across the little stream and on the other side I ran into a little forest and I was barefoot, because I can still feel how the moss felt under my feet." She stopped for breath, and they all sat quietly, listening. "And there were birds singing, and—oh, I wish I could remember, and make you all see how lovely it was!—and flowers, and everything was so gentle and warm and light; it is going to be so beautiful," and she looked around at all of them with tears in her eyes. "I don't think I ever really believed it, *completely*, before." She turned, half-laughing, to Essex. "I don't even hate *you*," she said.

Essex rose gravely and took her hand to lead her to the table. "Your shrine," he said, "will be set in a forest of ash trees. The oracle will manifest itself through the great movement of the leaves and the flights of clouds of starlings. I will cause to be constructed an image of yourself as a young goddess; offerings favorably received will be grapes and other sweet fruit, colored pebbles, and sweet grasses; acceptable sacrifices will include the otter and the young of soft-footed animals, such as the leopard."

Gloria smiled at Essex. "I will help you build it," she said. "I will show you the place where you can run down the hill and jump across the stream and go into the trees, and we will find an ash grove for our shrine."

"Are there reeds in the stream?" the captain asked. "We will make young Fancy here a flute, and she can pipe for us."

Fancy giggled. "You will all have to follow me and dance," and Maryjane added shyly, "We can put flowers in our hair, those red ones, and dance under the trees."

"Pagan abandon," said Mrs. Willow indulgently.

"Pagan abandon, indeed," said Mrs. Halloran dangerously from the doorway. "Can you not realize that you are *already* breaking my laws?"

Toward the end of August the weather turned strange; various and unusual phenomena were reported from one end of the country to the other: freak snow storms, hurricanes, hail from a clear sky. Around the big house there were thunderstorms every afternoon, coming with heavy regularity, the clouds beginning to mass blackly on the horizon shortly after four o'clock, and moving with speed until in an hour the sky was black, and, by six, clear again. If the first Mr. Halloran had been alive he might have pointed out that although everyone talked about the weather, no one did anything about it; there were cases of death from heat and death from drowning and death from wind in each morning's newspaper, along with statements that the earth's surface was being lowered into the oceans at the rate of two inches a century; a volcano which had been dormant for five hundred years erupted, blasted its surrounding countryside, and fell asleep again forever.

A woman in Chicago was arrested for leading a polar bear clipped like a French poodle into a large downtown department store. A man in Texas won a divorce from his wife because she tore out the last chapter of every mystery story he borrowed from the library. A television set in Florida refused to let itself be turned off; until its owners took an axe to it, it continued, on or off, presenting inferior music and stale movies and endless, maddening advertising, and even under the axe, with its last sigh, it died with the praises of a hair tonic on its lips.

Mrs. Halloran's crown arrived, and she wore it to dinner. "I expect you will soon be accustomed to seeing me wear a crown," she said amiably down the dinner table. "After all, it is not the least of the adjustments we will be called upon to make."

"It is less regal than I had anticipated," Essex said politely.

"My sister-in-law," Aunt Fanny told Essex, "has never been remarkable for her good taste or—what shall I call it?—family background; I think that tonight, however, she has surpassed herself."

"I kind of like it," Maryjane said. "I wish I'd thought of it first."

"Like calls to like," Aunt Fanny said darkly.

"Well, I don't understand *this* at all," Mrs. Willow said, looking in perplexity from one to another, "I just don't understand all this carping and good taste talk; stands to reason, far as *I* can see, that Orianna here is going to be the boss from now on, the way she's always been up to now, so why can't she wear what she pleases? Well?" She stared at Aunt Fanny. "Been taking a little too much on yourself, haven't you?" she demanded. "Maybe you thought *you* ought to be the queen and wear a crown?" and Mrs. Willow laughed shortly.

"My father—"

"*Your* father—I just guess we've heard about all we can take of your father—we don't even know it *was* your father."

"Mrs. Willow." Aunt Fanny rose in white-faced indignation. "Are you suggesting that I am illegitimate?"

Mrs. Halloran put in smoothly, "Aunt Fanny, sit down, please. Augusta, do not speak again without my permission; your warm support makes me doubtful of my own cause. Essex—Maryjane—Miss Ogilvie—if my lunacy takes the form of desiring to wear a crown, will you deny me? May I not look foolish in tolerant peace? Gloria—may I continue to wear my crown?"

"Since you *do* ask me, Mrs. Halloran," Gloria said, "I think you look like a damned fool."

"Indeed. Thank you, Gloria, for not troubling to spare my feelings; I wonder if it is not too late for you to join your father?"

"And tell him you're a crazy old lady who sits at her dinner table with a crown on her head?"

"I *wish* you all found my wearing a crown less annoying." Mrs. Halloran touched the crown tenderly; it was not, after all, of any great magnificence; if she had not persisted in calling it a crown Mrs. Halloran might very well have been suspected of wearing only a plain gold band around her hair. "Gloria," she said, "you are not to call me a crazy old lady. I am no older than Mrs. Willow, I am certain that I am not crazy, and Aunt Fanny will remove any doubts you have as to my being a lady. In any case, you were discourteous."

"I apologize," Gloria said sincerely. "I *am* your guest, Mrs. Halloran, and it was not right of me to call you names. I certainly don't like your crown, but I do not think that I have any right to stop you from wearing it."

"Are we going to go on worrying about Mrs. Halloran's crown all night?" the captain demanded. "I thought we were supposed to be making plans for the party." He nudged Arabella. "The last orgy," he said.

"Wicked." Arabella giggled.

15

Miss Inverness was wearing grey taffeta, and Miss Deborah Inverness was dressed in pink chiffon. Both had wide hats, flowered, because they had been invited for a garden party. They arrived early, anxious to admire any preparations which had been made for the party, and got out of the village taxi before the entrance front of the house, were met by Gloria and Mrs. Willow, and escorted along the garden path, past the barbecue pit where coals were already heating, to the terrace where Mrs. Halloran sat in a great chair. Mrs. Halloran's golden canopy had been extended a little, to make it more of a general shelter and less a personal tribute to Mrs. Halloran, but she was wearing her golden dress and her crown. The Misses Inverness approached, hands out, and greeted Mrs. Halloran, Aunt Fanny, Maryjane, and Essex, in scrupulous order.

"It is nice to see you again," Miss Deborah said to Aunt Fanny, timidly, because Aunt Fanny had been so very distressing the last time they met; Miss Deborah and, to a lesser extent, her sister, were anxious to make Aunt Fanny understand that they bore no grudge; did not, indeed, believe in letting the sun go down on their wrath; "So *very* nice to see you again," Miss Deborah said, and then, perceiving Miss Ogilvie in the background, "Miss Ogilvie; this *is* nice."

"Do you like my crown?" Mrs. Halloran asked directly.

"A crown?" said Miss Inverness, bewildered. "I confess I had not thought of it as a crown, Mrs. Halloran. It looked to me like a substitute for a hat."

"It is a crown," Mrs. Halloran said complacently.

"Well, I am sure it is very becoming. Although, of course, for general wear . . ."

"*I* certainly intend to wear it generally," Mrs. Halloran said.

"Perhaps not suitable for everybody . . . But very handsome, nevertheless. An heirloom?" Miss Inverness was puzzled for compliments.

"It will be."

"Of considerable value, I imagine. I am of course not inquiring the price."

"Of inestimable value," Mrs. Halloran said.

"Yes. You carry it well, Mrs. Halloran. My sister and I," Miss Inverness went on to Aunt Fanny, "were brought up to believe in nobility of character, and to disdain baubles of rank. But we would certainly not impose our opinions upon others."

"Not, at least," Aunt Fanny said, "on my brother's wife. Who was clearly brought up to value baubles of rank and let nobility of character alone."

"Are you still talking about my crown?" Mrs. Halloran asked.

"About your regal bearing, Mrs. Halloran."

"And what it covers," Aunt Fanny put in maliciously.

Mrs. Halloran laughed. "It covers a regal position," she said. "Had you ever thought of wearing a crown, Miss Inverness?"

Miss Inverness stiffened. "In Paradise . . . a princely diadem . . ." she said. "Although my father was an agnostic."

"It comforts me," Mrs. Halloran said, "to reflect upon the Misses Inverness inheriting their angelic crowns, but I must spare a moment's pity for the late Mr. Inverness. I remember him."

"Religious discussion is not for the drawing room, Mrs. Halloran. My father determined his own afterlife."

"You chide me, Miss Inverness. But I am still sorry for your father."

"*My* father," Aunt Fanny said, anxious to avert what seemed to her a rising crisis, "was a splendid man. I recall that he mentioned your father, Miss Inverness, most affectionately."

"In any case," Miss Deborah said gently, "it does not look so *very* much like a crown, sister. A simple gold band—"

Miss Inverness glanced at her sister, and then said firmly, "How perfectly beautiful the grounds look, Mrs. Halloran. You must be very proud of them," but Mrs. Halloran had turned to greet the schoolteacher and Mr. Armstrong the postmaster.

At first the lawn looked pleasingly empty under the japanese lanterns, with the Misses Inverness strolling with Miss Ogilvie, admiring the bushes, and then Mr. Armstrong and the schoolteacher, greeting the Misses Inverness and wandering aside to look briefly on the sundial, and then a group of the villagers who had arrived together in one car, and straggled out onto the lawn. Mrs. Willow turned over her position at the entrance front to Arabella, and joined the captain in the large tent on the lawn from which champagne was to be served. The beef roasts sizzled and splattered over the barbecue pit, and Julia was sent to supervise the setting out of additional food in the second tent, near the barbecue pit. Mrs. Halloran remained in her chair on the terrace, and each guest was brought to greet her individually. Aunt Fanny and Miss Ogilvie began gradually to steer the guests toward the champagne tent, where Mrs. Willow reassured doubters about the intoxicating properties of champagne, which, although largely unknown to the villagers, was, Mrs. Halloran had thought, the only appropriate beverage to serve. The captain, in contrivance with Essex and without Mrs. Halloran's knowledge, had laid in a great stock of beer and this combination, of beer with champagne, may have been responsible for the general feeling of well-being which was spreading swiftly along the lawn.

Essex and Gloria had seemingly determined to avoid one another. Gloria remained at the entrance and Essex hovered over Mrs. Halloran, running small errands and supervising, like a general from a point of vantage, the small skirmishes which made the great movements of the battle on the lawn. When Gloria brought guests to greet Mrs. Halloran she moved

silently past Essex, and Mrs. Halloran, amused, noticed each
small gesture of mutual indifference, but did not comment.

The general movement on the lawn was clockwise, guests
coming down from the terrace after greeting Mrs. Halloran,
entering into the circular turn of the crowd, going past the sundial, admiring the view and the japanese lanterns from midway
down the great lawn, which was as far as the party had strayed
so far, then on into the champagne tent and out again, to continue the same vague round. The Misses Inverness, each having touched a glass of champagne, sat to one side of the general
group on chairs provided for them by Essex, and old Mrs. Peabody, mother to the Mr. Peabody who kept the Carriage Stop
Inn, had been seated nearby; little groups of people paused to
speak to them and moved on.

The villagers, who knew one another intimately at home,
now behaved toward one another more formally, under Mrs.
Halloran's eye. Mrs. Peabody, who knew to the day which funeral had last brought to public view the blue serge suit of
Mr. Straus, the butcher, and why the younger Watkins boy
had come after all, and how much Mrs. Halloran had been
overcharged for the champagne, was highly amused by the
whole party and had been heard to observe that the first Mr.
Halloran had always had too much sense to invite the villagers
to his house. "And," she added to the captain, who was bringing her a glass of champagne, "in his time, *we* would have had
too much sense to *come.*"

"Baubles of rank," Miss Inverness observed to a little group.
"Baubles of rank and pride of place."

"My father always took such an interest in all of you." Aunt
Fanny beamed tenderly upon Mr. Straus, the butcher, and
Mrs. Otis, who gave dancing lessons. "He thought of you
as . . . personal *friends*, I really believe. He was a fine man."

"A fine man," Mrs. Otis said obediently, and Mr. Straus
nodded heavily.

"I remember," Aunt Fanny said, "when he first spoke of
building the big house, he thought at once of you villagers.

'We must take care of them always,' he said. 'They will look to us for guidance and security.'"

"Of course we do," said Mrs. Otis, and Mr. Straus nodded.

"I think you will have to concede," Aunt Fanny went on, "that we in the big house have always treated you well. Even now—our only thought in having this expensive lawn party was for *your* pleasure. My father, I think, would be pleased."

"I am sure he would," Mrs. Otis said, and Mr. Straus nodded.

"Of course," Aunt Fanny said, "and believe me, I am most reluctant to bring it up, but of course, you will see at once that, no matter how fond we have grown of all of you, we can hardly, *now*, persuade my father to include you. I am sure he will regret it as much as any of us; I am sure that losing you grieves him bitterly."

"He was a fine man," Mrs. Otis said, bewildered, and Mr. Straus nodded. "He was a man who liked a good roast of beef," Mr. Straus said.

"Miss Ogilvie?" said Essex politely, "Miss Ogilvie as a child was violated by a band of Comanche Indians in a lonely farmhouse on Little Wicked Bend River. It has left her taciturn."

"Good heavens!" Miss Deborah turned her head slightly to give Miss Ogilvie a quick, fleeting look; "I've known Miss Ogilvie for years," Miss Deborah said, "and she never breathed a word."

"It's not the sort of thing one mentions, you know," Essex said. "*I* only learned it quite by accident."

"Poor Miss Ogilvie; if we had only known, my sister and I, perhaps we could have done something. Ah . . . comforted her, perhaps. Do you think I might mention it to her?"

"Under no circumstances," said Essex with some haste. "I believe it would be extremely harmful, *extremely*. After all, the memory has been successfully buried for so long . . ."

"But bringing these things out into the open air—sister!" Miss Deborah called, "I really *must* tell you; Mr. Essex has just given me the most *alarming* information. Poor Miss Ogilvie! And we never knew!"

"I am doing all I can to make your party a success," Essex said, coming up to Mrs. Halloran on the terrace.

"All it lacks, actually," Mrs. Halloran said, "is the head of the Cheshire Cat looking down on us from the sky." She looked from the terrace onto the sizable crowd now moving more freely on the lawn. The sundial stood out clearly, since no one went really close to it, and it stood by itself, a small island, in the moving people. From the terrace the sound of voices was a little distant, murmuring, with now and then the clear round bellow of Mrs. Willow, saying, "The little bubbles tickle your nose," or, "The drink of angels, I promise you; fit for any king."

"If we had a Cheshire Cat," Essex said, pleased, "Mrs. Willow could be the Duchess."

"As I recall, the Duchess was under sentence of execution for boxing the Queen's ears." Mrs. Halloran laughed. "Off with their heads!" she said.

Gloria came up behind Mrs. Halloran and said, not looking at Essex, "They sent me to tell you that the barbecue was ready, and everything is ready to be served in the barbecue tent."

"Essex," Mrs. Halloran said, "can you communicate with these people?"

Essex came from the terrace down into the crowd. "The food is ready," he said to Mr. Straus. "Follow the path around to the left."

"Righto," Mr. Straus said. "Happen to know the quality of the meat." He took Aunt Fanny on one arm and Mrs. Otis on the other arm and made purposefully for the barbecue; Essex moved on, urging the Misses Inverness into action, turning people toward the right path, nudging, stirring, like a sheep dog turning a flock of sheep toward the fold: "The barbecue is ready," he said over and over, "follow the path to the left," and obediently, the people standing with champagne cups in their hands listened, nodded, and moved slowly and talking toward the barbecue pit and the second tent. "The old lady has done herself proud," Mr. Atkins from the hardware store said to the schoolteacher, and the schoolteacher, who had never tasted champagne before, nodded hazily and giggled.

"Now come on everybody," came the great voice of Mrs. Willow, who had tasted champagne before, "fill up your cups, and then eat hearty—it may be the last meal you ever get." People laughed, and asked one another what was in the salad dressing, and handed around plates; someone gave the schoolteacher a full plate of meat and salad and rolls and two little chocolate cupcakes and the schoolteacher, giggling and swaying, held it precariously for a minute or so and then set it down on a chair and went after more champagne.

"That's a good piece of meat," Mr. Straus said to Mrs. Willow, and Mrs. Willow slapped him on the shoulder and said richly, "You'll never eat better again, so go at it, my boy."

"Delicious," said Miss Inverness, tasting delicately of her potato salad. She and her sister held identical plates, with tiny servings at which they were nibbling with tiny bites. "Everything always tastes so much better out of doors," said Miss Deborah. She sighed, changing her plate from one hand to the other, and glanced longingly at the lighted windows of the big house.

It was growing darker; faces which had a few minutes ago been clearly visible were fading, so that only in the light of the great barbecue fire was an occasional countenance familiar, reddened and in many cases dirty. Mr. Straus hung lovingly over the man who, white-jacketed and sober, went on endlessly carving thin curling slices of meat onto a huge wooden platter; beyond him the fires flared and spattered when the barbecue sauce went onto the coals, and beyond the fires the silent darkness of the rose garden and the farther trees descended, hiding successfully the youngest Watkins boy and Julia Willow, who had taken a bottle of champagne and decided to skip dinner.

"Cuts like butter," Mr. Straus said, watching the carver with splendid approval.

On the terrace Mrs. Halloran stirred wearily, eyeing her untouched plate. "I have no appetite," she said. "Being a queen is a very public penance."

"Perhaps I could get you a little something from the kitchen?"

Miss Ogilvie, hovering solicitously, made little futile dabs at her own plate, clearly unwilling to seem to be enjoying her food.

Mrs. Halloran sighed. "Run along and get yourself some champagne," she said. "Dream of pressing your own grapes."

When Miss Ogilvie had gone scurrying down toward the champagne tent, where some few revellers still lingered, Mrs. Halloran rose. She looked once down the long fine sweep of the lawn, where the sundial was still faintly visible, white against the dark grass, and glanced at the pale shape of the tent, where faint laughter persisted. From the barbecue pit she could hear voices raised, the sounds of fire, and the touching of forks against plates; over it all Mrs. Willow urging, "Eat hearty, friends, you'll never see as good again." Mrs. Halloran set down her plate and opened the great door; she had set her chair against it as though guarding the house. She went into the black and white tiled entrance hall; "When shall we live if not now?" she read over the staircase, and it seemed all at once an echo of Mrs. Willow. Moving quickly, Mrs. Halloran went into the right wing where Mr. Halloran sat before his fire. His dinner tray was on the small table near him, untouched; "Nurse?" Mr. Halloran said, not turning around, "Nurse, I have not had my dinner yet."

"Good evening, Richard," Mrs. Halloran said.

"Orianna?" said Mr. Halloran, peering uncertainly around the wing of his chair. "Orianna, I have not been given my dinner yet. Nurse has not given me my dinner."

"She has probably been tempted by the party outside," Mrs. Halloran said, "but do not distress yourself, Richard; I am perfectly able to give you your dinner, and we will let Nurse celebrate while she can."

"I don't want oatmeal," Mr. Halloran said pettishly. "If it's oatmeal you must send it back and have them make me something else."

Mrs. Halloran lifted the silver cover from a bowl; "It's two splendid soft-cooked eggs," she said. "And I believe a nice hot broth, and a pretty little pudding."

"But Nurse is not here to feed me," Mr. Halloran said crossly.

"Then you will see how well *I* can do it." Mrs. Halloran tied the napkin under his chin, and opened the eggs carefully. Then she moved the nurse's low stool beside him, and sat down with the tray beside her. "Eggs first?" she asked.

"I want the broth," Mr. Halloran said.

"I think the broth may be too warm, Richard." Mrs. Halloran took up a little of the broth and blew on it to cool it. "Now," she said, and put the spoon to her husband's mouth. He accepted it obediently, and swallowed, and Mrs. Halloran took another spoonful and held it ready.

"It's too hot," Mr. Halloran said. "Nurse *always* gives me my eggs first."

"Then we'll try the eggs," Mrs. Halloran said.

"I want the pudding," Mr. Halloran said at once.

"Then we'll try the pudding."

"Why was I not sent oatmeal? They *knew* I wanted oatmeal tonight."

"They sent up a very pleasant dinner, Richard. Eggs, and broth, and pudding."

"Then *feed* it to me," Mr. Halloran said. "Nurse is *never* this slow."

"Open your mouth, then."

"Are they having a party?" Mr. Halloran said, when he had finished his mouthful.

"A big party," Mrs. Halloran said. "Ready with another spoonful."

"Why am I not going to the party?"

"If you eat every bite of your dinner, Richard, I will tell you about it, what everyone is doing."

"Are they going to ring the bells? Over the carriage house?"

"A splendid idea. Open your mouth, Richard. I think we must really ring the bells."

"Who has come to this party?"

"All the people from the village. The party is for them, a treat. Right now they are around the barbecue pit, having their dinners just as you are having your dinner, and they are drinking champagne; later, after you finish all your dinner, I will bring you a glass of champagne as a treat for you, too."

"No more egg," Mr. Halloran said. "I want pudding."

"Pudding, then. We have strung lanterns back and forth across the long lawn, little colored lights along the lawn. There is a corner of the terrace where we are going to put musicians, musicians I brought all the way from the city, and all the people will be dancing out on the grass under the lanterns."

"And drinking champagne."

"And drinking champagne. Since the night air is far too cool for you, I thought I would bring you into the drawing room and you may sit by the big window and watch. There, now, the pudding is gone; you ate your pudding very nicely, Richard."

"It reminds me of when Lionel died, and we rang the bells all night."

"More egg now? You will hear the bells, I promise you. And you will sit in the drawing room and drink a glass of champagne and watch the villagers dancing under the colored lights."

"I think not." Mr. Halloran sighed tiredly. "I would rather stay here. I can hear the bells, you know, and I think colored lights would be too bright for my eyes." He hit his hand irritably against the arm of his chair. "I *wish* Nurse would come back," he said. "Do you know, I have not had my dinner yet? Nurse went off without giving me my dinner, and I do not think that is in any way proper. You must find Nurse at once and tell her I want my dinner."

"Mr. Essex." Miss Inverness bore down heavily, glass in hand. "Mr. Essex, I must really ask an explanation from you. This distressing story which my sister has repeated to me—"

"Distressing indeed, Miss Inverness. I cannot tell you how we all deplore it."

"I think it most thoughtless and—yes, even *tasteless*—of Mrs. Halloran. One does not expect to meet, in nice houses, people of unsuitable background; I have permitted my sister to become intimate with Miss Ogilvie, even help her with small purchases in our little emporium. I think it very hard that we were not told of Miss Ogilvie's character."

"Surely not a story for general circulation," Essex murmured.

"Certainly not. I assure you that I will be the last to repeat it. But, Mr. Essex, *ladies* should know. One assumes, all too frequently, that the mere presence of a woman in a respectable family is enough to ensure that her reputation is above reproach. It will be very difficult, now, to know how to speak to Mrs. Halloran."

"It has *always* been difficult," Essex said, "to know how to speak to Mrs. Halloran."

"All I can say, Mr. Essex, is that Mrs. Halloran Senior would never have allowed a person of questionable character to enter her house. This is all very hard on her memory, and I shall tell Mrs. Halloran so when I say goodnight; naturally, my sister and I cannot remain at this delightful party. We stayed only long enough to take a little refreshment, in courtesy to our hosts."

"I hope you will not find it necessary to say anything to Miss Ogilvie."

"We were brought up ladies, Mr. Essex. My mother was not one to reproach an erring sister for her misfortunes. But further association will be, of course, out of the question."

"I believe, on the whole, that it will," Essex said.

"Good night, Mr. Essex."

"Before you leave," Essex said, lowering his voice, "there is something more I really *must* tell you. Since your association with this house is to be so irrevocably severed, you will want, I think, to hear the unsavory truth about Aunt Fanny? As you know, like Miss Ogilvie, she has never married."

Miss Inverness gasped. "Not Miss Halloran *too?*"

"Similar, although the circumstances were different," Essex said gravely. "I myself find Aunt Fanny's story the more pitiable. Do you recall the year that Aunt Fanny spent abroad? It was given out that she was in Switzerland."

"I remember," said Miss Inverness faintly.

"In actuality," Essex said, "she had been captured by pirates off the Mediterranean coast. It was upwards of seven months before a British man of war tracked them down and wrested Aunt Fanny from their clutches. A most horrible fate."

Miss Inverness sipped from her glass, her hand shaking. "Horrible, indeed," she said weakly; in the darkness she peered at Essex, leaning forward and almost whispering. "The worst," she said. "I suppose it *happened?*"

"Alas," Essex said. "May I bring you more champagne?"

Miss Inverness drained her glass. "I think yes," she said. "We *must* leave, my sister and I, but at the moment I think I am slightly ill."

"Aunt Fanny," Essex said, coming up beside her where she stood in the darkness outside the champagne tent, "Aunt Fanny, will you do me a favor?"

"Essex? Yes, certainly, my dear."

"If Miss Inverness asks you whether you were ever captured and held prisoner by pirates off the Mediterranean coast, I want you to say yes."

"To say what? Yes? All right, surely, Essex. I think that will be splendid. Has anyone seen my brother tonight?"

"He was to have been moved into the drawing room, so he could watch the party."

"I daresay his wife forgot. I must really go and see to it."

"A known murderer," Essex said happily to Miss Deborah. "Mrs. Halloran has been sheltering him from the law, or, worse, the outraged relatives of his victims. 'Captain' is of course an assumed name."

"Who—" gasped Miss Deborah.

"Whom did he kill? Old women, mostly. Mutilated them in a most shocking fashion."

"A . . . a sex murderer?"

Essex shrugged. "One can hardly *ask*," he said.

"Now the proper carving of meat is an art," Mr. Straus said heavily. "It takes a love of flesh. I've seen a man carve a roast of beef as though he hated every inch of it, and you can't tell me *that* meat made fair eating."

"Drink, brother?" asked Mrs. Willow.

"I have done too well already, ma'am. But yes, another small drop. If you see a man take up a piece of meat with care and fondness like he was lifting a baby, now, *that* man can carve meat. I remember a fellow—married man, of course—we used to have in the shop many years ago—"

Hidden in the rose garden, Julia began to cry drunkenly. "I just don't know why it's got to end," she said.

"What's got to end?" The youngest Watkins boy handed her a lighted cigarette and laughed. "I never been in here before," he said. "*Look* at those roses; I bet it costs plenty to keep this place going. But now I know the way," he said to Julia, "I figure I could get back here sometimes. Nights, sometimes. And you can always sneak off and get down to the village. So what's got to end?"

Lying in the grass under the roses, Julia laughed, and cried, and laughed.

"Captain," said the schoolteacher, moving up to him with a wavering intensity, "I hope you won't think me bold?"

"Not at all," said the captain. He glanced over his shoulder to the entrance of the champagne tent, clearly decided that it was too far to make in one leap, and submitted to the schoolteacher's firm clutch on his sleeve.

"I want to hear about your adventures."

"Adventures?" said the captain.

The schoolteacher laughed giddily. "For someone like *me*, little me," she said, fumbling, "*you* know, reading nothing but *books?* It really *means* something to man a meet who's had *real* adventures. Real real real real real real real *real* adventures," and she sighed.

"But I am afraid that I—"

"Like carrying struggling maidens across your saddle—across your *horse*'s saddle, I mean, across your saddle across your horse across some desert. Screaming and struggling and begging to get away because she *knows* what's going to happen, and screaming fruitlessly for help and struggling and begging and scratching at you with her fingernails and pleading—"

"Rarely," said the captain. "Most of my ladies come willingly. I have little use for any other kind."

"—and keeping her prisoner for long moonlight nights in a satin tent, with cushions." The schoolteacher sighed. "Turkish delight," she said. "Shishkebab. Ropes of pearls."

"Yes," the captain said, edging sideways. "Always ropes of pearls."

"The desert moon," the schoolteacher said, but he had gotten away.

"I was *what?*" Miss Ogilvie demanded, her mouth open.

Miss Deborah leaned over, and whispered.

"*What?*" said Miss Ogilvie.

"I'm *sure* you won't mind my mentioning it, dear. I only hoped—"

"Why," said Miss Ogilvie, her eyes shining, "how perfectly *marvelous!*"

"Well, of course, *I* didn't know who he was," Maryjane said earnestly. She and Arabella were sitting in a quiet corner of the terrace, not far from the spot prepared for the musicians, who were having their dinner. Maryjane and Arabella had set their empty dinner plates down on the stone floor and occasionally they stopped Mrs. Willow, who was by now travelling luxuriously among the guests with a bottle of champagne under each arm, and asked her to fill their glasses; "Here," Mrs. Willow was shouting, "Cupbearer of the gods!"

"And he didn't *say* anything?" Arabella asked.

"Well, what *could* he say? It was just like a movie, honestly. He came into the library one day and of course I was there at the desk and I thought the *minute* I saw him that he looked kind of unusual and sort of . . . well, not the least bit like the kind of fellows who used to be pestering me all the time for dates and things."

"*I* saw a movie where—"

"And I said to myself," Maryjane went on overwhelmingly, "that this was certainly the most *gentlemanly* fellow I had seen for a long time even though his name kind of put me off at first—Lionel, *you* know, and when he said Lionel I honestly thought at first I would have died, because after all how many men are called Lionel? But of course when it turned out he only wanted to use the reference books I was *sure* because who else would be looking things up? You see a lot of people in a library and if I do say so myself you get kind of particular, because *naturally* they were always around asking me for dates and things."

"But if it was love at first—"

"Well, of course no, dear. When *you* get married you'll know more about these things, I always think. We just kind of got to talking, because it turned out they were binding the volume he wanted—and remind me someday to tell you about the cute fellow from the bindery, because *he* was one you had to see to believe, honestly—and *I* said why didn't he come back in a day or so, never thinking he *would*, of course. He wanted to be a poet then, you know, but of course we came right back here when we were married, because of course I wouldn't *dream* of alienating his family; after all, I always think, what are families *for?* So of course he *did* come back the next day and the first thing I knew he was asking me to go roller-skating with him and *I* said—"

Mr. Atkins of the hardware store, and Mr. Peabody who kept the Carriage Stop Inn, and Mr. Armstrong the postmaster, sat on folding chairs in a little group somewhat aside from the general crowd. They still held plates on their knees, and they ate slowly and methodically.

"That was when my father had the shop." Mr. Atkins said. He waved generously with his fork. "Nothing here *then*," he said.

Mr. Peabody nodded. "The Inn was a real carriage stop those days," he agreed.

"I remember them digging the foundations," Mr. Atkins

said, "me, just a little kid. I used to hang around up here watching."

"There was a fellow got killed, wasn't there?" asked Mr. Peabody.

"Got run over by a wagon. I was here—just a little kid. I remember the old man come over and looked down at this fellow lying there and he said—I swear I can hear him now—*he* said, 'Get him out of the way,' he said, 'this is where the terrace has got to go.' I can hear him now."

"He wasn't one who cared a lot about other people getting in his way," Mr. Peabody said.

"I remember," Mr. Atkins said, "there was a little carnival came to town, two or three little wagons and a pony ride, maybe it was, and a fortune teller and what not; well, they set up their kind of little camp right down there where that rose affair is now, and folks were coming around, buying tickets and looking at the fortune teller—come to think of it, there was a tattooed man along with them—and they were giving the kids a pony ride, and *he* comes raging out with his gang of bullies and chased the whole pack right off down the road. 'Let 'em stay off *my* land,' he says, 'let 'em stay off *my* land.' "

"And then he built the wall," Mr. Peabody said.

"There was some around here didn't care much for *that* wall," Mr. Atkins said, grinning, and Mr. Armstrong, the postmaster, shook his head with a tired old anger.

"Once," he said, "I could walk you all around there where my father's fences used to be. My father's farm, and then one morning my father turned around and there was his farm, *inside* the old man's wall, and here my father always supposed it was going to be *outside*. 'Oh, no,' says the old man, 'it's *my* land now—leastways, it's inside *my* wall, and try and get it back.' My father thought he ought to take it to the law, and my mother thought so too, but come to find out, there wasn't a lawyer anywhere around wasn't working for the old man, and so all my father could do was sneak in sometimes and walk around what used to be his farm, checking away on his fences, and then the old man, he had to have a lake, and there's my father's farm now, under ten feet of water. 'Take it back, for all

I care,' the old man says once to my father, '*I* don't want it any more. Just go take it back. Course, it'll take some *draining.*' Then he figured to make it all up by sending me to high school in the city." Carefully Mr. Armstrong speared a piece of meat on his fork and put it into his mouth.

"Mr. Armstrong," said Aunt Fanny, coming up with quick little steps, "Mr. Peabody, Mr. Atkins—do you all have everything you want? You mustn't hesitate to ask for anything—we would be very much offended if you went away hungry, you know. My father always hated to see anyone leave his table with an appetite, and, after all, this party *is* in your honor; my father would be the first to say that you deserved a good treat."

"He was a fine man," said Mr. Armstrong tiredly.

"A fine man," Mr. Peabody agreed.

"Oh, yes," said Mr. Atkins. "A very fine man."

Fancy slipped softly through the great doorway and sat herself quietly down on the step beside her grandmother. "Is it nearly over?" she asked.

"About half," said Mrs. Halloran.

"They look like pigs and weasels and rats," Fancy said.

"They will be soon gone."

"Why do you bother to give them all that good food and stuff to drink?"

"One last indulgence. Now we can remember them as being happy and carefree."

"How much longer is there?"

"An hour or so, I expect."

"*Not* the party," Fancy said.

"Oh, I see. About twenty hours, I imagine. Perhaps a little less."

"Do you think they will know what is happening?"

"I doubt it. For a minute, perhaps, no longer."

"Will it hurt them?"

"I trust not."

"Will they be frightened?"

"I suppose they will, for a minute or so; there will not really be very much time, I hope, for being frightened. In any case, people are not really frightened until they know what is happening to them, and I hope all of this will be quick enough for them not to know."

"*Does* it happen quickly?"

"I can hardly say; it has never happened before, to my knowledge. I can only believe, in mercy, that it will not take very long."

"Do they know now?"

"I hardly think so."

"What would they do if they *did* know?"

"From what I have seen of them, I suspect nothing. They would stand with their jaws hanging, looking at each other and grinning in a foolish fashion."

"I wish we could watch it when it happens."

"I think, on the whole, that it is not the kind of sight fit for our eyes, or any others. I cannot imagine living on, with that picture before me."

"When can I have your crown?"

Mrs. Halloran turned slowly and looked at Fancy. From down among the crowd, over the beginning sound of the music, came Mrs. Willow's voice, no longer shouting anything intelligible; on the outskirts of the crowd a small group was singing, unrecognizably; there were still sounds of activity around the barbecue pit, and from the champagne tent great bursts of laughter.

"When I am dead," Mrs. Halloran said.

Miss Inverness was crying miserably in a corner of the champagne tent onto the shoulder of Mr. Straus, the butcher. She had been brought up a lady, Miss Inverness was wailing, and taught the right way of doing things and how to comport herself in a ladylike fashion, and where was her mother now? "She was the finest woman who ever lived," said Miss Inverness, sobbing, and Mr. Straus nodded sympathetically and patted her gently on the back. "*You*'re fine, too," Miss Inverness said, "I can always tell, always tell. You're the finest woman who ever lived."

———

Miss Deborah had the captain by one arm and the school-teacher, somehow still navigating, had him by the other.

"You're a wicked wicked man," Miss Deborah screamed joyfully, "you're a pirate and I have been taken prisoner and I bet you won't *ever* let me go!"

"Screaming and begging and pleading in a silken tent," the schoolteacher said, rolling out the words gloriously. "Screaming and pleading to be saved from a fate worse than death!"

"Ladies—" said the captain.

"*Is* it worse than death?" asked Miss Deborah, conversationally, leaning around the captain to look at the schoolteacher. "I always wondered."

"Ladies," said the captain helplessly, and they swung him between them out onto the lawn and around in great circles, beginning a dance which caught up the others, moving and cavorting and shouting behind them; Mrs. Otis, who taught dancing, attempted a complicated step with Mr. Atkins, and both of them fell, laughing and struggling, onto the grass, and Miss Ogilvie, dancing along behind in a lonely complex waltz, fell over them; in the champagne tent Mr. Straus stirred to the sound of the music and laughter, and Miss Inverness, her face buried in his shoulder, hiccuped. "I never knew how fine she was," Miss Inverness said. "Now, I could kill myself."

Under the colored lights they moved in a great circle, leaping, howling, hurling glasses, embracing. Essex slipped down into the darkness of the crowd and joined hands with Gloria; silently they followed the pulls of other hands against theirs, turning in a great unending circle. "Dance, brothers, dance," Mrs. Willow shouted, and Aunt Fanny, her hair down over her eyes, took hands with the youngest Watkins boy. Maryjane and Arabella ran down from the terrace, laughing, and fell into the crowd; Julia was doing a cakewalk with Mr. Peabody. "Drink, sisters, drink," Mrs. Willow yelled, and they went around and around, trampling the grass and shattering cups and glasses under their feet; "Repent, children, repent," Mrs. Willow howled, and the dance caught her up and she whirled and kicked, holding a champagne bottle under each arm.

On the terrace Mrs. Halloran in her great chair, and Fancy on the step below her, watched in indulgent silence.

Suddenly Miss Ogilvie broke from the dance, and threw herself up the terrace steps. "I don't *want* them to go," she said wildly, "they're kind and nice and they're happy and you *can't* let them go." She held out her arms to Mrs. Halloran, and Mrs. Halloran laughed and shrugged. "*Please* let them come with us," Miss Ogilvie begged, and Mrs. Halloran laughed. "You can't, you can't, you *can't*," Miss Ogilvie said, her voice breaking, and then, turning suddenly, she held up her arms; the music was silenced and the dancers hesitated and then, seeing Miss Ogilvie, turned their faces to her and waited.

"My dear dear dear friends," Miss Ogilvie said, "*please* listen to me, please *please* listen. You are going away from here tonight to a dreadful and terrible catastrophe and none of you will live unless you stay here with us, you will *die*; please *please* stay. Believe me, I beg of you—how can I make you believe me? It is too late now to repent or change your ways or find another place to hide; *we* have let things go most miserably—can any of you *believe* me?" Briefly, there was a little scatter of applause. "No," Miss Ogilvie said, more softly, "will you just *trust* me? I don't want to see you die, not any of you, and you just simply will *not* understand and how can I tell you? It was even hard for *me* to believe at first, and how can I begin to tell you?"

Below, on the lawn, people stirred restlessly, and spoke among themselves, and then Julia, calling from the crowd, said, "Come on, everyone, *we* want to dance."

"Please, *please* listen," Miss Ogilvie said, but Mrs. Halloran said "Music," to the little orchestra, and the music began again.

"But you must not *go*," Miss Ogilvie cried, and Mrs. Halloran, laughing, said to Fancy, "I have known hostesses like this, who could not bear to see the end of their parties."

"Dance, brothers," Mrs. Willow called. "Tomorrow we'll be sober!" The circle went round and round, hands joined, voices raised in what might have been song, feet tangling and slipping, and Mrs. Willow was drinking champagne out of the bottles she carried. On the terrace Mrs. Halloran sat silently. Then, without warning, it was finished. The dancers stopped, wondering at one another, pushing back their hair, gasping now for breath. People began to look for one another, and speak of going home; around the circle went a whisper about the time. Someone found Miss Inverness asleep in a corner of the champagne tent, her pocketbook beside her and her wide hat thrown over her, and carried her charitably to a car to drive her home. Miss Deborah, giggling wildly and clinging to the captain, was pried away and taken with her sister. Julia and the schoolteacher, saying goodnight tearfully to one another, were parted. The guests departed swiftly, melting around the corner of the terrace to the entrance front where their cars were parked, moving in the darkness with a sudden shocking recollection of where they were. Not one of the villagers said goodbye to Mrs. Halloran.

16

The sundial showed no hours at night. Thanks to the champagne, Mrs. Willow slept soundly, her dreams untroubled save for a certain buried nagging anticipation of illness in the morning. Julia cried herself to sleep, railing at the cruelty which afflicted her young life. Arabella and Maryjane put their hair up together, took each a sleeping pill, and dreamed jointly of tall dark handsome men. Fancy slept with the exquisite sleep of a child; Miss Ogilvie, determined to meet the new world clean, washed out her underwear and stockings, inefficiently because of the champagne, and finally fell into bed fully dressed. Aunt Fanny sat by her window, wearing her mother's diamonds, and looked with grief and longing at the garden by night. Essex and the captain sat very late in the library, telling lies about themselves and confessing long-forgotten sins. Mrs. Halloran, her crown set in its case on her dressing table, was unable to compose herself for sleep. She went once around the house, nodding to Essex and the captain in the library, opening the door upon Mr. Halloran sleeping fitfully and calling on his nurse. Finally, she sat down at her desk to straighten out her last few accounts, looking over bills she would never pay, adding debts she would never collect.

During the night the wind rose, although it was still very hot. There was a strong sense of thunder in the air, and the wind, increasing toward dawn, swept freely down the great lawn of the house and tangled the wires on which the japanese lanterns swung wildly. By a quarter to seven the rose garden was swept bare, and the hot wind carried with it a freight of bruised and torn rose petals. Far off, by the lake, the water was whipped into waves which beat restlessly against the shore, and even washed the floor of the grotto where the swans cowered.

In the secret garden a statue swayed, and fell, crashing through the flowers and cracking in half as it hit the ground. One of the empty arms of Anna-in-the-maze caught a flying branch, and comforted and rocked it. At seven Mrs. Halloran dressed herself and came downstairs, to meet Aunt Fanny in the breakfast room. Because Mrs. Halloran had been anxious for the servants to make an early start on their holiday, the house was already awake, and in the breakfast room the sound of the wind was lessened by the indoor sounds of activity. What had been left overnight of the party was now cleared, although the japanese lanterns were hopelessly tangled and the tents had been turned by the wind into live flying monsters; the barbecue pit had been cleaned, the dishes used by the villagers had been washed and sterilized in the electric dishwashers, and the breakfast coffee awaited Mrs. Halloran and Aunt Fanny at the table.

"Good morning, Aunt Fanny."

"Good morning, Orianna. Did you notice the wind?"

"Certainly. I confess it frightens me a little."

Aunt Fanny contemplated her grapefruit. "Strange," she said, "How one's mind insists upon noticing only small things; I daresay it will be long enough before I see another grapefruit, tamed and cut."

"Do you think to tear fruit from the trees and sink your teeth into it?"

"Probably. We never know how pagan we may be. The wind does not frighten me, exactly; I only know that I cannot bring myself to think of how it will be later."

"Yes," Mrs. Halloran said. "I thought of it a good deal during the night, hearing the wind rising and trying to understand that this time it would not die down. It is an ominous, almost unbearable thought, this realization that a state of weather we would ordinarily regard without unusual fear will this time not subside as it always has before, but will increase and finally—"

"Be still, Orianna. The servants are still here. And in any case the prospect sickens me."

Mrs. Halloran and Aunt Fanny took toast, and eggs, and bacon, and coffee; with small glances at one another and both thinking, without saying, that a last quiet breakfast, prepared for them and served daintily in colored porcelain and silver, was something to be dwelt on and cherished; they both sat longer over their food than usual, and certainly longer than they would before have spent in one another's presence. Once, looking at her heavy silver fork, Mrs. Halloran found tears in her eyes; what use will this be to me tomorrow? she was thinking, and she made no attempt to hide her tears from Aunt Fanny.

"My father will be here," Aunt Fanny said softly. "I have perfect faith in him."

While Mrs. Halloran and Aunt Fanny lingered, Arabella came downstairs, in curlers and housecoat, to say that Mrs. Willow was ill, and might she have, please, a tray with only coffee, tomato juice, and a bottle of aspirin. Mrs. Halloran instructed that the tomato juice be fortified with raw egg and worcestershire sauce; "It would not suit us to have your mother ill today," she told Arabella. Arabella carried up her mother's tray, and returned shortly, dressed, with her hair combed; by then Fancy had come to breakfast, and Gloria, and shortly afterward, Maryjane and the captain. Mrs. Halloran and Aunt Fanny sat on at the breakfast table, drinking coffee, and no one spoke. Miss Ogilvie, looking most unwell, came to breakfast, and refused with unusual vehemence Mrs. Halloran's offer of tomato juice with raw egg and worcestershire sauce; "It's the wind," Miss Ogilvie said, whimpering, "I think the wind will drive me out of my mind."

"It's hideous," the captain said.

Essex and Julia, the last to reach the breakfast table, found the others sitting in subdued silence, listening to the distant sounds of the wind. "Our own little coven, waiting together," said Essex in a tone of some strain, and Julia said, her voice only barely controlled, "I wish it would stop, I wish it would stop."

"Well," the captain said, "it won't."

The breakfast room was meant to be delightfully bright and lit with early morning sun, so it had tall glass doors opening out over the garden; even though the noise of the wind was muffled here, they sat at the table and could see the darkening of the sky. Slowly, over the farthest trees in the garden, the clouds moved, and the room grew dim, and the reflections on the silver coffeepot were greyed and dull.

"It's going to storm," said Julia, and began to giggle hysterically.

By noon Mrs. Halloran, oppressed now by the driving wind into an urgent sense of haste, had seen the servants off in the two station wagons; Mr. Halloran's nurse was reluctant to leave, believing that she ought to give up her holiday in case the oppressive weather should trouble Mr. Halloran unduly, but Mrs. Halloran insisted, almost raising her voice, and the nurse went with the others. When the two station wagons had gone down the driveway Mrs. Halloran took a deep breath.

"Now," she said, "we must search the house carefully to make sure that there is *no one* left; I assure you that I checked the servants carefully, but I should not like to find a drunken villager asleep in some corner. On Miss Ogilvie's invitation." Her eyes turned briefly on Miss Ogilvie, who winced, and made a repudiating gesture.

Fancy was sent to sit with her grandfather while the rest searched the house, and she told him "Peter Rabbit" and "The Three Bears," which he enjoyed hugely.

"The house is so empty," Essex said to Maryjane, meeting her in an upstairs hallway. "Somehow you never realize how many people there actually were in it, before."

"I don't mind *this* part so much," Maryjane said, and shivered. "This is like a game, hide and seek, or murder, or something. It's what is coming later that I think I am going to mind."

"At least, up here you can't hear the wind," Essex said.

When they reassembled in the drawing room Mrs. Halloran, assured that they were now alone in the house, said, speaking loudly over the rising noise of the wind, "I urge you all, most earnestly, to take a glass of sherry before lunch; we have a great deal still to do, and, I need hardly tell you, we need all the courage we can muster."

"We must have complete faith," Aunt Fanny said. "My father has given me his word. Anyway," she added vaguely, "it's too late now."

"I don't think I will be able to stand it," Julia said; her lips were trembling and she had trouble speaking.

"This is final." Mrs. Halloran's voice seemed to echo, now, in the big drawing room; although the weather outside was hotter than it had been for months, perhaps years, there was a chill and a kind of dampness over everything in the big room, and the people in it gathered closer together before the empty fireplace. "This is final," Mrs. Halloran said. "We have no time now, and certainly no patience, for hysteria or panic. We have all known about this coming day and night for many weeks, and we know, too, what we shall see tomorrow morning. Any one of you—and I mean you, Julia, particularly—who provokes or indulges in any emotional outburst, will be shut in a closet and kept there by force, if I find it necessary. You are my people," she went on more gently, "and I must bring you safely through this unbelievable experience; trust me."

"My father—"

"I want to go outside," said Julia, barely articulate. "I don't want to stay in here any more."

"We must try to think of ourselves," Mrs. Halloran went on, "as absolutely isolated. We are on a tiny island in a raging sea; we are a point of safety in a world of ruin. Think," she said urgingly, "today, right now, out there in the world, people are beginning to wonder. They notice the weather, of course, and perhaps even feel the first apprehensions already; there must be some people, even this early, who are beginning to fear for their homes and their property, and perhaps into one or two minds the thought of death has already entered. But it is the people out *there* who have to be afraid; *we*, inside here, are safe. Julia, at the risk of sounding like Miss Ogilvie, I beg you to listen to me. *This* is safety. During all the rest of this day and this night, in the face of all your fears—and I believe that we will be called upon to steel ourselves beyond belief; one does not survive a cataclysm easily; I think we none of us know how deep our fears will be before morning—but, I insist, in the face of all your fears, remind yourselves, say it over and over again: the peril is for others: we are safe."

"My father—"

"It's too soon," Julia said helplessly. "There's so much I wanted to see again, and do again . . ."

"I never wrote to my father," Gloria said. "I wish now I had said goodbye to him."

"Well, it's a world well lost, if you ask *me*," said Mrs. Willow bluntly. "I've seen all of it I can take, and *that*'s no lie."

"I wish we'd managed to get some roses from the garden, to wear in our hair," Arabella said to Maryjane, and Maryjane said resentfully, "If she hadn't sent the servants off in such a hurry . . . do you know," she went on to Arabella, "no one made my bed this morning?"

"It seems to me," Mrs. Halloran said, "that we would be wise to barricade the house as soon as we can. There does not seem to be any immediate danger, and as you all know we do not anticipate the full fury of the elements until tonight, but on the one hand it will spare us work we may not be able to find time for later, and on the other hand it will serve in some manner to muffle the noise of that wind. It seems to drive right through the house. After the house is as secure as we can make it—"

"And we know it will stand," Aunt Fanny said.

"—we will gather for lunch, and then retire to dress, to reassemble here at four o'clock. You will recall, of course, that we are to be together in the drawing room from four o'clock on."

"Action," said the captain. "Everyone get moving—*that*'s the secret; no panic if you're busy."

"Blankets over the windows, and particularly the glass doors," Mrs. Halloran said. "The furniture is to be pushed as well as possible against outer doors, to prevent their blowing open in the wind. Save a few blankets, of course, for our own use during the night; we have no conception of the extremes of temperature we may be called upon to endure."

"Candles," said Essex, moving close to her. "The electricity may go soon."

"Look at the chandelier," Julia said, and giggled crazily. "You will never see an electric light again."

"Now *there*'s a thought," the captain said. "While we work, let's have on every light in the house—no need to worry about bills *now*," and he laughed. "And a couple of you ladies better use our last few kilowatts to brew up some coffee and hot soup to put in thermos bottles, and anything else you can think of; it's going to be cold eating for the rest of the night."

"And radios," Arabella said. "Turn on all the radios."

"No," Julia said violently. "Not radios, *please*. There will be announcements and warnings and descriptions . . ." She shivered.

"True," Mrs. Halloran said. "We don't want to see any of it, and we don't want to hear about it, either."

"Containers of water," the captain said. "Best get plenty of water; the mains will be going, you know, and I can tell all of you right now that I, for one, am not going to be particularly anxious to stand outside and catch raindrops in a pail."

"I will oversee the coffee and the water, then," Mrs. Halloran said. "I suppose," she said, hesitating in the doorway, "that the blankets will have to be nailed over the windows?"

"I'm afraid so," Essex said. "Tight."

"The woodwork?" said Mrs. Halloran wonderingly. "The lovely window frames? They were carved especially for the house."

"The house is not so important today, Orianna."

"The house is always important, Essex. But I must reconcile myself, I see, to nail holes in the window frames. I suppose they will be repaired later?"

"At least," the captain said unsympathetically, "if you're making the coffee you won't have to watch. Belle, you get out the candles. This room is our headquarters, so put plenty of candlesticks in here. I suppose a fire would be a mistake?" he said to Essex.

"Most unwise, I should think," Essex said. "We can be sure the chimneys will go."

"And we can't call the fire department." Julia's voice was high, and she giggled when she spoke.

The captain glanced to be sure that Mrs. Halloran had left the room. "It seems to *me*," he said, dropping his voice, "that we haven't either the manpower or the equipment to make any try at covering the top floors—I'd be prepared to let those windows go, even it it means a chance of losing the furniture and what not up there. We just *can't* barricade the whole house, and after all, everything we need is stored away in the library."

"If we're going to keep everyone in the drawing room, I agree with you," Essex said. "*I* want the windows covered, not so much for protection as invisibility; I mean, we don't want to have to look outside. It's not anything any of us ought to be watching. Besides," he added, "we *know* the house will stand."

"That big window in the drawing room is going to take a lot of covering. But I don't want to see it any more than you do."

They started together up the great curving staircase, which was already shivering slightly under the impact of the wind, and the captain grinned up at WHEN SHALL WE LIVE IF NOT NOW. "You know," the captain said, "if the old boy had known what this house was going to go through, he might have built it some different."

"He built it solid, anyway," Essex said. "We can be thankful for that."

By three o'clock that afternoon the great windows downstairs, sparkling clean and shining, were covered entirely. Essex and the captain, with help from Gloria and Maryjane, had used blankets, bedspreads, tablecloths, sheets, and finally the huge canvas cover from the barbecue pit, which it cost them a struggle to bring in through the roaring wind. During all this time Julia had sat huddled in a big chair in one corner of the drawing room, crying a little and watching the big chandelier feverishly. The lights were still on, and several of them had remarked that it was no darker now, with the windows covered, than it had been before, with the sky black and furious outside. Fancy and her grandfather were playing checkers in his room. Mrs. Halloran had brought out a second bottle of sherry to accompany their cold lunch, but the captain, Essex, and a somewhat recovered Mrs. Willow were drinking whisky. Every available container in the house had been filled with water, and on the long drawing room table there was a line of thermos bottles, brought from the supplies in the library, each filled and labelled "Coffee" "Soup" or "Tea." Blankets were piled neatly on a corner table in the drawing room, candles were in all the candlesticks, and extra boxes of candles on the mantel, with packages of matches. Mrs. Halloran, with half-hearted assistance from Mrs. Willow, had made plates of sandwiches and covered them with wax paper; they sat on the drawing room table with the row of thermos bottles. Under advice from Essex, who liked his whisky with ice, Mrs. Halloran had also filled two insulated ice buckets and, amused, informed Essex that so long as the refrigerator kept running, he need not drink his whisky warm. "I plan to drink a lot of it tonight," said Essex. "And I am with you," Mrs. Willow said.

Except for Julia, most of their original apprehension had faded into a kind of grim humor. They had done all they could; they were almost used to the crash of the wind against the sides of the house; they were excited and festive, with a kind of picnic air.

"My hangover is gone," Mrs. Willow announced once with deep pleasure.

Maryjane laughed. "I am never going to have any more asthma," she said. "Do you know," she told Aunt Fanny, "I have been better today than any time since Lionel passed on."

"That," said Aunt Fanny sternly, "is because you got up and did a little hard work for a change. And I promise you, you will be active enough from now on."

"I am going to dress," Mrs. Halloran said. "I do not know how much longer the lights will stay on, and I am sure I would detest dressing by candlelight."

"Better take a candle with you anyway," the captain said.

Mrs. Halloran rose and stood in the center of the room. "Before I go," she said, "we must be sure that all instructions are clearly understood. I have already told you that I expect all of you to be here, in this room, suitably dressed, by four o'clock, and that no one is to leave this room after that time. I recommend that you dress yourselves as well as possible, with, of course, due attention to warmth and safety, but with an eye to our appearance tomorrow morning and the good impression we must create. When I step out of this house tomorrow morning, I want to know that I am bringing with me into that clean world a family neat, prepossessing, and well-groomed. Remember," and for a minute Mrs. Halloran hesitated, because her voice shook; she put one hand against her lips, and said, "Remember, this—this is the end we have waited for so long."

"*Very* true," Aunt Fanny said, bustling. "We must all look our very best."

"And hurry, too," Arabella said. "Julia, stop moping and *hurry.*"

"The light is dimmer," Julia said.

"More reason to hurry," Aunt Fanny said, and Julia rose wearily.

"Fancy?" Maryjane called down the corridor. "Fancy? Come and put on your party dress; it's time."

"My father always liked to see his daughter sweet and clean, although a pinafore until the party actually starts—"

"It irks me," Essex said to the captain, "to be required to greet our free bright world in a jacket and a tie."

"Feel a little out of place?" the captain asked.

"Like a businessman from the city walking into a summer camp," Essex said.

"I suppose we'll be allowed to dress informally now and then," the captain said. "Anyway, from what *I* heard, your hunting costume was *most* informal."

"Come along, my gels," Mrs. Willow said, shepherding Julia and Arabella, "you'll be the belles of the ball, and *this* is going to be a party, *this* is; Julia, you'll be more cheerful in your fine clothes; Belle, a lady must not linger on her way to her toilette; Aunt Fanny, take my candle, since I see you are without, and I shall use Belle's; *do* come, my beauties."

"Oh, dear," Miss Ogilvie said, wavering, "ought *I* to dress, too, Mrs. Willow? Am I to have a candle? Perhaps *I* am only expected to wait here? Or Mr. Halloran—I could perhaps go to Mr. Halloran?"

"Miss Ogilvie," Mrs. Willow said sternly, "you are to inherit with the rest of us, and you must not be remiss in your dress. Mr. Halloran will be well enough for half an hour, and Mrs. Halloran would be very much displeased if you were not here at four o'clock in your better clothes. It is like going to church, Miss Ogilvie, precisely like going to church—one dresses decently, you know. Although, sadly, unlike going to church to be married, Miss Ogilvie, although I expect *you* will not perceive the fine difference in degrees of felicity; Miss Ogilvie, I must stress our very great need for haste."

"If you would just step out of the doorway," Miss Ogilvie said with dignity, "perhaps *I* could get through."

The lights went out at last while they were dressing, and there was so much noise of laughter and running from one room to another and remarks shouted down the dark hallways that it was difficult to hear even the wind, much less the sound of Mrs. Halloran going down the staircase. At any rate, they all appeared considerably surprised when, gathering with their candles upon the wide landing, festively dressed, eager and excited beneath WHEN SHALL WE LIVE IF NOT NOW? they saw, all at once, Mrs. Halloran lying in her golden gown, crumpled at the foot of the great staircase. In the weak light of the candles the stuff of the golden gown shimmered richly; "Mrs. Halloran?" Miss Ogilvie called down anxiously, but Mrs. Halloran did not answer and, further, did not move.

"Good heavens," Miss Ogilvie said to the rest of them, and then called again, "Mrs. Halloran? Are you all right?"

"I expect somebody pushed her down the stairs," Mrs. Willow said. She nodded profoundly and added, "Live by the sword, die by the sword."

"I wonder how it could have happened," Aunt Fanny said. "Poor Orianna was always so careful of her footing."

"Somebody pushed her, of course," Mrs. Willow said.

"I was certainly *wondering* about all those instructions and rules of hers," Arabella said. "I kept *thinking* maybe she was going to a different place than ours. And so of course I *was* right, wasn't I?"

"My crown!" Fancy said suddenly, and bolted down the stairs.

"Fancy dear, be careful—you'll trip and fall," Maryjane called, but Fancy leaped down the last two steps, avoiding Mrs. Halloran, and tugged at the crown. "It's stuck," she said.

"One minute there." The captain came heavily down the stairs and bent over Mrs. Halloran. For a minute he looked at her carefully, taking her wrist to feel her pulse, and then he stood up, shaking his head. "Poor old lady," he said. And then, to Fancy, "I guess it's your crown all right." Gently he moved Mrs. Halloran's head and took off the crown to set on Fancy's head.

"*My* crown, now," Fancy said, pleased.

The rest were coming down the stairs, going carefully from one step to the next, with a certain tendency to eye with suspicion whoever was walking in back of them. "Live by the sword, die by the sword," Mrs. Willow kept saying. They gathered around Mrs. Halloran, looking down in silence for a minute, and then Gloria said, "I can't believe it. I am so sorry that I was rude to her."

Aunt Fanny smoothed the hair which had been disarranged when the captain took off the crown. "I am going to miss her," she said with some surprise.

"Well, *some*body pushed her down the stairs," Mrs. Willow said. "She never fell by herself."

"*That* hardly matters, does it?" Aunt Fanny said. "Poor Orianna."

"She wouldn't like having all of us standing around staring at her," Gloria said, and they all moved back a little, looking away.

Essex sat on the bottom step of the staircase and said, looking at Mrs. Halloran, "She said she would either come with us as a ruler, or not at all. I wish," he said, looking helplessly at the others, "that she had been able to change her mind."

"She was always a very firm woman," Aunt Fanny said. She sighed. "I *am* going to miss her."

"Perhaps," the captain suggested, with the air of one looking on the bright side, "perhaps she wouldn't have liked it anyway. Tomorrow, I mean."

"She might have felt *very* out of place," Arabella added.

Essex leaned down and touched Mrs. Halloran's cheek gently. Then he stood up and turned away. "Look at my *crown*," Fancy said insistently, capering up to him, "Essex, look at my crown!"

"It looks very nice on you, Fancy," Maryjane said.

"But vanity is out of place in a young girl," Aunt Fanny said. "Try to remember, Fancy, that earthly possessions do not make a noble soul; just because you have a crown you are not any better than other girls your age."

"Live by the sword, die by the sword," Mrs. Willow said again, standing over Mrs. Halloran. "I wonder who could have pushed her down the stairs? *Any*way, though, we can't leave her *here*."

"I don't like the idea of going up and down the stairs past her, and *that*'s the truth," the captain said.

"Well, she ought to be outside," Aunt Fanny said.

"True," the captain said. He frowned thoughtfully. "Door's barricaded," he pointed out.

Fancy, who was dancing a slow child's dance around the hall, carrying a candle and wearing her crown, called "But she didn't want to see what was happening outside."

"She won't be watching," the captain said. "No fear of *that*. The way *I* look at it, we just can't figure to keep her along with us, and plan to bury her or something tomorrow morning. Aside from everything else, it would put a damper on the whole first day."

"No," Aunt Fanny said, "outside is right; put her outside."

"But the door is barricaded," Mrs. Willow said.

"The upstairs windows—" the captain suggested, but Aunt Fanny shook her head emphatically.

"She was my brother's wife," Aunt Fanny said, "and as such, must leave the house with dignity. I cannot, for my part, consent to ejecting Mrs. Halloran from an upstairs window. Although, as I remember," she added thoughtfully, "the great door is not the one she first came in by; I think originally she used the servant's entrance. At any rate, she must go out the great door."

"Well." The captain sighed, and looked at Essex. "You game?" he asked.

Essex had been looking down at Mrs. Halloran. "Anything you say," he said slowly. "I rather liked her," he said.

"Why, Essex." Aunt Fanny came up and put a consoling hand on Essex' arm. "We all loved her *very* dearly, Essex. But we must look forward, and think of the morning; consider the others who will go tonight—consider her as only one of millions."

"Of course," Mrs. Willow put in, "somebody *did* push her down the stairs."

"Well, that is all water under the bridge now," Aunt Fanny said soothingly, "and you are not to grieve, Essex. Try to remember that we all share in this loss. And get her outside."

"I do dislike taking all that stuff down from the door," the captain said. "It was a hell of a job getting it up."

"Well, it must be done," Aunt Fanny said.

"I suppose so," said the captain grumpily, and he began to push at one end of the great chest with which they had barricaded the door. The others came to help him, working now with speed in the flickering light of the candles, while Fancy moved in graceful circles over the black and white marble floor, trying to catch reflections of her crown in the tall mirrors. The captain got onto a stepladder and pried loose the nails with which they had fastened the blankets securely to the top of the door frame and the blankets came loose and fell, and Mrs. Willow and Aunt Fanny caught them and heaped them onto the great chest, to be ready to put back up again after Mrs. Halloran was outside.

"Now, the wind is pretty strong," the captain said warningly. "Essex and I will take her out, but all you women stand by the door here, so you can get it closed after we go through.

And be sure to be ready to open it again when we come back. You carry her," he said to Essex. "You liked her better. I'll stand by to help if you drop her or something."

Essex lifted Mrs. Halloran, who seemed to him oddly bulkier than when she was standing erect, and moved toward the great door. "Now," the captain said, and the door was opened and the wind rushed in and up and down the great staircase. Essex and the captain slipped out, and the door was slammed shut behind them. "Where?" the captain shouted, and Essex, not hesitating, said, "Sundial—where else?"

Although the wind was strong, they moved with reasonable accuracy down the terrace and down the steps on the sundial side, skirting the edge of the ornamental pool and going across the grass, wet now with the waves the wind was pushing from the pool. When they came to the sundial, which said WHAT IS THIS WORLD? Essex stopped, still holding Mrs. Halloran.

"Well, put her down," the captain said, and Essex said, "you know, I don't know why we brought her here—she never liked the inscription. Allone," Essex said, "with-outen any companye."

At last, with the captain hurrying him, he sat Mrs. Halloran on the grass beside the sundial, facing out over the long lovely lawn, and arranged her feet together and her hands on her lap. The captain carefully spread the long golden skirt around her, and for a minute the two of them stood, admiring the way Mrs. Halloran sat by the sundial with her hands folded, quite as though it were still all her property she surveyed. The captain turned, Essex stayed to look once more, and then, with the wind behind them and almost rushing them back to the house, they came along beside the ornamental pool, up the marble steps, and across the terrace to the door. "All done, let us in," the captain yelled, pounding, and the door swung open and the wind rushed in and up and down the great staircase, and all of them leaned against the door and got it shut again.

"Well, *that's* taken care of," the captain said, sinking down on the great chest and wiping his forehead. "Pretty rough out there."

"Barricade the door again right away," Mrs. Willow said.

"Let us catch our breath," Essex said. "We went all the way to the sundial."

Aunt Fanny nodded. "Splendid," she said. "It was the only thing around here that really *looked* like her, if you know what I mean."

With less difficulty, now, since they had done it before, they put the blankets back over the door, stretched them tight, and nailed them firmly. Then, all together, they pushed the great chest across the doorway, laughing together because it was their last chore. When it was done they crowded into the drawing room and settled down comfortably. Aunt Fanny went into the right wing and brought back Richard Halloran in his wheel chair; Mr. Halloran was puzzled, but pleased at being brought into company, and inquired at once about a fire in the fireplace.

"You will have a fire tomorrow morning, Richard," Mrs. Willow said, "if you really want one then."

"I daresay I shall. I like a fire even in the mornings."

"You realize that you must stay in this room all night, Richard?" Aunt Fanny asked.

"I was told, I believe. I forget what is going to happen, but someone told me that I should be expected to be very strong, and sit up all night in the drawing room."

"We will all be right here with you."

"If I get very tired," Mr. Halloran explained, "I shall nap in my chair."

"Well." Mrs. Willow stretched her legs and yawned. "Too early for dinner," she said, "and a long night ahead. Anyone care for bridge?"

"Not I, thank you," Aunt Fanny said. "I believe we play in different styles, Mrs. Willow."

"But I think we are only five bridge players here, Aunt Fanny, so if we are to play at all in the future we must compromise our different styles."

"I'm too restless," Arabella said. "I keep feeling something is going to happen," and she laughed.

"I can still hear the wind," Julia said.

"Now, Julia," Mrs. Willow said, "there's no sense in getting yourself all nervous and agitated. You'll just be a wet blanket on the rest of us. Have yourself a drink."

"Good idea," Essex said. "We have plenty of ice, at least." He went over to the portable bar they had moved into the drawing room.

"I wonder if we ought to have clear heads for the morning?" Aunt Fanny asked, worried.

"Aunt Fanny, the time for clearing our heads is long past. Mrs. Willow—scotch?"

"I thank you, Essex."

"I thought I heard a crash," Julia said, turning her hands nervously.

"Probably one of the trees going down," Aunt Fanny said. "The best thing for you, dear, is to try not to notice. Try to think of something else."

"Mr. Halloran," Miss Ogilvie said, coming to the wheel chair, "are you quite warm enough?"

"Splendidly warm, thank you, Miss Ogilvie. And yourself? Should you not put on a shawl?"

"I am quite warm, thank you. I was only concerned about *you*."

"That was kind, Miss Ogilvie. You know, I expect, that I am to stay in my chair all night?"

"Yes. Mrs. Halloran—"

"Who?" said Mr. Halloran.

"May I wear your crown sometimes?" Gloria asked Fancy.

"No," Fancy said, and giggled. "But you can have my doll house," she said.

"Fancy is going to find that she is getting headaches from that crown, I believe," Mrs. Willow said. "I expect we shall soon find her taking it off."

"I like dancing in it," Fancy said.

"It wasn't the plot so much, you know," Maryjane was saying to Arabella, "it was the *acting*. I mean, it was so real you really got to thinking they were real people. Just *wonderful* acting. Of course, they used real natives, and most of the photography was done right there in the Oturi Forest, with the animals—you know? But I actually cried when they tortured—"

"My." Mrs. Willow stretched, and sighed. "It's going to be a long wait," she said.

"The first thing I will do," Essex said to Gloria, "is make *you* a crown of flowers."

MORE FROM SHIRLEY JACKSON

The Bird's Nest
Foreword by Kevin Wilson
ISBN 978-0-14-310703-3

Come Along with Me
Foreword by Laura Miller
ISBN 978-0-14-310711-8

Hangsaman
Foreword by Francine Prose
ISBN 978-0-14-310704-0

The Haunting of Hill House
Introduction by Laura Miller
ISBN 978-0-14-303998-3

MORE FROM SHIRLEY JACKSON

Life Among the Savages
ISBN 978-0-14-026767-9

The Sundial
Foreword by Victor LaValle
ISBN 978-0-14-310706-4

The Road Through the Wall
Foreword by Ruth Franklin
ISBN 978-0-14-310705-7

*We Have Always Lived
in the Castle*

Introduction by
Jonathan Lethem
Cover art by Thomas Ott
ISBN 978-0-14-303997-6